THE OLYMPIUM OF BACCHUS 12

BY

WILLIAM SPEIR

Published 2016 by Progressive Rising Phoenix Press, LLC
www.progressiverisingphoenix.com

ISBN: 978-1-946329-00-4

*

Printed in the U.S.A.

Illustration: "The Great Seal of the United Earth Planets Confederation" by William Speir

Cover Artwork: "Sojourn" by Tobias Roetsch, Dresden, Germany (http://www.gtgraphics.de). Used by permission of the artist, © Copyright 2012 Tobias Roetsch.

Book and Cover design by William Speir
Visit: http://www.williamspeir.com

DEDICATION

I want to thank my sister and editor, Linda Speir, for her tireless work in helping me shape my draft manuscripts into a polished, finished version worthy of reading.

Additional thanks go to Jennifer Cook, Ray Flynt, Zame Kahn, Jim Newman, Katherine Ramsay, and Pat Russell for helping to make the drafts better.

Thanks to Amanda Thrasher and Jannifer Powelson at Progressive Rising Phoenix Press for once again believing in my books. Both of you are wonderful!

Deepest gratitude goes to my wife Lee Anne for putting up with me. Every day I love her more than I ever thought possible. I am also grateful for my family, without whom there would be no words worth writing.

To all of the men and women who inspired me to reach for the stars. Godspeed.

CHAPTER 1

"It's amazing how quickly teenagers can take a perfectly beautiful morning and turn it into complete shit," Rick Douglas muttered to himself as he looked around the recently vacated dining table. He glanced at the letter in his hand and realized that he was still clenching it tightly. He put it on the table and tried to smooth it out. The letter had been the source of so much pride and joy just a few minutes earlier, and he wanted to keep it looking pristine – as if that might erase the memory of this latest confrontation. He saw the words, "We are pleased to inform you…" on the first line just below his son's name.

Rick winced when he heard a door upstairs slam shut. "Complete shit." He rose from the table to follow his wife to their son's room. He walked toward the stairs, hoping that he'd think of something constructive to say by the time he reached his son's door. As he put a hand on the cold metal bannister, he noticed the familiar car waiting for him on the street outside.

He hesitated, looking up the stairs. He wanted to be with his son – to make him understand how important the contents of the letter were to his future. But duty called. Rick reluctantly took his hand off the banister, grabbed the briefcase that he had set on the floor when he came downstairs for breakfast, and silently exited the house through the front door.

He stood on the front porch of his house for a moment, staring up at the planetary rings visible in the morning sky above him. *I know I'm forgetting something. What am I forgetting?*

Twenty minutes earlier, Rick had been sitting on the balcony off his bedroom, watching the sunrise and sipping a glass of fruit juice. This was his favorite time of the day – the time he spent collecting his thoughts and preparing for the pressures of his work.

He heard his wife, Beth, making breakfast downstairs. His son and daughter, Bret and Cindy, were down the hall in the washroom they shared – yelling at each other like they did every morning as they got ready for school.

"Door close," he instructed. The sliding glass door behind him slid closed, blocking out the sounds.

Sunrises on Bacchus 12 are spectacular this time of year. He saw the rings of the planet glowing in the morning sunlight, but the sky was still dark enough to see the two planetary nebulas clearly. Even after the sun rose above the horizon, the nebulas were still visible, but their brilliant colors faded into pale pastels.

As he watched the planet's shadow shift on the rings, the net-dev in his briefcase on the table announced that he had an incoming message. He turned away from the celestial beauty and looked over at the screen.

"Dear Mr. Douglas," the message began. "We are contacting you to inform you that your son's aptitude testing scores were sent to him two weeks ago, but we have not heard back from him concerning his advanced education plans. A copy of the letter that we sent to him is attached. Please have your son review the contents of the letter and respond with his intentions within the next two days to ensure his place for the next school term…"

Rick eagerly opened the attached letter, wondering why Bret hadn't responded.

"Bret Douglas, We are pleased to inform you that your aptitude scores have been reviewed, and you have been granted placement for advanced education in Theoretical and Applied Physics. Please respond to this letter confirming that you will be attending advanced education in the next school term…"

Theoretical and Applied Physics! Rick re-read the letter, feeling a profound sense of pride. Bret, who had recently turned 18, was a bright and likable boy. His school grades were always high, but Rick had no idea that his son's aptitude test scores would earn him the right to study the hardest advanced education program in the Confederation.

Why didn't he say something to us? Rick printed the letter so Beth could read it.

He finished his juice and took the letter from the printer in his briefcase. Then he stood. The sliding glass door separating the balcony from his bedroom opened silently as he walked toward it. He finished getting dressed before stepping back onto the balcony to retrieve the letter and his briefcase.

Rick smiled as he walked down the stairs. He put his briefcase on the floor next to the front door and walked toward the dining room next to the large kitchen on the main floor – letter still in hand. He couldn't stop thinking about his son's achievement. *Theoretical and Applied Physics means he'll either get a job in the Advanced Weapons Division here on Bacchus 12 when he graduates, or he'll be relocated to Trinity 7 to work at the Fleet shipyards designing new ship propulsion systems. What a fantastic set of options my son has!*

Beth and the two children were sitting at the table when he reached the dining room. Bret and Cindy were too busy communicating with their friends on their net-devs to notice that he had entered the room. Neither of the children looked up as he walked around the table.

Beth looked up at him with a curious expression on her face. Rick kept smiling and silently handed her the letter. She took it and read it carefully. Rick saw her eyes open wide. She looked up and handed the letter back to him. Then they both looked at Bret.

"Bret, why didn't you tell us about your aptitude score letter?" Rick asked, sitting down in the empty chair between his children.

"What?" Bret asked absently, still staring at his net-dev screen.

Rick leaned forward and took the net-dev from Bret. "I'm talking to you, son," he said gently but firmly.

"Hey, give that back!" Bret demanded, reaching to grab the net-dev away from his father. "I'm talking to Peter about our trip to Manis 2."

"In a minute," Rick said. He held up the letter. "Why didn't you tell us about your aptitude scores?"

"Because I'm not going to study Theoretical and Applied Physics," he stated.

"Then what are you going to study?" Rick asked.

"Nothing," Bret replied. "I'm going to be an artist like Mom."

Not this again. "We've talked about this before, Bret," Rick said. "Art is not a career. It's a hobby."

"Well I want it for my career," Bret said, raising his voice.

Rick fought to maintain his composure. "Bret, there haven't been any full-time career artists in the history of the Confederation."

"I don't care!" Bret snapped. "It's not your decision; it's mine. I don't care if it hurts your position as Administrator of Bacchus 12. I don't care if it embarrasses you. If I want, I'll be the first career artist since Earth was abandoned and the Confederation was founded. Art is what I love, and it's what I want to do with my life. You and the Confederation will just have to get over it."

"Son," Beth began, "Your sculptures are beautiful, as are your paintings. You know how proud we are that you've been invited to show your work at the Confederation Art Festival on Manis 2. It's a great honor, and it's well-deserved. But art isn't supposed to be something that you do to earn your way through life. It's something you do to make you a well-rounded person – to reduce stress, to give your creativity an outlet. Look at me. I've been an artist for most of my life, but Bio-Botany is my career."

"But you gave it up," Bret countered, getting red in the face. "All you do is art now."

"I didn't give up my career to do art," Beth reminded him. "I gave it up to raise you and your sister. Art is what I do to keep me busy during the day while you and your sister are at school. Once the two of you are set on your careers, I'm going back to Bio-Botany full time."

"Son," Rick interjected. "We're not telling you that you can't be an artist. Your work is amazing, just like your mother's. But you have to work in an approved field for your career, and they're offering you one of the greatest career opportunities in the Confederation. Very few people have the aptitude for the kind of work you'll be doing. It's a great honor to be selected, and it's something you need to do."

"No!" Bret shouted, standing up and taking back his net-dev. "God damn it, Dad, you're not listening. You never listen. I'm going to be an artist. Period!"

"Bret, come back here!" Rick shouted as Bret stormed out of the dining room. "We're not finished!"

Beth stood up and walked around the table. "I have to take him to the spaceport in a little while," she said, putting a hand on her husband's shoulder. "I'll tell him to think about it while he's on Manis 2, and we'll discuss it when he gets back."

"They need an answer by tomorrow," Rick reminded her, holding up the letter.

"Then I'll tell him to think about it on his flight, and we'll discuss it tonight by vid-com."

Rick nodded, and Beth left the dining room to follow her son upstairs.

Turning to Cindy, Rick asked, "Is there anything *you* haven't told me that I need to know?"

Cindy looked up from her net-dev. She looked slightly annoyed that her dad interrupted her from her eight-way conversation with her friends. "I'm pregnant, but I have no idea who the father is. Does that count?" she asked with a straight face.

Rick glared at her. "I'm really not in the mood, Cindy."

"Relax, Daddy," she said, getting up from the table and smiling. "I'm not pregnant… not yet."

She gave him a quick kiss on the cheek and dashed out of the dining room to finish getting ready for school. As she ran up the stairs, he heard her say, "I told him I wasn't pregnant yet." She giggled, and he heard her friends giggling through the net-dev's speaker.

Rick sat there by himself, wishing that he had stayed upstairs watching the sunrise.

Rick walked down the front steps of his house to the circular drive where his car waited. He returned the salute of the Fleet Marine corporal who served as his escort when he was outside the house.

"Good morning, sir," the corporal said.

"Morning, Corporal," Rick responded as he got into the car. The corporal closed Rick's door and joined the driver in the front of the car.

"Good morning, Administrator Douglas," Natalia Komarov said from the seat next to Rick.

"Morning, Natalia," Rick said absently to his administrative assistant as the driver accelerated the car away from the house. "What's on my agenda for today?"

CHAPTER 2

"You were a little hard on your father, don't you think?" Beth said to her son as the small motorcade headed for the spaceport.

Bret glanced out the back window at the two trucks carrying his artwork and said, "I don't want to talk about it, Mom."

Beth raised the partition so the driver and the Fleet Marine escort in the front seat couldn't hear their conversation. "He only wants what's best for you. So do I."

"Then why won't you let me be an artist?" Bret shot back, glaring at his mother.

"Honestly, didn't you learn a thing in your Earth History and Confederation History classes?"

"Mom, *no one* learns a thing in history classes. I used that time to study."

"Well then, maybe you need a quick refresher," Beth replied firmly. Bret knew from her tone that he had to listen to what she said or face another long, drawn-out lecture about his attitude. He nodded sullenly.

"Before the cataclysm that forced mankind to abandon Earth, there were all kinds of professional artists – painters, sculptors, musicians, architects, photographers, digital artists, performance artists... Earth society supported artists for centuries, and it was possible to pursue art as a career, although very few artists ever earned enough to support themselves."

Beth glanced out the window as the car passed the planetary administration complex where Rick worked. "None of the original twenty-one planets of the Confederation had everything that Earth had. Some were well-suited for agriculture while others were better suited for mining or manufacturing. That's when the decision was made to have each planet specialize in a single purpose or a small set of purposes. The original refugees who founded the Confederation arrived on their new worlds with few tools, minimal building materials, and very little time to get shelters built, food supplies organized, and industries set up. There was no room for professional artists, or professional athletes for that matter, when every day was a fight for survival. By the time Bacchus 12 was discovered and added to the Confederation, people were accustomed to careers that served the needs of their planets and the Confederation as a whole. Art and athletics were considered hobbies to enjoy, rather than careers to pursue."

"But the Confederation was founded 206 years ago, and we're not fighting to survive anymore," Bret pointed out. "Maybe it's time to start allowing hobbies to become careers again."

"Maybe it is, but you can't change society overnight. Not even your father can do that. Besides, history isn't the only reason we don't want you to pursue art as your career."

"What's the other reason?"

Beth smiled at him. "Because it's important for people to utilize *all* of their talents, not just some of them. You're a gifted artist, but you're a gifted physicist as well. You school scores show that you have a strong aptitude for math and sciences. If you were to pursue art instead of physics, you'd be using only half of your gifts, and that's a waste. If you pursued physics and forgot about your art, you'd still be using just half of your gifts. By pursuing both, one as a career and one as a hobby, you'll be using all of your gifts, and it's those gifts that make you who you are. Your life will have meaning, but more importantly, it will have balance. Your father and I don't want to see you waste any of your potential. That's why we want you to take the opportunity you've been given to study physics. You already know how to be an artist. Now it's time to also learn how to be a productive member of the Confederation."

Bret silently watched the city move past the car window. "How did you know you wanted to be a Bio-Botanist?" he asked softly after several minutes.

"I didn't," Beth replied. "I didn't really want to do much of anything when I was eighteen. But my aptitude tests suggested bio-botany, so I decided to give it a try. I ended up loving it! And, oddly enough, my art improved once I started working."

"How is that possible?" Bret asked incredulously.

"Because work inspired me. It gave me things to paint. And art helped me relax and deal with the stress of work. I did my best paintings and sculptures when I was working. I still love art, but what I create now isn't anywhere near as good as what I used to make."

Bret sat silently, thinking about what his mother had said, when his com-dev alerted him to an incoming message. He looked at it and read, *Bret, Have a safe trip to Manis 2 and good luck at the exhibition. See you when you get back. Jen.* Bret smiled, typed a quick reply, and put his com-dev away.

"Who was that?" Beth asked.

"No one, Mom," Bret replied.

"It must have been someone, or you wouldn't be smiling like that."

"It was just a friend wishing me a good trip," Bret said.

Beth looked at her son, wondering who could make him smile that big by just wishing him a good trip.

The spaceport loomed ahead through the windshield. Beth saw two medium freighters taking off and a large starliner landing. *I wonder if that's the same starliner Bret will be taking.*

The Fleet Marine escort lowered the partition. "I'm sorry for interrupting, Mrs. Douglas. The spaceport is just ahead. The trucks will deliver the artwork to the cargo terminal, and we'll drop your son off at the passenger terminal."

"Thank you, Corporal," Beth said.

Once the partition was back up, she looked at her son. "Will you at least consider the offer to study physics? The Education Service needs an answer by tomorrow. Think about it on your flight, and give your father and me a call in the morning and let us know what you've decided."

"There's no need," Bret said calmly as they approached the passenger terminal. "I'll send my acceptance to the Educational Service once I'm on board the starliner."

Beth hugged her son. "Are you sure?"

Bret nodded. "I understand what you're saying about wasting my talents. I've always been good at science, and it'll be interesting to learn what advanced physics is all about. I can always change my mind later."

"Why don't you call your father and let him know what you decided. I think he'll appreciate hearing it from you."

"OK, Mom. I'll call him after I transmit my acceptance."

They pulled up to the passenger terminal, and the Fleet Marine escort jumped out and opened the back door. Bret exited the car, followed by Beth. Another Fleet Marine stepped out of the shadows of the terminal arrival portico and took his position near Bret.

"You have all of your boarding passes and identification?" Beth asked him as he grabbed his bags from the car's cargo compartment.

"Yes, Mom. I've double-checked everything."

"When will you reach Manis 2?" she asked.

"Sometime tomorrow morning," he replied. "The art exhibit starts the next day, so I'll be spending all day tomorrow getting everything set up."

Bret saw two familiar faces pulling up to the terminal, and he waved. Five artists from each of the twenty-two Confederation planets had received invitations to exhibit their art at the Fire Moon Resort on Manis 2, and two of the five from Bacchus 12 were Bret's best friends, Peter and Silas.

"Gotta go, Mom," Bret said, giving her a quick kiss on the cheek. "I'll see you in two weeks."

"Have fun," she said. "I love you!"

"Love you too, Mom." He hurried to greet his friends. The Fleet Marine stayed close to Bret, and soon Bret, his friends, and the Fleet Marine disappeared into the terminal building.

"Where to now, Mrs. Douglas?" the corporal asked, holding the door for her.

"Home, please," she replied, getting into the car.

The car pulled away from the terminal. *Thank you, God!* She reached for her com-dev and called her husband.

Rick felt like pulling his hair out. *How long can one man drone on? I've always liked the man, but he could bore the dead.*

Nigel Canterbury, Bishop of the Interplanetary Ecumenical Church on Bacchus 12, had been rambling for the past twenty-five minutes, and Rick waited for him to take a breath so he could interrupt and get the bishop back on topic. Canterbury was Rick's second meeting of the morning, and it was almost time for his third. *If he doesn't stop talking soon, we'll never get to the point of this meeting. He'll want to schedule another meeting and another meeting, and we'll still never get this issue resolved.*

Realizing that the bishop was getting farther and farther off topic, Rick raised his hand. "I have to stop you there, Bishop. We have only five more minutes, and we still need to make a decision on your budget for the next year."

"The budget? I thought that was settled," the bishop stated.

"No, it's not settled. You think it's settled because you submitted the request. But the request hasn't been approved."

"Why not?"

"Bishop, we discussed that in our last meeting. You were supposed to come here today with the information I requested to justify the budget increase, but instead you've been talking at length about the conference you attended on Trinity 5. That's not going to help me understand why you need so much more money next year."

"Well I can't possibly explain that in five minutes. We'll need to schedule another meeting."

Dear God, No! "That's unacceptable, Bishop. You agreed to provide the information this morning. You didn't. Under the circumstances, I can't possibly approve your budget request."

"Now, see here, Administrator Douglas," the bishop sputtered, getting to his feet. "This is the *Church* we're talking about here. You can't just dismiss us like we're irrelevant."

"You know me better than that, Bishop. I'm not dismissing the church. I'm dismissing your request for a budget increase. You know the rules of the budgetary process as well as anyone. It's the same rules that every other planet in the Confederation has to follow. There's a deadline for submitting requests, and there's a deadline for submitting additional information. You failed to provide the additional information by the deadline, so your request

11

for an increase is denied. That's the rule. It's not my rule. I just administer it."

The bishop began sputtering again, and Rick got to his feet and escorted the bishop to the door. He gently propelled the bishop out of the office and into the waiting area.

Natalia quickly stepped past the bishop and entered Rick's office. They both heard the bishop still sputtering in the waiting area as the office door closed.

Rick gestured toward an empty chair. "What's next?" he asked.

"Enrique and Karl are on their way up. They'll be here in ten minutes."

"It's not like them to be late for a meeting," Rick commented.

"They knew that you were meeting with the bishop and wanted to make sure you had enough time to finish the conversation."

Rick laughed. "Remind me to commend them for their foresight."

Natalia was about to say something when Rick's com-dev alerted him to an incoming call from his wife.

"Hold that thought, Natalia," he said, picking up the com-dev.

"Hi, Honey," he said when he answered the call. "Did Bret get to the spaceport okay?"

"No problem," Beth replied. "We had a good talk on the way."

"Has he agreed to think about the physics training?"

"No."

"What do you mean 'no'? How could it have been a good talk if he won't think about the training?"

"Because he decided to go ahead and accept," Beth replied. "He's transmitting his intention as soon as he gets settled on the starliner. I told him to call you and tell you personally, but in case he forgets, I wanted you to know."

Rick leaned back and smiled. "Outstanding, Honey! You've always had a gift for helping people see things clearly. Sometimes I think you'd be better in this job than I am."

"No, thank you!" she said. "Administering our family is one thing. Administering the entire planet is something else altogether."

Changing the subject, she asked, "Will you be home for dinner?"

"I don't know. Let me check." Turning to Natalia, he whispered, "Will I be home for dinner tonight?"

Natalia glanced down at his schedule and nodded.

"Yes, I'll be home for dinner tonight," he said to Beth.

"Good. I have something special planned."

Rick knew not to ask what it was. Beth never revealed her plans until she was ready. "I can't wait," he said.

"Good. Gotta run. Tell Natalia I said hello and to make sure you get out of there on time. Love you!"

"Love you, too," he said, ending the call.

Natalia tried to say something again when there was a knock on the door.

"Come in," Rick said.

Enrique Fuentes, the Assistant Administrator for Bacchus 12, and Karl Pitowski, the Director of Planetary Services for Bacchus 12, walked into his office. "Are you done with the bishop already?" Enrique asked, taking a seat across from Rick.

"I'll bet he forgot the information you requested," Karl stated as he sat down.

Rick nodded. "He did. I told him his request for a budget increase is denied. I think he started having some sort of fit."

The three of them laughed, and Natalia handed them copies of the agenda for the meeting.

Rick looked at his assistant. "Natalia, you started to say something twice. What is it?"

"It can wait," she said, moving toward the door.

"No, I want to know what it is."

"I was just going to wish you and your wife a happy anniversary. Wasn't the wedding twenty-three years ago today?"

Rick slapped his hand to his forehead. "*That's* what I was forgetting! I need to get a present for Beth."

"I can handle that for you," Natalia offered.

Rick shook his head. "Thank you, Natalia, but no. I need to do it. I already have it picked out; I just need to purchase it. Please tell my driver that there'll be a couple of stops on the way home tonight, and make sure I get out of here a few minutes early."

"Yes, sir," Natalia replied, closing the door behind her as she left the three men alone.

"Very well, gentlemen," Rick said, turning his attention to Enrique and Karl. "Let's get started."

"Beth! Cindy! I'm home," Rick said as he walked through the front door that evening.

It had been a busy day, but he was happy. On the way home, he bought Beth what he thought was the perfect anniversary present. He also got her two dozen of her favorite flowers. They were her favorite because she had created the plant species the year that she and Rick met, and the plants grew in only one place on Bacchus 12.

He put his briefcase down next to the stairs and carried his gifts into the dining room. He saw that the table was set for two. He put the gifts down by Beth's side of the table and went in search of his wife.

He found her in the kitchen, putting the finishing touches on the meal. "Happy anniversary, Honey," he said, giving her a kiss on the cheek. "It smells wonderful."

"Thank you," she said, smiling. "You remembered! I'm impressed."

"I would have wished you a happy anniversary this morning, but in all the confusion, I forgot."

She kissed him. "You're forgiven. Now go wash up so we can eat."

Rick walked over to the sink. "Where's Cindy?"

"Out with friends. She won't be home until tomorrow afternoon."

"Do I know any of these friends?" he asked, washing his hands.

"I don't think so. She's trying to keep their identities a secret. She doesn't want you to run checks on them or have security details following her while she's trying to have a good time. She says it embarrasses her."

"She'd better not try to ditch her security detail." Rick dried his hands. "It's UEPC regulations for Planetary Administrators and their families to have security escorts at all times. I assume Bret's detail met him at the spaceport."

"No, she didn't ditch her detail. Yes, Bret's detail met him at the spaceport. And don't you dare quote regulations to me on our anniversary when I've been cooking something for you for hours."

"Yes, dear," he said, grinning at her.

"Hey, did Bret call you from the starliner?" Beth asked.

Rick nodded. "Sort of. I got a vid-com message from him telling me that you two talked and he had just transmitted his acceptance to the Educational Service. He must have sent me the message just before the starliner lifted off. I could hear the pre-launch announcement in the background."

"Well, at least he told you himself, even if you couldn't talk to him," Beth said, handing Rick a serving platter.

"I sent him a vid-com message reply and told him how happy and how proud of him I am. I imagine he's seen it by now."

Beth smiled, picked up the other serving platter, and headed for the dining room. Rick followed her, picking up a bottle of wine with his free hand.

Beth squealed with delight when she saw the flowers on the table. She set the platter on the table and immediately put the flowers in a vase filled with water. "Do you mind if I wait until dessert before I open your present?" she asked. "I don't want dinner to get cold."

"That's fine with me," Rick replied.

Dinner was excellent. Rick cleared the dishes while Beth brought dessert to the table. Once Rick sat down again, she opened her gift. Inside the box was a beautiful necklace made of Baris and Equus gemstones. Baris 2 was a water planet, and at the bottom of its oceans, the water pressure helped form the most amazing luminescent blue stones. Equus 6 was primarily an agricultural planet, but it had great deposits of brilliant clear stones that were similar to Earth diamonds.

"Thank you, Honey! It's beautiful!" she said.

Rick got up and came around the table. He took the necklace and put it around her neck, fastening the clasp in the back

15

before nuzzling her shoulder-length brown hair. "I saw it and immediately thought of you."

Beth jumped up and gave him a hug and a kiss. "I can't believe you remembered! We saw one just like it in that little boutique on Trinity 5 when we were there for the Administrators' conference, but I didn't think you were paying attention."

Rick just smiled at her.

"Your gift is upstairs. You can open it when dessert is finished."

They both sat down and ate dessert. Rick finished quickly and started clearing the dishes from the table.

Beth joined him in the kitchen, smiling. "What's so funny?" he asked as he started washing the dishes and putting them away.

"Mr. Planetary Administrator washing his own dishes... What would the people think of their fearless leader?"

"Hopefully they'd remember that the Planetary Administrator isn't their leader – quite the opposite," Rick replied. "He administers the Confederation's planetary services, and he serves the needs of the people of this planet based on specific guidelines established for all planets in the Confederation. And that includes serving the needs of his own family – especially his beautiful, loving wife."

Beth laughed and started putting away the food. "So that means I'm *your* leader, right?"

"Always have been and always will be, Honey. And for the last 23 years, I wouldn't have had it any other way."

Beth gave him a kiss on the cheek, and they went back to cleaning up the kitchen together. Once they were finished, Beth asked, "Why don't we go upstairs to relax for the rest of the evening?"

Rick smiled and followed her to the staircase, picking up his briefcase as he passed it.

"Don't even think about opening that tonight," Beth warned with a grin as they reached their room on the upper floor.

"I'd never do that to you," Rick promised. He put the briefcase on his dresser and walked into the closet to hang up his clothes.

"So where's my present?" he called, wondering why Beth had disappeared.

"It's right here," Beth said from behind him.

He turned, looked at her, and smiled.

"Happy anniversary to me," he whispered as he picked her up and carried her to the bed.

At the Fleet headquarters on Trinity 7, a technician stared at his monitor in confusion. A red warning flashed along the bottom of the screen.

"Proximity Detector AX-4661-3997-RT no longer transmitting. Contact lost."

The technician checked the logs for the proximity detector. The detectors, which were located all around the Confederation to watch for the marauders and raiders who attacked shipping every now and then, were designed to send a burst transmission if any ships were discovered approaching Confederation space. According to the logs, this proximity detector had just started sending its burst transmission when communication was lost.

The technician checked the other proximity detectors in the same area. None of them reported any problems, and none had detected the approach of any ships.

The technician shook his head. He tried to reestablish communications so he could run diagnostics on the detector, but there was no response.

Frustrated, the technician turned in his chair toward the duty officer, "Lieutenant? I have a failed proximity detector in sector A-X."

"Did you try to reestablish communications?"

"Yes, Lieutenant. There's no response."

"Did you check the other proximity detectors in the area?"

"Yes, Lieutenant. They're all working fine."

"Have there been any transmissions from that detector lately?"

"No, Lieutenant. It had just started sending a burst transmission when communications were lost."

The lieutenant stared at the screen for a moment. "Okay. Send a probe, and schedule a maintenance order to repair the detector as soon as possible."

"Yes, Lieutenant. A probe should reach the proximity detector in about seven hours."

"Good. Keep me posted."

"Yes, Lieutenant."

The technician keyed in the command to launch the probe as the lieutenant returned to his desk. When the monitor confirmed the launch of the probe, the technician keyed in a maintenance request for the proximity detector.

Nothing to do now but wait. The technician leaned back in his chair and stared at the warning still flashing at the bottom of his screen.

CHAPTER 3

"Wow, would you look at that!" Bret exclaimed as they approached the Fire Moon Resort on Manis 2.

Bret, along with his Fleet Marine escort and friends Peter and Silas, rode in a long transport along with the other two artists from Bacchus 12. Bret sat next to the window, watching the lush landscape go past as they traveled from the spaceport to the resort. Six large trucks followed the transport, carrying the art of all five Bacchus 12 artists for the exhibition.

The resort loomed in the distance, but even from afar, it seemed gigantic. "How many rooms does that place have?" Bret asked.

"Over two thousand," the driver of the transport replied. "Plus over two hundred and fifty suites and dozens of meeting rooms and exhibition halls. This is the second-largest resort on Manis 2, and it's the most popular conference and exhibition destination in the Confederation."

The driver started going through his well-rehearsed speech on the history of the resort and the Manis 2 recreation planet, but Bret wasn't listening. He was too busy staring at the expertly manicured lawns and the topiaries that all looked like big green creatures.

The transport pulled up to the grand entranceway, and the passengers disembarked. Several uniformed hotel staff members appeared from hidden alcoves to lead the arriving guests through the lobby to the check-in lounge. In less than ten minutes, Bret and his Fleet Marine escort were on board a travel pod taking them from the lobby to the station just down the hall from their suite.

"Have you ever been to a place like this?" Bret asked the Fleet Marine.

"No, sir," Corporal Jim Burgess replied. "I've never been on leave long enough to make the trip here worthwhile."

Bret nodded and unlocked the door. As the son of a Planetary Administrator, his room was a VIP suite. The suite had two bedrooms – one by the door for the Fleet Marine escort, and one at the far end of the suite for Bret. Corporal Burgess entered the suite first, made a quick inspection of each of the rooms, and motioned for Bret to come inside.

"All clear, sir," he said as Bret reached the living room in the center of the suite.

"Thanks, Corporal," Bret said, disappearing into his bedroom to drop off his luggage. Corporal Burgess stowed his bag in his room and returned to the living room to wait for Bret.

Bret reemerged a few minutes later. "I have to go to the exhibition hall to start setting up my display area."

"Very well, sir," the corporal said.

Bret and Corporal Burgess left the suite and walked down the hall to summon another travel pod to take them to Exhibition Hall 14. In spite of the fact that the resort was a single building, Exhibition Hall 14 was over two miles from Bret's room, making the travel pods the easiest way to reach the exhibition hall from the suite.

Less than a minute later, the travel pod arrived. Soon, it was whisking them across the resort to the exhibition halls.

The technician at Fleet headquarters on Trinity 7 watched the probe's telemetry data on his screen. The probe was less than five minutes away from the last known location of Proximity Detector AX-4661-3997-RT, which had stopped transmitting several hours earlier. The technician was anxious to see the data from the probe – especially since five other detectors in two different sectors had also stopped transmitting. Their red warnings flashed along the bottom of his screen.

"How close is the probe now?" the lieutenant asked.

"Three minutes at present speed," the technician replied.

"What about the probes sent to check on the other proximity detectors?" the lieutenant's commanding officer asked.

"They're all at least four hours away from their destinations, Admiral," the technician responded.

Fleet officers filled the Proximity Detector Command Center – all wanting to see what the probe had to report. Losing one proximity detector was rare, but losing six in one day was unprecedented.

"The probe is decelerating," the technician reported. "It will reach Proximity Detector AX-4661-3997-RT in one minute."

The crowd watched the large monitor on the wall, which displayed the same information that was on the technician's screen. The countdown clock in the upper corner flashed the number of seconds remaining before the probe would show them what was going on.

Just as the countdown clock reached 00:00:20, the screen went blank. The vid-feed was lost, and all telemetry data disappeared.

"What happened?" the admiral asked, sounding annoyed.

"I'm not sure, Admiral," the technician answered, busily typing in commands to try to reestablish contact with the probe. After a minute, he said, "I can't raise the probe, Admiral. It's stopped transmitting."

"What does that mean?" the admiral demanded.

"It means that the probe either malfunctioned or was destroyed, Admiral," the technician said. "Either way, I can't restore contact with it."

"What do we do?" the lieutenant asked.

"I say we send a ship to investigate," one of the Fleet captains suggested.

"I think we need to investigate all of the proximity detectors that stopped transmitting," another captain said.

"I agree," the admiral said. "Send out six Heavy Cruisers with full escorts immediately – one Cruiser group to each of the proximity detectors that malfunctioned. I want to know what's going on out there."

"Yes, Admiral," the officers said.

The Fleet officers quickly left the Proximity Detector Command Center to carry out the admiral's orders, leaving only the technician and the lieutenant in the room.

"Do you really think that the probe was destroyed?" the lieutenant asked.

"I'm not sure, Lieutenant, but I don't see how we could lose a proximity detector and a probe in the same place in less than ten hours. I don't have proof, but I think there's something out there that doesn't want us to see it."

"Something… or someone?" the lieutenant asked.

"How late will you be tonight?" Beth asked as Rick finally got out of bed to get ready for work.

"Possibly a little later than usual," he replied, picking up the blanket, comforter, and pillows strewn around the floor and putting them back on the bed. "I have a vid-conference with the other Planetary Administrators this afternoon to review the final budgets. I have no idea how long that will take."

"Sounds like loads of fun," Beth said, getting up to help Rick straighten the bed. "I'll make something that you can heat up for dinner when you get home."

"Thanks, Honey," Rick said, walking into the bathroom to take a shower. "Don't forget to question Cindy about the friends she was with last night. And don't be afraid to question her protective detail if she doesn't give you straight answers."

"Relax," she said, walking into the bathroom to start her bath. "I've got it covered."

"I know you do, Honey," Rick said, getting into the shower.

"I think the painting of the landscape showing the waterfall and the rings and the nebulas in the background should go in the center of the display," Bret said to the exhibit staff assigned to him. "It's the largest piece, and it's the one that best represents Bacchus 12. It's what I want people to remember when they go through my exhibit."

"Yes, sir," the senior staff member said. He pointed to two workmen who picked up the painting and placed it on the center display stand.

"Perfect," Bret said. "Now let's put the two largest sculptures on either side, and then we'll figure out where the rest of the pieces go."

Bret glanced over at the other Bacchus 12 displays. Peter and Silas were busy getting theirs set up on his left, and the two artists he didn't know very well were setting up on his right. Bret had the center position of the Bacchus 12 artists, which was the prime location – reserved for the artist whose work had scored the highest among the judges organizing the exhibition.

He turned back to see one of the workmen almost drop the painting of his sister sitting in a field of flowers. "Be careful with that!" he said, walking up to the workman. "My sister will kill me if this one gets damaged."

"Is there any word from the ships sent to investigate the proximity detectors?" the technician asked.

"Not that I've heard," the lieutenant replied. "Let me check on that."

The lieutenant walked over to his console and picked up his com-dev. A moment later, he said, "Fleet Command Center? This is the Proximity Detector Command Center. Is there an update on the ships sent out to investigate the six proximity detectors that stopped transmitting?"

The lieutenant listened for a moment. "You'll let us have real-time access?" he asked.

He keyed several commands into his console and a new image appeared on the large monitor on the wall. "I have the display on my monitor. Thank you."

He put down the com-dev and turned to the technician. "They're allowing us to watch the communications between Fleet Command and the Heavy Cruiser Groups."

The technician and the lieutenant watched the section of the monitor that displayed data from the Heavy Cruiser approaching the last known location of Proximity Detector AX-4661-3997-RT and the probe. The Heavy Cruiser had an escort of six smaller Cruisers. Two of the escort Cruisers were visible just ahead of the Heavy Cruiser.

The technician watched the monitor intently, looking for some sign of the missing proximity detector or probe. Suddenly, the escort Cruiser on the left of the Heavy Cruiser exploded.

"What was that?!" the lieutenant asked, startled.

"I don't know, Lieutenant. It looked like…"

Before the technician could finish his sentence, the escort Cruiser on the right exploded. Unknown objects streaked past the front of the Heavy Cruiser, but the technician couldn't identify them. A moment later, the Heavy Cruiser shuddered and the image from its front monitor began gyrating. As the image spun around, the technician saw that the Heavy Cruiser had broken into two pieces. The front half was spinning out of control, and the back half was burning as the fuel cells ignited. The images from the Heavy Cruiser vanished, leaving only static.

"Could you see if any of the ships survived?" the lieutenant asked in a hoarse whisper.

"No, sir. It looks like they were all destroyed."

The lieutenant stared at the technician with a shocked look on his face.

Alarms sounded throughout the building. The illuminated panels around each of the doors changed from the standard blue to red. "Red Alert! Repeat, Red Alert! All Fleet personnel to battle stations. This is not a drill!"

"I think that the pieces are where they should be," Bret said to the senior staff member and the workmen assigned to him. "Thank you all for your assistance."

Peter, Silas, and the two other artists from Bacchus 12 had just finished walking through Bret's exhibit, and he saw from their faces that they were excited about his display.

Bret was about to say something to the other artists when a strange noise distracted him. He turned toward Corporal Burgess and saw the Fleet Marine looking at the readout on the Fleet-issued net-dev that he carried.

Suddenly, the corporal drew his sidearm. "Come with me," he said sternly, putting away the portable device and grabbing a startled Bret by the arm.

"What's going on?" Bret demanded. He had been through the required training that every member of a Planetary Administrator's family goes through, but he had never seen one of his escorts execute the protocol that meant there was imminent danger.

"I need to get you to a safe location," the corporal said, moving quickly across the exhibition hall floor.

Bret had to run to keep up with the Fleet Marine. He glanced back at the other artists and workmen. They all had surprised and shocked looks on their faces.

They reached the service entrance to the exhibition hall, and Corporal Burgess pushed past the security guard who stood at the doors to keep unauthorized personnel from exiting that way. Before the guard could protest, Bret and Corporal Burgess were through the doors and heading down one of the service corridors that went underground.

Bret was about to ask the corporal where they were going when he heard an alarm going off. Alarm bells in every corridor began ringing.

"What's going on? Where are we going?" Bret asked as the floor began to shake and loud booming noises echoed through the corridors. Debris started falling from the ceilings, and dust filled the air all around them.

Corporal Burgess said nothing and kept moving forward, going deeper into the subterranean part of the resort.

"Excuse me, sir," Natalia said as she stuck her head into Rick's office. "The vid-conference with Trinity 5 begins in a few minutes. Do you want me in here?"

"Yes, Natalia, thank you," Rick replied. "Could you access the secure link for me? I need to check on a couple of the numbers one more time before the meeting."

"Yes, sir," Natalia said. She walked over to the vid control console and keyed in the Bacchus 12 access code. The vid system allowed the Planetary Administrators to talk with each other at the same time without having to travel to one of the Confederation Planets to meet in person. The annual budget conference was one of the regularly scheduled vid-conferences and was the final chance for the Planetary Administrators to look at the entire Confederation budget before it went to the Confederation Council for approval.

"I can't access the vid-conference," Natalia said a minute later.

"Do we have an outdated access code?" Rick asked, putting down his papers and walking over to the vid control console.

"No, sir. It's the access code they sent us last week when they forwarded the meeting agenda."

Natalia entered the access code again. The screen on the console repeated the same message as before. "Vid Link Cannot Be Established At This Time."

"'Cannot be established'?" Rick asked. "Sounds like the problem is on Trinity 5, not here."

Rick walked over to his com-dev and entered a number. "Jen, can you come in here please?"

A minute later, Jen Peterson, Rick's Communications Specialist, walked into the office. "You needed to see me, sir?" she asked.

"Yes, Jen. We're trying to access a vid-conference with Trinity 5, but the console says the link can't be established at this time. Are any of the other com-channels with Trinity 5 open?"

"Let me check, sir," she said, opening her notebook and keying a command into the keypad.

She stared at her screen with a puzzled look on her face. She entered another command. Her puzzled look turned to a look of frustration as she sat down and began keying several commands into the keypad.

"I can't reach Trinity 5 on any of the normal channels, sir," she said finally.

"None of them? That's strange, isn't it?"

"Yes, sir. It's never happened as far as I know."

"Could it be solar flares from Trinity?" Natalia asked.

Jen shook her head. "There haven't been any reports of solar flares strong enough to knock out communications anywhere in the Confederation."

"What about Darius 13? It's the closest planet to us. Try them."

"Yes, sir." Jen entered several commands on her keypad. "Nothing, sir. I can't raise Darius 13 or Darius 8. Do you want me to try to raise your son, Bret, on Manis 2?"

Rick was confused. *Why can't we raise the Trinity or the Darius system? And why did Jen suggest contacting Bret?* "Try every planet in the Confederation," he said aloud. Turning to Natalia, he said, "Get me Colonel Monroe with the Fleet Marines."

"Yes, sir."

26

Colonel Paul Monroe commanded the Fleet Marine detachment on Bacchus 12 and served as Rick's military advisor. Natalia dialed his number, and he answered immediately. "Colonel Monroe here."

"Colonel Monroe, please hold for Administrator Douglas," Natalia said before handing the com-dev to Rick.

"Colonel, this is Rick Douglas," Rick said into the com-dev.

"What can I do for you, Administrator Douglas?" Monroe asked.

"We've lost the vid-com link and all other communication channels with Trinity 5, the Darius system, and several other planets in the Confederation. Are you receiving Fleet communications?"

"Let me check on that. Can you hold for a minute?"

"Yes, Colonel."

Colonel Monroe pressed the hold button on his com-dev and walked out of his office into the Fleet Marines Operations Center, the military headquarters for personnel assigned to Bacchus 12. The room was usually fairly quiet with each staff member performing an important, yet routine function.

Not today.

The room was chaotic. All of the personnel were either on their com-devs, running from console to console and shouting at each other, or staring at the monitors around the room with shocked looks on their faces.

Sergeant Major Thomas Kirkland saw Colonel Monroe and rushed over to his commanding officer. "Colonel, I was just about to get you."

"What's going on, Sergeant Major?" the colonel demanded.

"We're not certain, Colonel. The Fleet just went on full alert. All interplanetary communications are down throughout the Confederation, and the Fleet communications channels are jammed with reports of ships and planets under attack. I can't get any facts yet. There's too much happening at the same time to understand the full scope of the situation."

"Do you know how many planets are under attack?"

27

"No sir, but reports are coming in from the other seven star systems. So far, the ships in orbit around Bacchus 12 haven't reported anything."

Colonel Monroe looked at the sergeant major for a moment. He glanced up at the star chart projection of the Confederation slowly rotating over the center of the room. *For years, we didn't know that there was a planetary system here. The nebulas hid Bacchus and its fourteen planets until one of our ships accidently stumbled across it. If we didn't know that there was anything here besides the remnants of two exploded stars, maybe whoever is attacking doesn't know that we're here either.*

He made a decision. "We're going dark. Immediately. Stop sending transmissions of any kind except to the ships already within the Bacchus system. Continue monitoring transmissions from the other systems and Fleet Headquarters, but do not send any signals that could alert someone that we're here. If we're not being attacked yet, it may be because no one knows that we exist."

"Yes, sir. What about civilian communications?"

"I'll handle that. You just stop any of our people from sending transmissions. Also, alert the ships in the Bacchus system as to what we're doing, and order them to stop all transmissions outside the Bacchus system as well. And order all ground troops to deploy immediately. This is a Code Black situation."

"Yes, sir!"

Colonel Monroe pressed a key on his com-dev. "Administrator Douglas, I need you to stop any attempts at interplanetary communications immediately."

"Why? What's happening, Colonel?" Rick asked.

"The Confederation appears to be under attack. I don't know by whom. We have reports coming in from every other star system, but it's very confused, and we can't get a clear idea of what's going on out there. It's possible that no one knows we're here; no one has attacked us yet. I've ordered all interplanetary communications stopped – we're in communications with the Fleet ships in the Bacchus system, but no one else."

"Colonel, you know I don't have the authority to shut down all interplanetary communications."

"Administrator Douglas, *I* have the authority," Colonel Monroe stated, sounding exasperated.

Rick thought about this for a minute. The Confederation Charter clearly stated the limits of a Planetary Administrator's authority. Even in a time of emergency, the Planetary Administrator had almost no authority to define or implement any policy not handed down by the Confederation Council.

But what happens if the Confederation Council no longer exists? Do planetary decisions fall on me or the military? I guess for now they lie with the military.

"Very well then, on your authority I'll shut down all interplanetary communications," Rick said, feeling overwhelmed by the implications. "What do we need to do next, Colonel?"

"I'm ordering the planet to go dark," Monroe replied. "You can receive messages, but don't attempt any transmissions until further notice. We're now in a Code Black situation."

"Code Black?" Rick asked, his face ashen from the information he just received.

"Yes, Code Black. I've already ordered the Fleet Marine detachment on Bacchus 12 to be deployed immediately. That's going to alert the civilian population that something's up. Let me try to figure out what's going on. I suggest we meet later this evening – say… two hours from now. I also recommend convening the Planetary Council. After that, we can decide what we're going to tell people."

You know I don't have the authority to summon the Planetary Council either. But you do. "Very well, Colonel," Rick agreed. "Two hours in my office."

Rick was about to end the call when he thought of something. "What about the navigation beacons?"

"Shut them down, too," Colonel Monroe ordered. The navigation beacons marked the two safe passages through the outer rim of the star system so Fleet and civilian ships wouldn't collide with debris from the nebulas while traveling to Bacchus' planets.

Rick slowly put down his com-dev. Natalia and Jen were staring at him with questioning looks.

"We're in a Code Black situation. The Confederation is under attack. Colonel Monroe is ordering the planet to go dark. We're to stop making any attempts to send interplanetary communications, and the navigation beacons are to be shut down immediately. The colonel thinks it's possible that whoever is attacking doesn't know we're here, so we need to make sure we don't do anything to change that."

Turning to Jen, he said, "Jen, I want you to deal with the navigation beacons and communications channels. All of the interplanetary communications are to be shut down except for this building and the Fleet Marines Operations Center. I want you and your staff to monitor any signal you can receive and start piecing together what's going on."

"Yes, sir," Jen said, shocked.

"Natalia, we need to convene the Planetary Council in three hours. Can you alert the Council Secretary? I want Enrique and Karl up here in ten minutes, and I want Allan O'Connor, the director of the Advanced Weapons Division, and one of his senior engineers here within the hour."

"You want me to summon Director O'Connor?" Natalia asked, sounding surprised.

"Yes."

"Yes, sir."

Jen and Natalia left Rick's office. Rick picked up his com-dev and called Beth.

"Hi, Honey," he said when she answered the phone.

"Did your vid-conference let out early?" she asked

"No, it never happened. Look, I need you to grab our go-bags from the downstairs storeroom. You and Cindy are to come here to the administration complex. Make sure your driver and escorts are with you."

"Why?"

"No questions, Honey. Just trust me. And do it quickly."

"Rick, you're scaring me."

"You should be scared, Beth. We all should. Just get here as soon as you can. I'll explain it all as soon as I can."

"Rick, is this a Code Red?"

"No. It's a Code Black."

"A Code Black?" Beth gasped. The tome of her voice told Rick that she understood the urgency. "All right. We'll be there as soon as possible."

Rick put down the com-dev. *A Code Black. The one situation listed in the Confederation procedures manual that I never thought I'd see implemented. I knew that Code Reds might happen if there were a planetary disaster, but none of the Planetary Administrators believed a Confederation-wide disaster would ever really happen.*

Does Beth understand what's happening? I couldn't go into details over the com-dev. I hope she remembers what a Code Black is. I hope she remembers reading about it in the procedures manual when I became Planetary Administrator. I hope she understood what I was telling her – that the entire Confederation is in jeopardy.

Because it is.

CHAPTER 4

Cindy complained throughout the entire ride to the administrative complex. "Mom, I don't want to go to Daddy's office. I'm supposed to get together with my friends tonight," she said for the fifth time as they drove into the city. "This is so unfair! I already promised everyone that I'd be there. They're expecting me. I can't back out now. Just let me meet them for a few hours, OK? I'll have my escort bring me straight to Daddy's office after that. Can I go? God, Mom, why are you being so mean? Why can't I meet with my friends tonight?"

Beth tried to ignore her. *How can anyone whine so much? There's no way I was so self-centered when I was her age.*

Two Fleet Marine escorts sat in the passenger compartment of their transport vehicle, while a third Fleet Marine sat with the driver in the front compartment. All of the Fleet Marines were dressed in full tactical gear and carried weapons that Beth had never seen before.

"This is just another way you and Daddy are trying to control who I spend time with, isn't it?" Cindy demanded. "You don't want me to go out and have fun with people my age. Well, you don't understand what it's like to be the daughter of a planetary official, do you? I have expectations placed on me, too, you know. My friends depend on me the same way people depend on Daddy. It's not fair to them when I have to cancel plans with no explanation. What do I tell them when they ask me where I was? How do I apologize for something that's not even my fault? Why can't I go out tonight?"

Beth reached her limit. "Oh for the love of God, SHUT UP!" she snapped at her daughter. "Stop thinking of yourself so much. This has nothing to do with you."

"Then what is it?" Cindy asked, sounding hurt from the way Beth spoke to her.

"It's a Code Black."

"What the hell is a 'Code Black'?"

Looking at the Fleet Marines in the seat in front of them, Beth asked, "Would you like to answer that, Corporal?"

"Yes, ma'am," the corporal replied. "A Code Black is a Confederation-wide emergency. It means the Confederation itself is threatened – in this case by an unknown force that has attacked the other seven star systems."

"Yeah, right," Cindy said sarcastically.

"I'm completely serious, ma'am," he stated firmly.

Cindy stared out the window. Squads of Fleet Marines dressed in tactical gear were deploying near key locations as they drove toward the administration complex. She reached into her pocket and took out her com-dev.

"What are you doing?" Beth asked.

"I've got to tell Lisa and Tammy about this," Cindy said.

The corporal reached forward and grabbed the com-dev out of Cindy's hand.

"Hey…" Cindy protested.

"Sorry, ma'am," the corporal said. "Emergency protocols are in place. That means no personal communications of any kind."

Cindy glared at her mother, enraged. Beth just shook her head, but said nothing. Cindy crossed her arms and snapped her head away. "This is *so* not fair," she mumbled as she looked out the window.

"It's not supposed to be," Beth said quietly.

They arrived at the administrative complex, and the Fleet Marines on duty waved them through the security checkpoint and directed them to the ramp that led to the underground entrance. The Fleet Marines took Cindy and the go-bags to the living quarters in the shelters underneath the main administrative building. Beth was escorted to Rick's office.

Beth had been to Rick's office many times and always found it neat as a pin. Even with a Confederation-wide emergency, she wasn't prepared for what she saw when she walked in. Rick, Enrique, and Karl sat around Rick's desk, while Natalia, Jen, and several other technicians and planetary officials sat around the conference table with com-devs in one hand and net-devs in the other. It seemed more like a crisis center than the office of a Planetary Administrator.

"Beth, thank God you're here," Rick said when he saw her enter his office. He got up and hugged her. "Where's Cindy?"

"She's down in the emergency quarters," Beth replied.

Rick looked at her face and guessed how Cindy had reacted. "She's not very happy is she?"

"She'll get over it. So why did you want me up here?"

"I need your strength right now," he said softly. "Plus, I have an idea that you might be able to help me with, and I need someone with your background to help me figure out what to do."

Beth nodded and took a seat next to Karl.

"Notifications have gone out to all planetary services staff members," Karl began, "and orders have gone out recalling key personnel to work. Emergency protocols are being dusted off and put into effect. All services are functioning properly for now, but that won't last."

"Why not?" Enrique asked. "If we're not attacked, there's no reason why planetary services should break down."

"Yes there is," Karl replied. "We don't produce food on this planet, remember? In fact, apart from our own energy, we don't produce much of anything that'll help sustain our population for long."

Standing up, Karl pointed to the map of the star system cluster that comprised the Confederation. "The Confederation was settled so that each planet served a specific purpose, because none of the planets had everything that Earth had before the cataclysm. All of our meat comes from Equus 4, Manis 5, and Baris 8, except for the fish and sea proteins from Baris 2. Vegetables, fruits, and grains are grown on Trinity 6, Felis 2, Canis 4, and Piris 3. Felis 5 and Darius 13 provide our timber and fabrics. All of the ores we use for construction materials, and all equipment and spare parts come from Felis 3, Piris 6, and Darius 8, not to mention the Fleet shipyards on Trinity 7. Trinity 5, Equus 6, Felis 8, Canis 7, Manis 2 and 6, and Piris 9 are all government, small fabrication, and residential planets that provide most of the goods and services not provided by the Planetary Services Administrations. And that leaves us here on Bacchus 12. All we produce on this planet is Olympium and advanced weapons systems."

Rick saw the fatal flaw in the way the Confederation had been organized. *Unbelievable! In the two hundred years the Confederation has existed, no one ever thought to make sure that each planet could stand on its own in an emergency?* "All of the planet's energy is generated by hydro and solar power, and the Olympium refineries can provide plenty of fuel for space travel," Rick noted. "How long before we run out of food?"

"The routine shipments arrived yesterday, so we have enough food for about three weeks, assuming we don't add to the population."

"Why would we do that?" Enrique asked.

"What are we going to do about survivors throughout the Confederation?" Karl asked. "Ships could have survived the attack. People on the other planets could have survived the attack. They could be stranded out there. What are we going to do with them?"

"Are you saying that we should evacuate them and bring them here?" Rick asked.

"No, I'm saying we *can't* evacuate them and bring them here," Karl corrected him. "We can't support any increases in our population until we can arrange for more food shipments. Besides, we don't know if we're going to be staying here or not."

"What do you mean?" Enrique asked. "Abandon Bacchus 12? Where would we go?"

"I'm just saying that it's a possibility," Karl replied. "Before we start bringing people here, we need to decide if we're staying here, and we need more food."

"And what if there are no more food shipments?" Rick asked. "What do we do then?"

No one said a word.

Beth cleared her throat. Rick looked at her. "Yes, Beth?"

"I had a thought, but we can talk about it later..." Beth said, looking uncomfortable at having interrupted the conversation.

"No, it's OK. If you have an idea, let's hear it."

"Well, Karl is right up to a point. The original twenty-one planets of the Confederation didn't have everything that Earth had before we abandoned it. But then Bacchus 12 was discovered. It has almost everything that Earth had. There are entire continents on this planet that are perfect for farming and raising cattle, and they're largely uninhabited. Our water supply is able to support a population twenty times our current size. If we can get our hands on seeds and flocks, we can start a self-sustaining agricultural system on this planet that will make us self-sufficient within a season."

"Are you sure?" Enrique asked.

"Positive. That was focus of my research when I got pregnant with Bret. I had already proved it conclusively, and I was getting ready to begin a pilot project on one of the southern continents when I started my extended leave of absence. It should be easy enough to resurrect my research and implement it on a large scale."

"But what do we do for food in the mean time?" Karl asked. "And where do we get seeds and flocks?"

"I think the answer to both questions is the same," Beth said. "We need to send ships to the agricultural planets to get enough food to keep us going until we can start our own food production, and we need to gather as many seeds, transplantable food plants, and flocks as we can carry back here."

"That's crazy!" Karl snapped. He looked at Rick. "I'm sorry, Rick, I know she's your wife, but we can't do that. We don't have the authority to create farms and ranches on this planet; we don't have the ships, and even if we did, we need every ship for the defense of the planet!"

"I know," Rick conceded. "But the Planetary Council might have the authority. Besides, we have to plan for the long-term as well as the short-term. If we put all our focus on defense, won't we all starve to death?"

Turning to Beth, Rick added, "How long will it take to find your old research and create a proposal detailing what it would take to implement a self-sustaining agricultural system?"

"The research is here in the archives, so I should be able to locate it within an hour," Beth replied. "I can have a complete proposal ready in a day or two."

"I need it in two hours for the council meeting."

Beth stared at Rick for a moment. "I can't promise it will be very detailed, but you'll have something before the meeting."

"Thank you," Rick said with a tired smile.

Beth nodded and left the office along with one of the staff members that Rick asked to go with her and help create the proposal.

"I'm pretty sure the Planetary Council doesn't have that authority, Rick," Karl said after the office door closed. "Only the Confederation Council can re-task a planet's purpose."

"And what if there is no more Confederation Council?" Rick asked. "Who has the authority then?"

Beth walked down the hallway that led to the elevators. The archives were four floors down, and Beth didn't feel like taking the stairs.

When she reached the elevators, the doors of the closest car opened. Allan O'Connor got off the elevator with another man. She shuddered slightly as he walked toward her. *Every time I see that man, it's like watching a snake moving through tall grass.*

As the Director of the Advanced Weapons Division, O'Connor was the principal employer on the planet. As the wife of the Planetary Administrator, Beth had met him socially many times.

"Director O'Connor, how are you?" Beth asked with a smile that belied how she felt about that man.

"As well as can be expected under the circumstances, Mrs. Douglas," he answered smoothly. "This is George Buchannan, my senior engineer. George, this is Beth Douglas, the wife of the Planetary Administrator."

"I'm pleased to meet you," George said.

"Likewise," Beth answered, introducing the staff member to the two men. Turning to O'Connor, she said, "I assume you're here to see Rick?"

O'Connor nodded curtly.

"Then I won't keep you," Beth said, gesturing towards Rick's office.

O'Connor and his senior engineer strode down the hall toward Rick's office. Beth entered the elevator, followed by the staff member, and pushed the button for the floor of the archives. *I've never liked that man.*

"What's this meeting about, Natalia?" O'Connor asked when he reached Rick's outer office.

"I don't know, Director O'Connor," Natalia answered, trying to keep her voice professional. "Administrator Douglas said that he wanted to talk to you and one of your engineers as soon as possible. I assume it's related to the emergency Planetary Council meeting he called."

"*He* called an emergency Planetary Council meeting? He knows better."

Natalia stood up and walked around her desk to Rick's office door. "He's waiting for you, Director O'Connor."

O'Connor sighed and gave Natalia a flash of a smile. "Very well. Let's not keep him waiting."

Natalia nodded. She knocked on Rick's door and felt O'Connor's hand brush against her thigh. Her face felt hot as she blushed, and she turned her head so Buchannan wouldn't notice. *I wish he'd save that for when we're alone.*

Rick heard a knocking on the door. "Come in," he said loudly.

O'Connor and Buchannan walked into the office.

"Thank you for coming," Rick said, getting to his feet.

"Not at all, Administrator Douglas," O'Connor answered coldly. "This is my senior engineer, George Buchannan. We got here as quickly as we could. How bad is it?"

"What have you heard?" Rick asked, motioning the two men to sit down in the chairs that Enrique and Karl had just pulled over to the desk.

"That we're in a Confederation-wide state of emergency."

"We are," Rick admitted. "Colonel Monroe declared the Code Black. He's still trying to figure out what's going on. He said he'd be here in an hour or so to brief us."

"Did you also call an emergency Planetary Council meeting?" O'Connor asked – his piercing eyes staring at Rick.

Rick nodded, noting the rebuke in O'Connor's tone. "At Colonel Monroe's request. As you're well aware, he's the only one with the authority to summon the Council during a crisis."

"So what do you need from me?" O'Connor asked, appearing to relax somewhat and leaning back in his chair.

"I need to know what sort of planetary defenses we have available and how many ships you're currently working on either in space dock or on the planet. The Council will want to know what's available to us if we're attacked."

"I'm afraid that's classified, Administrator Douglas."

Rick expected that answer. "Yes, but under the circumstances, the Council will need to know what defenses are available."

"Then I'll attend the Council meeting and answer any questions that don't violate our security policies."

"Director O'Connor, we're in a state of emergency," Rick said, unable to hide his irritation with the man. "Doesn't that take precedence over your security policies?"

O'Connor looked down his nose at Rick with disdain. "How can you even ask such a question? The Advanced Weapons Division is the most top-secret organization in the Confederation. What we do is classified at the highest level. To reveal what we do and what ships we're working on is a breach of security that can only be authorized by the Confederation Council."

"And if the Confederation Council no longer exists?" Rick asked.

"Then there is no one left to authorize an exception to our security policies."

Arrogant bastard. You know we need the information, but you're hiding behind rules and procedures. I'd like to shove your rules and procedures right up your ass.

"Very well." Rick stood. "I'll see you at the Council meeting."

O'Connor and Buchannan got up and left Rick's office.

"That went well," Karl said sarcastically.

"Just like always," Rick said. "He manages almost 80% of the planet's adult population. He has more power than this office and Colonel Monroe's combined, and he knows it."

Colonel Monroe arrived almost an hour later. He brought two Fleet officers with him: Captain Janet Thompson of the Fleet Cruiser *Montreal* and Captain Patrick Ryan of the Fleet Destroyer *St.*

Petersburg. Their ships were part of the squadron assigned to protect Bacchus 12. Everyone in the office sat in silence as the colonel projected a holographic three-dimensional star chart of the Confederation and gave his report.

"From what we've pieced together, the Confederation was invaded by an unknown alien force. They took out several of our proximity detectors, and when we sent ships to investigate, they destroyed our ships. The Fleet deployed into three battle groups and engaged the enemy in sector A-X near the Canis system, Sector B-D near the Baris system, and Sector A-B near the Trinity system. All three battle groups were wiped out. I'm getting reports of some ships surviving the engagement, but I don't have confirmations at this time."

The location of the three Fleet battles appeared on the holographic projection. "Shortly after the Fleet was destroyed, we started getting reports that Confederation planets were being attacked. They wiped out the shipyards and Fleet headquarters on Trinity 7 first, and the capital on Trinity 5 was leveled. Trinity 6 was hit next. Canis 4 and 7 were attacked at the same time as Baris 2 and 8. From there, the invaders moved to the other star systems. We were getting reports from Equus 4 and 6, and from Felis 2, 3, 5, and 8 before communications were lost."

Rick looked at the holographic projection highlight the Confederation planets that were attacked. His eyes lingered on Manis 2, and he thought about Bret. Finally, he asked the question he had wanted to ask ever since Colonel Monroe arrived. "What do you know about Manis 2?"

"All of the major resorts were levelled," Monroe replied. "I don't have any reports about survivors."

Rick heard a strange sound and glanced over to where Jen and Natalia sat. Jen appeared to be listening intently to Monroe, but Rick noticed her lower lip quivering and tears forming in her eyes. *Why is Jen so upset about the Manis 2 resorts being destroyed? Maybe she's just in shock about the Confederation being attacked.*

Monroe continued. "Just before I left to come here, we received flash reports from Fleet Marine units on Manis 2, as well as Manis 5 and 6, Piris 3, 6, and 9, and Darius 8 and 13. All of the reports tell the same thing."

Please, God, protect and take care of my son. "What did the reports say?" Rick asked.

"The aliens leveled all major metropolitan areas, population centers, industrial complexes, power generators, and planetary defenses, but they left the smaller communities and remote centers alone. Also, no alien ground troops have been deployed yet."

"So this was just a bombardment?" Rick asked. "Why? What's their endgame?"

"It's a classic strategy," Monroe replied. "Knock out the bulk of the defenses and the population in the first wave. That way the ground troops have an easier time doing whatever they came to do."

"And what's that, Colonel?"

Monroe shook his head. "We have no idea, Administrator Douglas. We don't know who they are or what they want. They ignored all attempts to communicate. They just came in, killed over 80 percent of our population, and withdrew."

"Do you think they're coming back?" Rick asked.

"Let me put it to you this way, Administrator Douglas. Why else would they destroy our Fleet and bombard our planets? Either they want our planets or they want something from our planets. Nothing else makes sense."

"Is there any indication that they're coming here?"

Monroe shook his head. "Not yet. The Bacchus system is well-hidden. It's possible they don't know we're here. But if they take one look at our flag, they'll know that they missed something."

"Our flag? What are you talking about?"

Monroe pointed to the flag in the corner of Rick's office. "The flag has 22 stars on it, and the center star has eight points. They only attacked 21 planets in seven star systems. The aliens are eventually going to figure out that a star and a planet were missed."

CHAPTER 5

It was so dark when Bret regained consciousness that he wasn't sure he was actually awake. He moved his arms and legs slowly – not sure if they were still working or if any parts of the ceiling were on top of him. His mouth was dry and had a chalky taste in it. He cautiously sat up and felt something on his face. Reaching for his cheek in the darkness, he felt dust residue from the ceiling. He carefully brushed the dust off his face and clothes.

"Corporal Burgess?" he whispered hoarsely. "Are you there?"

"I'm here, sir," a reply came from the dark.

"Are you all right? Can you move?"

"I'm fine, sir. Just a couple of scrapes. Nothing serious. You?"

"I have a headache and dust in my mouth, but nothing else. What happened?"

"Part of the ceiling collapsed," the corporal replied.

"I *know* that. I mean what happened up above us?"

Bret heard the corporal stirring. "The planet was attacked. My net-dev's tied to the planetary Fleet Marine net. I got the alert just as the attack started."

"Who attacked the planet?" Bret asked.

"No idea, sir. I barely had enough time to check the emergency evacuation procedures and get you out of the exhibition hall. We're too far underground to link to the net, so I don't know what's going on topside."

"Why did you lead us down this corridor?" Bret asked, carefully crawling in the direction of Corporal Burgess' voice.

"Because this corridor connects to a power tunnel that comes out near the lake on the far side of the resort. I figured we could escape that way if the resort itself were damaged or destroyed."

Bret bumped his head several times as he crawled. Large chunks of debris littered the floor. *I didn't realize that anything could damage pressed stone like this. The manufacturers claim that their processes for compressing various kinds of stone together into prefabricated shapes will help construct buildings that can withstand anything. I guess they never planned for an attack like this.*

Bret kept crawling toward the sound of the corporal's voice until he felt the Fleet Marine's leg. "There you are," he said, sitting up next to Burgess. "Do you think the resort is all right?"

"No. For the ceiling in this corridor to collapse, the resort must have received more than one direct hit. My guess is that most of it was destroyed."

A blinding light shone in Bret's face, and he quickly covered his eyes. "Sorry about that," Burgess said. "I found my emergency light."

Bret nodded and carefully opened his eyes. The light showed large chunks of pressed stone all over the floor for as far as he could see. Dust covered Burgess, but Bret couldn't see any serious injuries. Looking at himself, he saw that his clothes were ripped, but he wasn't bleeding.

"What do we do now?" Bret asked as Burgess got to his feet.

"Try to find a way out of here," Burgess replied, making his way around the rubble on the floor.

Bret stood and followed the corporal.

The Council Chamber was eerily silent when Colonel Monroe finished his report on the situation throughout the Confederation. Monroe took his seat and nodded to Rick.

Rick stood and walked to the podium. "Ladies and Gentlemen, you now know the details of the crisis facing the Confederation. We seem to be the only planet spared from attack. Planetary services are fully staffed and working properly, but we only have enough food for three weeks. There are sporadic reports

43

of survivors across the Confederation, but we have no way to confirm the information at this time. There is a squadron of fifteen Fleet ships assigned to the protection of Bacchus 12, and these ships constitute the only known defenses of the planet, apart from Colonel Monroe's Fleet Marine detachment."

"What about the Advanced Weapons Division?" one of the Council members asked. "What do they have that can help defend the planet?"

"I asked Director O'Connor that question two hours ago," Rick replied. "He told me that any such information is classified and only the Confederation Council can authorize him to release the information."

The Council Chamber erupted with angry shouts at Director O'Connor, who sat in his chair with an emotionless expression on his face. After a moment, Rick held up his hands. The Council members stopped shouting and took their seats.

"Since we don't know if there even is a Confederation Council at this time," Rick said, glancing at O'Connor, "I see no way to compel the Advanced Weapons Division to share with us the number of ships docked in their facilities or the weapons systems they're currently working on that could provide additional defenses to the planet. We can only hope that Director O'Connor's sense of self-preservation will induce him to come to our aid before the planet is bombarded like the other Confederation planets were."

There were muted chuckles and laughs from the Council members.

"What are we going to do about food?" another Council member asked.

"We've been giving that some thought," Rick answered, gesturing toward Beth. "You all know my wife, Elizabeth Douglas. What you may not know is that she's a Bio-Botany researcher here on Bacchus 12 who discovered several years ago that this planet has everything needed to establish a self-sustaining agricultural system that could provide the food we need long-term. All we lack are the seeds, seedlings, and flocks to get the system started, as well as the agricultural manpower and equipment needed to plant, cultivate, and harvest the crops."

"How does she suggest we obtain what we need, and what do we do for food until then?" the Council member asked.

"She proposes that we send ships to the agricultural planets, bring back as much food as possible to sustain our population, and bring back as many seeds, seedlings, and flocks as the ships will carry, along with any survivors from those planets who know how to work in an agricultural system."

"Do we have any ships that can do that?" the Council member asked.

"I don't know," Rick admitted. "I'm having difficulty getting accurate counts of the military and commercial ships in the Bacchus system at this time – other than the Fleet squadron assigned to the system."

"I think we're forgetting something," another Council member said. "The Planetary Administrator has no authority to create agricultural systems on this planet. Neither does this Council. Only the Confederation Council has the authority to do that."

"Is there still a Confederation Council?" another Council member asked.

The Council Chamber erupted again as the Council members speculated on the idea that the Confederation government no longer existed.

Rick looked at Colonel Monroe. Monroe stood up and joined Rick at the podium.

"Do we know if there still is a Confederation government, Colonel?" Rick asked softly.

Monroe shook his head.

"Can we find out?"

Monroe thought about it for a moment. "We could send a Scout ship to check out the situation on Trinity 5," he whispered.

"How long would it take to get there, scan the planet, and get back here?"

"A day."

"Do you have enough Scout ships to scan the agricultural planets as well? We need to know if any of the food and crops have survived before we even think about sending out ships."

Monroe nodded.

"Good," Rick said. Turning to the Council, he held up his hands. The Council members quieted down and took their seats again. "Colonel Monroe has agreed to send Scout ships to Trinity 5 and to the agricultural planets to investigate the situation. He'll have the reports of the Scout ships tomorrow. Should the Council recess and reconvene tomorrow at this time to hear those reports? I think we need more information before making any decisions."

The Council members agreed, and the meeting recessed until the next night. The Council members filed out of the chamber. Rick and Colonel Monroe headed back to Rick's office, followed by Karl, Enrique, and Director O'Connor.

"I don't appreciate the way you made me look like the bad guy in front of the Council, Administrator Douglas," O'Connor said angrily when they reached the elevators. "I'm only doing my job."

Rick stepped into the waiting elevator without saying a word. Once Colonel Monroe, Karl, and Enrique had stepped in, Rick faced O'Connor and held up his hand to keep the director from entering the elevator.

"Bullshit!" Rick snapped at O'Connor. "You're not doing your job, you're hiding behind it. Wake up, Director O'Connor! Over three quarters of the entire human race was just wiped out by an unknown attacker. What are you going to do when they come for us? Will the epitaph for the human race be that you were just following your damn security policies? If you don't want to look like the bad guy, then stop acting like a machine and start figuring out how to help us protect the people on this planet!"

O'Connor didn't respond. He just stood there staring at Rick with his mouth open as the elevator doors closed.

"Nicely handled, Rick," Karl said softly as the elevator started moving.

Captain Octavio Garcia, Commander of the Fleet Scout Ship *Galileo*, felt a surge of adrenalin as his ship reached the Trinity star system. In the five hours since he received his orders to investigate the situation on Trinity 5 and Trinity 7, his crew had been unable to use their scanners for fear of alerting the enemy of their presence. As a result, they entered the Trinity system without any idea of what waited for them. They were flying blind.

"Approaching Trinity 7, Captain," the helmsman stated.

"Wait until the space docks are in view before activating the scanners," Garcia ordered.

"Yes, Captain."

The Scout ship entered the planet's orbit close to the atmosphere. They reached the space docks a couple of minutes later, and Garcia and his crew looked in horror at the sight in front of them.

"What could have done that?" Garcia's executive officer asked softly as the space docks appeared on the forward monitor.

The space docks of Trinity 7 were usually a magnificent sight. Its lattice of docking bays and facilities could accommodate up to thirty Fleet ships at any time. The docks provided space for anything from simple maintenance and repairs to major upgrades and propulsion system overhauls. The space dock orbiting Trinity 7 handled everything but weapon system upgrades. Those upgrades were handled by the Advanced Weapons Division on Bacchus 12.

The space dock was now just mangled and twisted bits of metal. Mixed with the debris of the space dock were the broken and shattered hulks of several Fleet ships. Parts of the dock were falling out of orbit, leaving bright trails of molten metal as the parts superheated when they entered the atmosphere.

"Scan for survivors," Garcia ordered.

"No signs of life anywhere in the wreckage, Captain."

"Try to raise Fleet headquarters."

"Yes, Captain."

The communications technician tried to contact the Fleet Operations Center, but there was no response. He tried short-range communications on all Fleet and Fleet Marine channels. There was nothing but static.

"No response on any Fleet channels, Captain."

"Any signs of life on the planet at all?" Garcia asked.

"Hard to tell, Captain," the scanner technician responded. "The cities were all demolished, but I can't tell if any of the smaller communities could have survivors."

Garcia nodded. "Launch two orbital probes to scan for life on the surface and relay the information back to Bacchus 12." Turning to the helmsman, he said, "Set course for Trinity 5."

"Admiral, we're picking up something!" The scanner technician on board the Fleet Heavy Carrier *Yorktown* adjusted the controls on his console to make the image clearer.

Admiral Harold Longstreet, senior officer on board the *Yorktown*, looked up. "What is it?"

"It appears to be a Scout-class ship, Admiral," the scanner technician responded.

"One of ours or one of theirs?" Longstreet asked.

"I can't tell yet, Admiral."

Longstreet hit a button on his console. "Beta Squadron to alert stations. Prepare to launch!"

Longstreet looked at the squadron status monitor to his right. The *Yorktown*, one of the largest and most powerful ships in the Fleet, was home to eight fighter squadrons and could carry as many as 250 short- and medium-range fighters and bombers. Alpha Squadron was busy flying a defensive formation around the *Yorktown* and the *Waterloo*, one of the Fleet's last surviving dreadnaught-class Battleships. Beta Squadron would handle the Scout ship if it turned out to be one of the enemy's.

The monitor showed that Beta Squadron was ready to launch when the technician said, "Admiral, it's one of ours!"

"Contact that ship, and find out where the hell it came from," Longstreet ordered.

"Yes, Admiral."

"Captain, there's a signal coming in," the communications technician on board the *Galileo* exclaimed.

Garcia looked at the technician. "From where?"

"It's coming from behind Trinity 5's fourth moon. It's a Confederation Fleet signal, Captain."

"Hail them."

"Yes, Captain."

"Admiral, the Scout ship's hailing us."

"Put it on the speaker."

"Yes, Admiral." The technician hit a button.

"This is Confederation Scout Ship *Galileo* to unidentified ship above Trinity 5. Please respond and identify yourself."

The communications technician looked at the admiral.

"Respond to their hail," the admiral ordered.

"Scout Ship *Galileo*, this is the Confederation Carrier *Yorktown*," the technician transmitted. "Switch to visual communications."

A moment later, Captain Garcia appeared on the communications monitor. "*Yorktown*, it's good to see you. How did you survive the attack?"

"Good to see you, too, *Galileo*," the admiral replied. "This is Admiral Longstreet. We were on patrol along the perimeter of Confederation space when the Fleet went on alert. We were ordered to stay in our patrol sector in case the Fleet needed somewhere to regroup. Those were the last orders we received. When we couldn't raise the Fleet, we came here looking for answers. Who are you and what are you doing here?"

"This is Captain Garcia, Admiral. We're assessing the situation here in the Trinity system."

"The situation?" the admiral asked sarcastically. "Here's the situation, Captain. The Confederation got its ass handed to it by an unknown force. The Fleet's wiped out, the civilian population on all three planets is dead, and we have no idea who or where the enemy is. Who ordered you to assess *the situation* in the Trinity system?"

"The Planetary Council and the Fleet Marine commander on Bacchus 12, Admiral," Garcia answered.

"Bacchus 12 survived?" Longstreet asked.

"Yes, Admiral. The enemy never reached the Bacchus system. We were sent to see what happened to the Fleet and whether the Confederation Council or any other civilian authority survived the attack."

Longstreet shook his head. "The Council and the President were killed in the first moments of the attack on Trinity 5, Captain. There's no Confederation civilian government left. In fact, there's no longer a Confederation at all. And as near as I can tell, I'm now the ranking Fleet officer."

"Understood, Admiral. That makes Bacchus 12 the only inhabited planet in the Confederation that hasn't been attacked. I'll need to report back immediately. The Planetary Council on

Bacchus 12 will need to establish a new government. Will you be remaining here?"

Longstreet stared at the monitor. "I don't like the idea of abandoning the Trinity system to the enemy, but if Bacchus 12 is the new Confederation capital, then our place is there. We'll follow you back to Bacchus, Captain."

"Very well, Admiral," Garcia said. "Do you know if any other Fleet ships survived?"

The admiral nodded. "We've been in contact with a few. Some ships were never in the fight to begin with. Several ships were damaged and are being repaired. They're keeping hidden so they can relay information about enemy movements back to us. I'll alert the ships that can reach Bacchus to head there at once."

"Order Alpha Squadron to return to base immediately," Longstreet said to his Flight Operations Officer. Turning to the communications technician, Longstreet added, "Send a message to Captain Marshall on the *Waterloo* and the captains of the other Fleet ships that can still travel between star systems. Tell them we're redeploying to the Bacchus system."

CHAPTER 6

Bret and Corporal Burgess crawled out of the power tunnel and looked around. It had taken several hours to reach the tunnel through the debris that littered the corridors underneath the resort, and two hours more to crawl through the tunnel to reach the surface. Parts of the tunnel had nearly collapsed, but Bret and his Fleet Marine escort were finally through.

"Look at that!" Burgess exclaimed.

Bret looked across the lake at what remained of the Fire Moon Resort. The second largest hotel on the planet was now a smoldering pile of twisted metal and debris.

"Could anyone still be alive inside there?" Bret asked.

"I don't know," Burgess replied. "Right now, we need to find food and water. I doubt we can drink the water from the lake, and I have only enough emergency rations on me to last us through today. Under the circumstances, I think our best bet is to see if anything can be salvaged from the hotel."

Bret nodded. Survival was the most important thing to worry about at the moment. He followed the corporal down the ridge toward what was left of the resort.

"The Scout ships have reported in, Administrator Douglas," Colonel Monroe said. "They located a Heavy Carrier, a Battleship, and a number of smaller ships from the Fleet, as well as several freighters. The ships that are able to reach us are on their way here to help with the defense of the planet."

Rick nodded. He checked the time. It was two hours before the Planetary Council planned to reconvene. Colonel Monroe,

Karl, Enrique, and Beth sat in Rick's office, making the final preparations for the council meeting.

"What about the Confederation government?" Rick asked.

Colonel Monroe shook his head. "The civilian government no longer exists. It didn't survive the attack. Neither did anyone else living in the Trinity system. The space dock at Trinity 7 was destroyed, as was Fleet headquarters. Admiral Longstreet is the only surviving flag officer in the Fleet. He'll be here in an hour."

"What about the other planets?" Rick asked.

"The Scout ships sent to the agricultural planets reported that the cities are all destroyed, but the crops and flocks away from the cities seem to be unharmed. The weapons used by the aliens weren't nuclear, so there's no radioactive fallout to worry about. And there's no indication that the alien weapons have any residual effect on plant or animal life. All of the Scout ships launched probes to determine which planets have survivors. We should have that data by tomorrow morning."

"So if we had the ships, we could gather food and agricultural supplies to bring back here, right?" Beth asked.

Monroe nodded. "Yes, ma'am. As long as the enemy doesn't return anytime soon, we could do that."

"What about survivors?" Enrique asked. "We can't just leave them out there defenseless. They don't have food, shelter, power, or the other things they need to survive on their own. And if the enemy comes back, there's not enough of a Fleet left to protect them."

"And put them where?" Karl asked. "We have no excess housing for them, and we've already talked about the food situation."

"We're going to start planning for those contingencies," Rick stated flatly, not wanting to rehash the argument. "We have a responsibility to save as many people as we can, but we can't save anyone at the risk of the people already here."

"If we rescue people on the agricultural planets first, we can use them to get the agricultural systems up and running," Beth suggested.

"That's true, but we have to figure out what to do with the other survivors," Rick pointed out.

"We'd better hope there are survivors who understand maintenance, manufacturing, fabrication, and the like," Enrique said. "Even if we can feed the expanded population, we're going to run out of other things quickly if we can't get those other industries duplicated. We need construction equipment, spare parts, building materials, appliances, fabrics, ores, new ships… everything that we used to get from the rest of the Confederation."

"We should talk about a new civilian government," Monroe added. "The Planetary Council will have to be responsible for the entire Confederation since it's the only council that survived the attack. A new president and Cabinet must be appointed to lead the people. During times of crisis, strong leadership is critical to help civilians remain calm and to keep the military focused on the job at hand."

"Shouldn't the military take over leadership of the Confederation under the circumstances?" Rick asked.

The colonel shook his head. "The military will have its hands full just keeping the planet safe. Someone else needs to be responsible for coordinating rescue operations, transforming the planet to be self-sustaining, and making sure that the military remains focused on the needs of the civilian population."

"Why is it important to keep the military focused?" Enrique asked.

"Because the military will want revenge for the attack," Monroe stated. "Senior officers will want to hunt down and teach the attackers a lesson. That would leave Bacchus 12 undefended and potentially lead to the loss of the rest of the Fleet. The military must put all its efforts into protecting Bacchus 12 and any rescue operations that are undertaken. A civilian leader is needed to keep that firmly in the minds of the Fleet officers."

"Who do you think should be the new president?" Rick asked.

"You, of course," Enrique said. Karl and Monroe nodded.

"Hey, wait a minute," Rick objected. "I'm just a Planetary Administrator. I don't make decisions; I implement policy. You're talking about leading the remnants of the entire human race while an enemy's out there trying to destroy us. I've never done anything like that before!"

"No one has, Administrator Douglas," Monroe pointed out. "This is the first serious crisis that the Confederation has ever faced. At least the Earth government had several years to plan for the evacuation. No one has experience leading people in our current situation. And it's not experience we need. It's the competence to organize an effective government to handle all of the things that have to get done, and it's the compassion, wisdom, and judgment to care enough to do the best job possible. That's you."

Everyone in the room nodded in agreement, but Rick looked doubtful. *Lead the Confederation? Take charge of the human race when it's on the verge of extinction? How am I supposed to do that? I can't even get my children to do what I want them to do. How can I get the entire planet to focus on what has to be done to survive? How would I even know where to start?*

Rick's mind filled with thoughts of Bret and Cindy. He hadn't seen much of Cindy since she and Beth came to the Administration complex. He had checked in on her briefly after the Council meeting, but he hadn't seen or spoken with her since. And then there was Bret. *I wonder if he survived the attack on Manis 2. Was his escort notified in time to get him to safety? Will anyone find him when the Manis system is searched for survivors?*

"I appreciate your confidence," Rick said, "but I still don't think I'm the right person for the job. I'm sure the Council will select one of its own to be the president, and I'll be here to help implement whatever the new president needs done."

"Colonel Monroe's right, you know," Beth said later after she followed Rick into the washroom adjacent to his office. "You are the right person to be president."

"How can you say that, Beth?" Rick asked. "You know I've never been in a leadership position like that before. I don't have the first idea what to do!"

"Yes, you do," Beth said gently. "How many times have you talked to me about what you'd do if you could set policy? Look at how many great ideas you've come up with and submitted to the Planetary Council and the Confederation Council that were accepted! You love the people more than any man I've ever met.

Everything you've done throughout your whole career is to make things better for the people who depend on you. You can do this."

Rick shook his head. "I don't know the first thing about the military," he protested. "How can I govern them? What do I tell them?"

"Rick, look at me," Beth said firmly. He obeyed. "Governing is not about one person knowing everything that has to be done. Governing is building coalitions of people who know the individual parts to be done, and persuading them to work together to direct all the parts toward a common goal. The military has its own leadership. The planet has a Planetary Services Administration. The Advanced Weapons Division has its own management. Each of the major parts has key people already in place. Your job will be to work with those key people and get them to move as one."

Rick thought about this. "What about the refugees and your efforts to set up a way to feed the people going forward?"

"You'll appoint a leader over those two initiatives, and you'll work with them just like you'll work with the other key people," Beth replied. "And if you're wondering how you'll know who to pick as the leaders, remember that you have your staff and the Council to help you figure that out. As president, you won't be alone. You'll be at the center of everything, and that's a position you've been in for most of your life."

Rick smiled and gave his wife a kiss. "You've always had faith in me, haven't you?" he asked.

"Of course," she replied. "I *know* you. And I have no doubt that you'll make the best president the Confederation has ever had."

"Thanks, Honey," Rick said. "I doubt I'll be chosen, but it's good to know I have your support."

Checking the time, he added, "We'd better get back to the others before they wonder what we're doing in here."

Beth smiled and followed him back to his office.

Rick sat with Enrique, Karl, Beth, O'Connor, Monroe, and Admiral Longstreet on the dais. The Council Chamber on the first floor of the Planetary Administration complex was filled to capacity. Rick had briefly met with Longstreet for the first time when the Admiral's shuttle landed. Longstreet supported the formation of a new civilian government, but as the ranking military officer in the Confederation, he felt he needed to remain impartial during the Council meeting. At Longstreet's request, Colonel Monroe provided the reports from the Scout ships to the Council.

"There is no surviving civilian government for the Confederation," Monroe concluded. "From my understanding of the Confederation Charter, a new government must be formed before any of the critical decisions can be made regarding what to do about survivors, food production, and the defense of Bacchus 12."

Rick stood and joined Colonel Monroe at the podium. "Are there any questions?"

One of the Council members stood. "Is the military going to assume control over the Confederation during this state of emergency?"

Rick looked back at Admiral Longstreet. "Admiral, do you want to speak to that?"

Longstreet nodded and joined Rick and Monroe at the podium. "No, the military will not assume control of the Confederation. Our responsibility is to defend what's left of the Confederation – specifically, this planet – as well as to support any efforts to rescue survivors on the other Confederation planets. We have no capacity to take on the extra work of planetary administration, refugee assimilation, or setting up agricultural and manufacturing operations to support the population."

Longstreet and Monroe took their seats. "I believe the first order of business is the creation of a new Confederation government," Rick said. "Once that's done, the other issues can be addressed by the proper authority."

Another Council member stood and began distributing a bundle of papers to the other members. "I've been going through the Confederation Charter, just in case," he said, "and with the exception of the clauses that deal with the administration of multiple planets, we should be able to adapt the Charter to our current situation very easily. As we are the only surviving Planetary Council, I move that we elect ourselves as the new Confederation Council and adopt the version of the Confederation Charter that I'm passing out."

"I second the motion," one of the other Council members shouted.

"The motion has been moved and seconded," Rick stated. "Is there any discussion?"

Several Council members stood in support of the motion as the rest of the Council members read the proposed version of the Confederation Charter. After more than an hour of discussion, the Council members voted, and the motion passed unanimously.

"Now the Council needs to elect a president," Rick stated.

One of the younger members of the Council jumped to his feet. "I nominate Director O'Connor. He already manages most of the planet's population, so leading the entire planet should be no problem for him."

Rick glanced at O'Connor and saw a smug grin on the man's face. *So that's what he's been up to since last night. He made sure that several of the Council members would turn to him for leadership if the Confederation government no longer existed. What an ass. I hope the Council nominates other candidates.*

"I don't think we should select a president who understands only the Advanced Weapons Division," one of the female Council members said. "Director O'Connor has managed the division well, but he's no leader. We need someone who will unite and inspire us to action. We need someone who can build cooperation between the military, the Advanced Weapons Division, the rescue operations across the rest of the Confederation, and the efforts to set up agricultural systems and industries here on the planet to support our population. I nominate Administrator Richard Douglas to be our president. I don't think anyone else in the room understands the full scope of what must to be done and how little time we have to get it all done."

Oh, shit!

Several Council members rose in support of Rick's nomination while other Council members shouted their disapproval. Rick glanced at O'Connor and saw the director glaring at the standing Council members. Rick let the conversation go on for several minutes until he felt that no one had anything new to say. "Are there any additional nominations?" he asked, hoping that someone else would be nominated.

No one spoke. *Damn. I guess I need to call for a vote.* "Very well. All those in favor of electing Director O'Connor as president, please stand." A dozen Council members stood.

"Please take your seats. All those in favor of electing Administrator Douglas as president, please stand." Three dozen Council members stood. Rick noticed that O'Connor sat red-faced, glaring at the Council members who had voted against him.

Oh dear God, I don't believe it! Why did they choose me? Is it too late to have the military take over?

The sound of applause filled the Council Chamber and interrupted his thoughts. He looked up to see the entire Council standing in support of his election as president. He smiled weakly, but inwardly he felt like throwing up. Finally, he held up his hands.

"I appreciate the confidence you've shown in me, and I will do my best to serve you and the Confederation during this time of crisis." He hesitated, and the Council members applauded again.

Bishop Canterbury came forward to administer the oath of office. Rick raised his right hand and repeated the bishop's words. "In the presence of every person assembled here, and in full realization of the high calling I assume as President of the United Earth Planets Confederation, I, Richard Douglas, swear that I will be faithful to the Confederation, and will obey, observe, uphold and maintain the Constitution and all other laws of the Confederation; and I solemnly swear that I will always promote all that will advance the Confederation, and oppose all that may harm it; protect and promote the welfare of all Confederation planets and citizens; discharge my duties faithfully to the best of my abilities; do justice to all; and devote myself to the well-being of the Confederation and all of its planets and citizens. This I swear before God."

The Council Chamber erupted into thunderous applause. Bishop Canterbury turned to the Council members, instructed them to stand, and administered the oath of office to the Confederation Council.

Rick mentally went through the list of items to present to the Council. *I know there's no way we can evacuate the planet, but it needs to be the Council's decision if we're going to stay here on Bacchus 12. That needs to be the first item of business to discuss.*

Rick raised his hand to signal the Council members to quiet down and retake their seats.

"We have a critical decision to make before we do anything else," Rick began. "Do we evacuate the planet and find somewhere safe to start over, or do we stay here and defend what we have?"

"How could we transport all of our people off Bacchus 12?" one of the Council members shouted. "Do we have enough ships for that?"

Rick gestured for Admiral Longstreet to join him at the podium. "We have a limited number of warships and civilian transports," Longstreet stated. "The Fleet hasn't had any arkships since the exodus from Earth. It would take a huge number of trips to transport the people from Bacchus 12 to wherever our new home would be, and I doubt we could completely evacuate the planet before the Bacchus system was discovered and attacked."

"Even if we had enough ships, where would we go?" one of the elder Council member asked as Longstreet sat down.

"I have no idea," Rick replied. "Earth had mapped the locations of a few other habitable worlds before we discovered the star systems that make up the Confederation, but those records were in the Archives on Trinity 5, and I think we have to assume that they no longer exist or are inaccessible. And there were no more explorations of deep space once the Confederation was established. The other Confederation planets are obviously out of the question, so unless one of you knows where a habitable planet is located, I'm not sure there's anywhere we *can* go."

"It sounds like the only practical solution is to stay here and defend ourselves the best way we can," the first Council member commented. There were nods of agreement around the Council Chamber.

"Shall we put it to a vote?" Rick asked. "All in favor of staying here and defending our planet, please stand."

There was silence in the room. No one moved. Then one Council member stood. Two more stood. Rick looked from the podium as more of the Council members stood. Soon, they were all standing.

Good. They made the right decision. Rick nodded and motioned for the Council members to sit down. "Very well. We stay here and defend our planet."

The Council members nodded, but several looked concerned with the implications of their vote.

When they were just the Bacchus 12 Planetary Council, they didn't usually make decisions of any importance – those had always been left to the Confederation Council. The Council members would debate for days over the most trivial of issues. The crisis must be forcing them to take their new responsibilities seriously and make important decisions quickly. Rick decided to test his theory and see if he could get them to approve his plans for moving forward.

"In light of your decision," Rick continued, "there are a number of initiatives that must start immediately and require your authorization to proceed. First is authorization to compel the Advanced Weapons Division to reveal all of their classified projects and information to me so Admiral Longstreet and Colonel Monroe will know what's available for the defense of the planet. Second is to re-task some of our continents for agriculture, fabrication, manufacturing, mining, and refugee housing. Third is to begin the evacuation of survivors from the other Confederation planets to Bacchus 12, and to begin transporting food, seeds, seedlings, and flocks for agricultural purposes. Fourth is to send out a broadcast to our population, informing them about what's happened and what's going to be happening in the coming weeks and months. And fifth is to form a new Cabinet to help me manage all the work that has to be done. Do I have your authorization?"

There was a lot of discussion regarding Rick's proposed initiatives. Several of the Council members who supported O'Connor for president tried to create confusion and conflict between the Council and Rick, but eventually the Council members who supported Rick were able to regain control of the meeting. They voted to give Rick all the authority he needed to move forward. Rick promised to keep the Council informed, and he then adjourned the meeting.

Rick left the Council Chamber and retreated to his office before anyone could follow him. He ran into his washroom, shaking, and closed the door. He turned on the faucet and splashed water in his face.

What do I do now? God, please tell me what I do now!

"Rick? Are you in here?" It was Beth's voice.

Rick turned off the water and opened the washroom door. "I'm here," he said.

Beth ran over to him and gave him a hug. "You can do this," she whispered when she felt him trembling. "I know you can do this."

Rick shook his head, feeling overwhelmed. "What if I can't."

"Do it anyway, Mr. President," Beth said firmly. "It's like you've said a hundred times… when you have no choice in the matter, you jump in and do the best you can. Did you mean it, or was that just bullshit?"

"I meant it," Rick said, smiling.

"Then it's time to jump in and do your best, Mr. President."

Rick nodded and gave Beth a kiss. "What would I do without you?" he asked.

Before she could answer, Enrique, Karl, O'Connor, Colonel Monroe, and Admiral Longstreet entered his office with Natalia and Jen.

"What are your orders, Mr. President?" Longstreet asked.

Rick looked at Beth and sighed. *It's too late to make a run for it now.* He took a deep breath, put a determined look on his face, and turned around.

Rick strode across the room to his desk and motioned for everyone to sit down. "Let's get to work. We need a plan for how we're going to save what's left of the Confederation."

CHAPTER 7

Bret and Corporal Burgess carefully made their way through the wreckage of the once-beautiful resort. In addition to the mangled metal-and-pressed-stone structure, the debris included human remains. Bret had to stop several times to throw up as they searched through the rubble for food, water, and other supplies that they could use to stay alive. Bret had never before seen anything so gruesome.

"How can you stand to look at all of this?" he asked the corporal after getting sick for the third time.

"I can't, sir," the corporal replied grimly. "But I have a job to do. Protecting you, finding supplies, and getting us to a place of safety are the only things I can focus on right now. I'll mourn the dead later."

Bret nodded. *That's why I could never be a Fleet Marine.*

Corporal Burgess moved off to the right, but Bret continued forward, trying to remember the layout of the resort. From what he could recall of the resort map he had seen on the wall of the travel tube, Bret guessed that they were close to where the exhibition halls had been. He remembered smelling one of the kitchens nearby when Burgess pulled him into the underground corridors. Keeping Burgess in sight, he climbed over a large chunk of rubble and looked around.

A glint of light on his left caught Bret's attention. He climbed up onto a metal beam and walked along it until he reached a pile of brightly colored shattered glass. "Corporal, come here!" he called.

Burgess made his way over to Bret. "What did you find?"

Bret pointed to the glass. "I think this was that giant light fixture from the exhibition hall. It hung right above my display. I remember thinking that the colors looked like one of my paintings." He pointed to the right. "If it is, then the doors you pulled me through are over there, and I remembered smelling a kitchen just off the first corridor we ran through."

"Let's see if we can find it." Burgess headed for the wreckage of the kitchen.

Bret followed Burgess across the wreckage. "Right behind you."

A copy of the press release naming the new Cabinet members sat on Rick's desk, surrounded by piles of reports, requisitions, and proposals.

OFFICE OF THE PRESIDENT

FOR IMMEDIATE RELEASE
New Confederation Cabinet Formed. Today, President Douglas appointed the following individuals to serve on his Cabinet:

Vice President and Bacchus 12 Planetary Administrator: Enrique Fuentes
   Director, Bacchus 12 Planetary Services: Karl Pitowski
   Director, Refugee Services: Michael Thatcher
   Archbishop, I. E. Church: Nigel Canterbury

Confederation Fleet Commander: Admiral Harold Longstreet
   Fleet Operations: Admiral Fletcher Marshall
   Fleet Marine Commander: General Paul Monroe
   Director, Advanced Weapons Division: Allan O'Connor

Director, Agricultural Systems: Elizabeth Douglas
Director, Manufacturing and Fabrication: Wallace Myerson

Director, Communications: Jennifer Peterson
Assistant to the President: Natalia Komarov

UNITED EARTH PLANETS CONFEDERATION

Rick and his new Cabinet had been meeting for hours. Selecting the members of his new Cabinet was the easy part. Now Rick tried to get the group to work together to plan the steps that needed to be taken immediately. The new Cabinet members quickly identified the tasks that had to be done, but they couldn't agree on the priority of each task.

Rick looked around the room. *They all seem so sure of themselves, but none of them knows what the right thing to do is. In fact, there's no way to know for certain what's right or wrong until we get started and see what happens.*

Rick listened to the Cabinet members' arguments carefully and realized that the group was never going to reach an agreement. *No one in this room is used to actually making decisions. Authority in the Confederation has been so centralized that they only know how to make suggestions and let someone else decide. I guess it falls to me to make the final decisions. If I make the wrong decisions, I could be signing the death warrant of the entire human race. If I make the right decisions, we could still lose a lot of people, but we might just save our species.*

Finally, Rick cleared his throat, and the members of his Cabinet quieted down. "I appreciate your input, and I've made my decision. The work to be done is about ensuring our survival – not just for the people of Bacchus 12, but for the survivors on the other Confederation planets as well."

Gesturing to Beth, he continued. "Our immediate problem is food. The people on this planet will starve in less than three weeks if we don't do something to increase our food supplies. No military response can change that. We must send freighters to the agricultural planets first, or we risk losing the existing population on Bacchus 12, not to mention making it impossible to bring refugees here. Now there are three planets that produce vegetables, fruits, and grains: Felis 2, Canis 4, and Piris 3. We need to go there first and gather any harvested crops that survived the attacks. We also have to gather seeds and seedlings that can be transplanted here, and equipment that can be used to prep the ground and harvest the crops. And we have to find people who know how to work in an agricultural system.

"Next, while the seeds and seedlings are being planted here, we need to go to the three planets that produce meat: Equus

4, Manis 5, and Baris 8. We have to locate any meat that's already been butchered and is still good, and we have to gather herds, meat processing equipment, and people who have experience ranching and butchering.

"Darius 13 and Felis 5 produce mostly fabrics and lumber. We're going to need to go there next if we're going to clothe and house the refugees."

"Do you want military escorts for the freighters going to these planets?" Admiral Longstreet asked.

"Yes, Admiral," Rick replied. "Not the entire Fleet, of course, but escorts to provide protection and extra cargo space for what the freighters can't hold."

"Protection from what?" Karl asked. "Our ships are no match for whoever attacked us, so what good would it do to send warships to escort the freighters?"

"There are other species of intelligent life out there besides the one that attacked us," Admiral Marshall pointed out. "We've encountered a few over the years, not to mention the raiders that have been harassing our shipping for the last decade or so. It's possible that those other species will look at our destruction as an opportunity to pillage what's left of the Confederation. Escorts are necessary to protect against them."

"I agree," Rick said. "Once we have our food problems under control, we can start building temporary shelters for the refugees and sending out the freighters to look for survivors. The Fleet ships that can't make it to Bacchus and the probes left behind by the Scout ships have identified survivors on most of the planets outside the Trinity system. Only Baris 2 and the heavy manufacturing planets of Felis 3 and Piris 6 appear to be devoid of life. However, these planets may have equipment that we can use. We'll send the freighters there last."

"In what order do you want to attempt to rescue survivors on the other planets?" Michael asked.

"In the order of what that planet has that we may need," Rick said. "I don't want to sound cold, but the planets that make spare parts for our ships, appliances for food preparation and storage, tools, and construction equipment have a higher priority than primarily residential or recreation planets."

"So Manis 2 is near the bottom of the list?" Beth asked, her voice shaking slightly.

Rick looked at her and realized that she understood the implication of his comment. "I know our son is there, Beth, but there's more at stake than the needs of our family. Manis 2 may have refugees, but there's little else there of value. It must be ranked near the bottom of the priority list." *God, did I actually just say that aloud to my wife?*

Beth nodded, but Rick saw tears form in the corner of her eyes. Glancing over at Jen, he noticed her trying to hide the fact that she was crying, too. *That's the second time I've seen her cry when mentioning Bret and Manis 2. Is there something going on between Jen and Bret?* Rick pushed that thought out of his head and focused on the work to be done.

"Beth, I want you, Michael, and Wallace to spearhead the efforts to bring what we need from the other Confederation planets back here. I want the three of you to go draw up your operational plans as quickly as possible and present them to me for final approval. We'll coordinate your plans with Enrique, Admiral Marshall, and General Monroe. I want Fleet Marines on those freighters to handle security on the planets and to help with the heavy lifting."

Beth, Michael, and Wallace agreed. They stood up and left Rick's office.

Turning to the people remaining in his office, Rick said, "Now, in addition to the efforts with the other Confederation planets, let's start working on the defense of Bacchus 12. That means we need ships, weapons, and plans."

Looking at Admiral Marshall, Rick added, "Admiral, you mentioned raiders a moment ago. Didn't we deploy some sort of weapon systems along the primary shipping lanes to help deal with them?"

Admiral Marshall nodded. "We set up minefields along the parts of the shipping lanes that are difficult to defend against an ambush."

"What kinds of mines were used?" Rick asked.

"Proximity nuclear mines, Mr. President. Ships must have a Confederation security code when approaching one of the minefields to keep the system from activating. Otherwise, mines will converge on the approaching ship and detonate. It's been an effective deterrent against the raiders for some time."

"So those mines are still out there?"

"Yes, Mr. President."

"Can we recover them and deploy them around the Bacchus system?"

"Yes, Mr. President. That's easy to do, but it will take time and ships."

"And it's not enough to defend us from attack," O'Connor pointed out, sounding much more cooperative than he had in the previous days. Pointing to the holographic chart of the Bacchus system floating nearby, he continued, "The Bacchus system is quite large. We can't put mines just around Bacchus 12. The mines were designed to remain in a fixed point in space until activated. They were never designed to hold position over a planet because of the gravitational forces involved, nor were they designed to move with a planet as it orbits its sun."

O'Connor stood up and walked over to the Bacchus system holograph. "When Bacchus' two adjacent stars exploded millions of years ago, they each created planetary nebulas that now mask Bacchus and its fourteen planets. The planets orbit Bacchus between the two nebulas. Navigation through the nebulas is difficult because of gasses, dust, debris, and the gravitational forces from the remnants of the two exploded stars in the nebula centers. So the best place to put the mines would be around the outer edge of the Bacchus system along the approach between the two nebulas where the navigational beacons are located."

O'Connor pointed to the outer ring of the Bacchus system on the chart. "But there aren't enough mines to blockade the entire approach to Bacchus. We can produce more, but it'll take time. We need other weapons to help defend the approaches into the Bacchus system."

"Is it impossible to approach through the nebulas?" Rick asked.

"No, just difficult," O'Connor replied. "We send ships through the nebulas all the time, but navigation systems don't work well, and it's hard to see where you're going. It's like trying to fly through water. The navigation systems think that you're inside a solid object, so the proximity detectors are useless. Gravitational forces from the star remnants can pull a ship off course easily, and there's debris in the nebulas large enough to destroy a Heavy Carrier if the two collide."

"Would the enemy risk coming through the nebula to get to us?"

"If they wanted to get to us badly enough, then yes, Mr. President, they would risk it."

"What can we do to stop them?"

O'Connor smiled. "Oh, we have a few ideas that might work. If you don't mind, why don't we reconvene at the Advanced Weapons Division offices tomorrow afternoon? My engineers can show you what we have that might help keep the enemy away from Bacchus 12."

O'Connor glanced over to Natalia, who quickly entered a notation about the meeting into her net-dev.

"Where is everybody?" Cindy demanded to the empty room.

Cindy was frustrated. She had been cooped up in the underground quarters for what seemed like days. She hadn't seen anyone in her family in quite a while. Her net-dev had been taken from her, and she had no way to communicate with her friends. Every time she tried to leave the quarters to go outside, the Marine escorts politely but firmly told her that she had to stay inside.

"I feel like a prisoner here!" she shouted at the wall.

She angrily activated the vid-com monitor on the wall. The capital news feed gave information about the local weather and how spectacular the planetary rings would look that night. She checked the other feeds.

No one's talking about any kind of emergency. If this were really a Code Black, wouldn't they be broadcasting emergency procedures or at least showing information about what happened?

Cindy turned off the vid-com monitor and leaned back on the couch. *Why are they keeping people from knowing about what's going on? Is this just a drill?*

The thought that she was stuck underground away from her friends because of a drill made her furious. But she remembered the serious looks on the face of her mother and the Marine escorts when they told her about the Code Black. *No, I don't think this is a drill. Whatever it is, it must be serious enough that the people can't be told yet.*

Cindy thought about Bret. *I wonder if he knows what's going on?* She turned the vid-com monitor back on and accessed the interstellar communications link.

"Contact the Fire Moon Resort on Manis 2 and connect me with Bret Douglas," she said when the interstellar communications link prompt appeared.

"All Interstellar Communications Are Unavailable," appeared on the screen.

Cindy stared at the vid-com monitor for a moment and turned it off. *All interstellar communications are down? That's never happened before.*

Cindy looked around the room, as if the blank walls would provide some clue about what was happening across the Confederation. She thought about her friends. Getting together with them and hanging out was no longer the most important thing to her. For the first time, she wondered if they were safe.

Are any of us safe? What's going on?

Two hours later, Jen dropped off a draft of Rick's first official statement to the people of Bacchus 12 about what was happening across the Confederation. His broadcast announcement was scheduled for the first thing in the morning.

As she turned to leave his office, Rick stopped her. "I couldn't help but notice that you've been getting upset when we talk about Manis 2, Jen. Is everything okay?"

Jen's face began to turn red.

"Is there someone on Manis 2 that you're worried about?" Rick asked.

Jen nodded.

"Is it Bret?"

Jen's face became even redder. She nodded.

"I didn't know that you two were involved."

"We're not, Mr. President. Not exactly. We flirt when he comes here to visit you, and we send messages to each other, but it's never gone beyond that."

"But you wish it would?" Rick asked.

69

Jen looked down and nodded. "He's a great guy, Mr. President. I know he's younger than I am, but great guys like him are few and far between. I hoped that, when he got a little older…"

"I understand, Jen," Rick said gently. "Don't lose hope. If he survived the attack, we'll find him and bring him home."

Jen nodded and left Rick's office. Rick watched her leave and smiled. *I wonder how I missed that Bret and Jen like each other. Does Beth know?*

Feeling exhausted from the day's events, Rick decided to read Jen's draft in his quarters. On his way to the elevators, he stuck his head into the conference room next to his office to see if Beth and the others had finished for the night. They were still working on their detailed plans for the evacuation of the other Confederation planets. He quietly closed the conference room door so he wouldn't disturb them. He took the elevator to the underground complex where he, Beth, and Cindy were staying.

Cindy was still awake when he walked into their quarters. "Hi, Daddy!" she said, jumping up and running to hug him when he walked in.

"Hi, Cindy. What are you still doing up?"

"I haven't heard anything from you or Mom since yesterday, and I was worried."

Rick sat down on the couch and motioned for Cindy to sit next to him. "I'm sorry about that, Cindy. Things have been happening so fast that I haven't been able to stop long enough to make sure you're OK."

"Can you please tell me what's going on? I tried to contact Bret, but the link said that all interstellar communications are down."

Rick looked at her, wondering how much to tell her. He finally decided she should know everything that was happening. He told her about the attack on the other Confederation planets. He talked about the loss of the Fleet and the Confederation government, the food situation, and the plans to rescue the survivors and feed the planet. Once he finished telling Cindy about the crises that had been keeping him busy, he added, "Your mother is now in charge of setting up crops on the planet so we can feed ourselves. I was appointed as the new President of the Confederation, or what's left of the Confederation. I'm broadcasting a message in the morning to tell everyone else what I just told you."

Cindy just stared at her father. "You're the *what*?"

"The president."

Cindy shook her head slowly. "Do we know anything about Bret?" she asked.

Rick put his hand on her shoulder. "No, we don't. We know there are survivors on Manis 2, but we don't know who or how many."

"You're going to send someone to find him, aren't you?"

"At some point, yes. But the first priority is to gather as much food as possible so we don't all starve."

"NO!" Cindy said as the tears started. "You need to send someone for him now!"

"It's not that simple," Rick said softly. "There are other priorities at the moment..."

"But he's my brother!" Cindy snapped.

"And he's my son!" Rick said. "But I can't put the needs of our family ahead of the needs of the people on this planet. We have to have food. If we run out, it doesn't matter if we find Bret or not. Once we know that we have enough food to keep us alive until the crops start growing, then we'll go out and look for survivors on all the rest of the planets."

Cindy began sobbing. Rick tried to comfort her, but she jumped up and ran to her room, slamming the door behind her. Rick stared at the door for several minutes.

How do you explain to a sister that finding her brother isn't the most important thing right now? How do you explain it to a mother about her son? I have to put the needs of the Confederation before my own needs, don't I? Will Cindy ever understand that? Will Beth? Will Bret?

Not knowing what else to do, Rick took Jen's draft out of his briefcase to read through it. But no matter how hard he tried to concentrate, two questions kept running through his mind. *Is Bret still alive? Will I ever see my son again?*

CHAPTER 8

"Over here," Corporal Burgess shouted.

Bret crawled over a large pile of debris and carefully made his way to the Fleet Marine. "What did you find?"

"Your kitchen, I think." Burgess pointed to a section of the rubble partially buried under broken glass and metal. Three large metallic cases that looked like refrigeration units lay on their sides. Nearby, an open flame rose from a pile of debris.

"I think the fire is from a ruptured gas line," Burgess said. "It's probably where the stoves were. If so, then the pantries should be over behind the refrigerators. Hopefully, we'll find something to eat over there."

"I'll check the refrigerators," Bret offered.

"OK. I'll look for the pantry. Listen for the hissing of gas escaping. We don't want to set off any more fires and risk burning up the supplies or ourselves."

"Right," Bret agreed.

Rick woke up and realized that he was still on the couch. The notes for his broadcast lay next to him, alone with a document that Rick didn't recognize. He picked it up and scanned the cover page. It was the draft operational plans from Beth, Michael, and Wallace.

She must have come in and decided not to wake me.

Rick looked at his watch. *Two hours until the broadcast.* He got up and walked to the washroom to make himself presentable for his first appearance to the people of Bacchus 12 as their new Confederation President.

Cindy watched her father's broadcast on the vid monitor. Even though she had already heard most of the information the night before, seeing her father deliver it officially over the com-net made it seem more real – and more frightening.

This is really happening. Dad wasn't lying. The human race was nearly wiped out, and we're the only planet that survived.

Cindy saw her mother when her father introduced each of the new Cabinet members. She always knew that her mother loved her father, but the look on her mother's face was one of complete trust. Cindy had never seen that look before.

Mom believes in him and is helping him. What did I do? I yelled at him and threw a tantrum. He's trying to keep all of us alive, and I acted like a spoiled brat.

Cindy watched her father outline the initiatives that he and his Cabinet were working through. He ended his remarks with a promise to keep everyone on the planet informed. The Great Seal of the Confederation appeared on the screen, and the voice-over began giving a recap of the president's remarks.

Cindy thought about her brother. *If Bret were here, he'd be upstairs looking for ways that he could help. He was always like that. He had his own interests, but he always put the needs of others first.*

Cindy turned off the vid-com monitor. *I've been acting like a brat for a long time, haven't I? I've been living a life where the most important things I had to worry about were what to wear and where my friends and I were going to hang out next. Now the only thing that matters is whether or not we're going to survive.* She looked around the room. *I can't just stay here underground and do nothing. I need to step up like Bret would if he were here.*

She knew what she needed to do. She quickly got dressed and went looking for her mother.

The Fleet Marine escort took his position beside her as soon as she left her quarters. "Good morning, ma'am," the corporal said.

"Good morning, Corporal," Cindy replied.

"Where are you off to?"

"I need to find my mother."

"One moment, please," the corporal said. He pulled out a hand-held net-dev and typed in a few commands. He returned the net-dev to his pocket and gestured toward a nearby bank of elevators. "This way, ma'am."

The elevator stopped on the floor below Rick's office. Cindy had never been on that floor before and was amazed at how busy it seemed. Military and civilian personnel sat wherever there was space. No one took notice of Cindy and her escort.

The corporal led her down a long hallway to a conference room with the words "Situation Room" embossed on the door. The corporal pointed to the door.

"She's in there, ma'am. I'll wait for you out here."

"Thank you, Corporal," she said. Taking a deep breath, she opened the door and stuck her head inside.

Hidden projectors displayed three-dimensional star charts around the room while enlarged images of Confederation planets hovered nearby. There were about two dozen people crammed into the conference room, grouped around the three-dimensional projections. Everyone seemed to be talking and keying into his or her net-devs at the same time.

Cindy looked around and saw Beth talking to a well-dressed middle-aged man near one of the projected charts. Cindy entered the conference room and closed the door behind her. She waited quietly until her mother finished her conversation.

Beth finally noticed Cindy standing by the door and walked over to her. "What are you doing here, Cindy?" she asked.

"I saw you on the broadcast this morning, Mom," Cindy said. "I didn't realize there was so much going on."

"There's a lot happening, and it's a busy time right now. What did you need to see me about?" Beth's voice sounded kind, but Cindy could tell that her mother had a million things on her mind.

"I want to help, Mom," she replied.

"Help with what?"

"Help with setting up an agricultural system on the planet." Before Beth could respond, Cindy continued. "Botany is one of the subjects I tested well in. Even though it's two years before I take my final tests, you know I have the aptitude for bio-sciences. I can't just sit underground, waiting to find out if we're going to survive and spending my days thinking about Bret. I need to be working – doing something worthwhile. I may not have a lot of expertise, but I'm willing to do anything. I want to help. I *know* I can help."

Beth looked at her daughter thoughtfully. "What brought this on?" she asked after a moment.

"I finally realized how childishly I've been acting. I yelled at Dad last night about Bret. He's got the entire Confederation to worry about, and I yelled at him. I watched him on the broadcast this morning, and I knew that I had to step up. I think working with you is the best way I can contribute."

Beth nodded slowly. "OK. We'll give it a try. You're our first volunteer. We're going to need lots of volunteers if we're going to establish an agricultural system in time. Do you know how you want to help?"

Cindy shook her heard. "I'll do anything you need me to do."

"Well, I divided the team into six groups: manage the food supplies, find the best place to plant crops and build the farms, find the best place to graze cattle and get the ranches set up, rescue seeds and seedlings from other planets, rescue flocks from other planets, and gather food from other planets. I don't want you leaving Bacchus 12 to rescue food from the agricultural planets, so which of the other groups do you want to work with?"

"I guess helping to find the best place to plant crops and build the farms," Cindy replied. "Or helping to find the best place to graze cattle and get the ranches set up."

Beth smiled and gave Cindy a quick hug. "Those groups are meeting right across the hall. Come on, I'll introduce you."

They left the Situation Room and walked across the hall to Conference Room L. Cindy's Fleet Marine escort followed them and took up his position outside the conference room door.

"We have a volunteer here to help," Beth said to the people crowded around the two conference tables.

O'Connor sat in the large conference room adjacent to his office on the top floor of the Advanced Weapons Division's central office, located on a sprawling, secured campus east of the capital. Two sides of the conference room were glass, giving the senior engineers gathered in the room an unobstructed view of the Division's campus and Bacchus 12's capital city in the distance.

O'Connor had called the meeting to make sure that everything was ready for the president's visit later in the day.

"So that's the situation," he concluded. "The president and several members of the Cabinet will be here in four hours to see what we have that can be used for the defense of the planet."

"I wish you had given us more time to prepare a proper VIP tour," George Buchannan, the Division's ranking senior engineer, said with a troubled look. "I guess we can take him to the Olympium testing grounds. People love watching things blow up out there. But we can't get any of the other factory areas ready in four hours. Can you have him come back later in the week?"

"What are you talking about?" O'Connor demanded. "The president doesn't want a tour. He wants to see what we have in inventory that will help keep the invaders away from the Bacchus system!"

Buchannan looked at him with a puzzled look. "I don't understand. The president wants us to show him *what*?"

O'Connor shook his head. *How can some people be so brilliant and so thickheaded at the same time?*

"We are the Advanced Weapons Division, right?" O'Connor asked, deciding he needed to take a different approach.

"Yes," Buchannan answered as senior engineers nodded enthusiastically.

"We make weapons here, right?"

"Of course we make weapons here. Toasters are made on Felis 8." Several of the other senior engineers chuckled at Buchannan's comment.

O'Connor ignored Buchannan's sarcasm. "Well the president wants weapons. He believes the aliens who destroyed the other planets of the Confederation will eventually find Bacchus 12, and he wants to see what we have here that will stop them. So what do we have that will stop them?"

Buchannan's puzzled look returned. "I don't understand."

"What's not to understand?" O'Connor exploded.

"Well that's not how we work. We create new ideas for weapons, we create one or two prototypes, we present them to the military and the Confederation government, they tell us which ones they want, and we build and install the new weapons. We've never had a government official come and ask us to build weapons for a specific purpose before. We have no procedures for that, and we can't put together a new procedure like that in four hours."

O'Connor felt his blood pressure rising. "What about the weapons that we have in inventory?"

"We don't have anything in inventory that he can use," Buchannan stated. "All weapons already constructed are earmarked and scheduled to be installed across the Fleet and on the defense platforms of the other Confederation planets."

"Weren't you listening to what I told you at the beginning of the meeting?" O'Connor asked angrily. "The other Confederation planets have been destroyed. The Fleet has been destroyed. Eighty percent of the human race has been destroyed. It doesn't matter what the weapons are earmarked and scheduled for; it only matters what's still warehoused that can be used to defend this planet from attack! Can you understand *that*?"

Buchannan and the other senior engineers looked at each other for a few moments. "So you want us to show the president all of the weapons that haven't been installed yet?"

"YES!" O'Connor said, raising his hands in the air. "Can you do that when he gets here?"

"If you want us to," Buchannan said with a tone of resignation in his voice. "Do you also want us to show him the prototypes that we're working on?"

O'Connor nodded. "I think that would be a very good idea. Also, he and the military may ask you what it would take to build specific weapons that we may or may not have in inventory at the moment. Even though you have no procedures for that, can you find a way to accommodate that kind of request?"

"You mean they're going to describe a weapon they want and ask us to build it?" Buchannan asked incredulously.

"Of course," O'Connor replied. "Why not?"

Buchannan had a pained look on his face. "It's not how we do things, Director. We'd need to have a brainstorming room reserved and staffed, I need to have our sales reps there to help with pricing…"

"Sales reps?!" O'Connor wanted to throw a chair at his ranking senior engineer. "Why the hell do we need sales reps at this meeting?"

Buchannan looked startled. "Well how else are we going to put together a pricing proposal for the weapons they order?"

Oh dear God! Spare me from this lunacy! O'Connor leaned forward and put his hands flat on the table. His eyelids were slits and his face grew redder by the minute. Lowering his voice to a growl, he said, "We're not putting together pricing proposals for the weapons, understand? We fall under the military now, and the entire planet is in a state of emergency. Whatever the president and the military want, we're going to build it for them. Quickly, efficiently, and with the highest quality we can achieve in the limited time available. They tell us what they need, and we give it to them. That's how things will be working around here from now on. Do you understand? It doesn't matter how we did things before. It doesn't matter that we don't have procedures in place. All that matters is giving the military what it wants and making suggestions for ways to defend this planet from attack."

Buchannan looked at the other senior engineers in the room. They nodded reluctantly. Buchannan turned back to O'Connor. "Very well, Director. We'll make it work."

"Thank you," O'Connor said. His tone made it clear to everyone in the room that there would be dire consequences if they didn't.

CHAPTER 9

"Damn it!" Bret shouted, shaking his right hand in pain.

Burgess, who had been pushing debris aside to reach the kitchen pantry, looked up. "What's wrong?" he asked.

"I can't get this refrigerator door to open," Bret replied. "I tried to pull it open, and that didn't work. I tried to use a piece of pressed stone to force it open, but all I managed to do was hit my right hand instead. The door won't budge."

"Try to find something you can use as a lever to pry it open," Burgess suggested. "It's only two hours before sunset, and I don't want us in the ruins of the resort after dark.

Bret nodded and looked around for a piece of wood or metal that would work. Burgess returned to his digging through the debris. After several minutes, Bret found a broken metal pipe with one end pinched flat. He grabbed it and made his way back to the refrigerators. He was about to wedge it into the first refrigerator door when he heard an explosion in the distance.

Bret and Burgess both looked up at the same time. "What was that?" Bret asked, staring at a narrow jet of flame rising some distance away.

"It looks like a gas line ignited," Burgess answered. "I'm surprised more lines haven't caught fire."

Bret worked faster. He jammed the flat end of the pipe underneath the refrigerator door and pushed down on it with all of his strength. The door wouldn't budge. Bret tried moving the pipe to other places underneath the door, but he couldn't pry it open. Frustrated, he jammed the pipe underneath one of the refrigerator door's corners and pushed down as hard as he could. At first, the door didn't move, but he felt the seal begin to give. A moment later, the door popped, and Bret was able to lift it all the way open.

The stench of rotted meat and vegetables was intense. Bret held his breath and looked for anything salvageable before slamming the refrigerator door shut.

"It's all rotting," Bret shouted to Burgess.

"Well, it's been in there more than three days without power," Burgess said. "Check the others."

Another explosion caught their attention. Looking up, Bret saw a second gas jet rising out of the debris – this one closer than the first one.

Burgess looked at Bret and said, "We need to hurry!"

Bret managed to open the other two refrigerators, but the food inside was just as unusable as the food in the first refrigerator. He slammed the third refrigerator door shut in frustration. Another explosion sounded.

"They're getting closer," Bret shouted as the newest flame jet rose from the wreckage.

"There must be fire in the gas line itself," Burgess speculated. "Keep looking for anything we can salvage."

Bret crawled past the refrigerators and moved aside some of the debris. Underneath what looked like a crumbled wall were several transport crates. Bret pushed the debris off the crates and grabbed the side of one of the lids. He lifted the lid and looked inside.

Slime covered the upper pallet inside the crate, which smelled like the inside of the refrigerators. Bret was about to put the lid back on, but he decided to check the lower pallets. He pulled out the upper pallet and threw it aside. The second pallet had no slime on it anywhere. Stacked in neat rows on the pallet were several dozen pouches. He pulled one out and looked at it. The logo at the top of the pouch had the words "Travel Meals" written above a picture of a plate filled with food.

"What are 'Travel Meals'?" Bret shouted.

"They're the commercial version of military rations that we eat on patrol or on maneuvers," Burgess replied as he threw a large piece of debris out of his way. "They're self-heating meals for people who need to carry their food with them. We use them when we're going to be away from the barracks for a day or more. Why?"

"I just found a crate of them," Bret answered. "Some of the pouches were damaged, but the rest look like they're still sealed."

Burgess quickly made his way over to Bret. Bret handed the corporal one of the pouches. Burgess turned the pouch over and pointed to the expiration date printed at the bottom. "These must have just arrived," he commented. "They're good for another three years."

Looking at Bret, he added, "This is exactly what we need! Nothing to cook, easy to carry, and all the nourishment we'll need. See if there are any more crates, and I'll try to find something we can use to carry the pouches."

Bret saw several similar crates and opened each of them. Each crate contained more pouches, and while a few had opened and leaked, most were still usable. There was quite a variety of food options in the crates. "There's enough here to keep us alive for months! But what are they doing here? This resort had three of the best restaurants in the Confederation. Why have pre-packaged meals in a kitchen?"

"Travel Meals are popular with people who enjoy hiking, camping, boating... things like that," Burgess said. "According to brochures, this resort has miles of riding and hiking trails, several rivers, and camping areas. It's probably easier to have a guest carry one of these than a fully-prepared meal from the kitchen, and the pouches are waterproof."

Burgess opened a small shipping container labeled "Go Bags." He reached inside and pulled out a dense fabric zipper bag. "Perfect," he said, holding up the bag so Bret could see it. "These are like the bags we use to carry supplies for the platoon."

He grabbed a handful of the neatly folded bags and brought them over to Bret. Before he could say anything, another explosion rocked that part of the resort. A new flame jet rose nearby. Handing Bret several of the bags, he said, "Fill these up fast. We need to get out of here."

Bret nodded and started filling the bags with the pouches from the crate next to him. Burgess moved to one of the other crates to fill his bags with pouches. In less than five minutes, they had eight bags filled.

"Leave the rest and come on!" Burgess said, grabbing four of the bags.

Bret put the pouches in his hand into the last open bag. He stuffed several of the empty Go Bags into the one he was filling, zipped it up, grabbed the rest of the bags already filled, and followed Burgess across the debris away from the kitchen.

It was difficult to walk through the ruins carrying four bags filled with food pouches. Bret looked at the horizon and saw the sun setting quickly. *I hope we can get away from the ruins before nightfall. It's hard enough to get through the debris in the light. I don't want to chance it in the dark. And we need to be clear of the kitchen before another gas line explodes.*

As the sun sank lower in the sky, the shadows made it even more difficult to navigate through the debris. Bret saw the edge of the ruins in the distance, and then he saw a bright light and heard an explosion behind him. Before he could react, he felt a tremendous force shove him forward. He fell but never let go of the bags of food.

Looking back, he saw a massive fireball rising into the air over where the kitchen had been. He looked around for Burgess.

"Are you all right, sir?" he heard the corporal ask him from nearby.

"I'm fine," Bret replied. "You?"

"Fine. It looks like we got out of there just in time."

"That explosion was larger than the others," Bret observed.

Burgess nodded. "I'm guessing that the gas lines from the stoves were leaking. The gas must have filled pockets underneath the debris, and when the line exploded, the gas pockets ignited."

The sun had reached the horizon, and the shadows lengthened around them. "We'd better keep moving," Burgess said. "It'll take us another twenty or thirty minutes to clear the debris field."

Bret nodded, got to his feet, and followed the corporal.

"You know, I've never even been to the main offices of the Advanced Weapons Division," Rick said to Admiral Longstreet as their military transport drove through the Division's outer security gates with the other Fleet Marine vehicles in the motorcade.

"Few visitors are ever allowed inside," Longstreet commented. "The Division values security highly. I've only been here once myself, and that's was for a briefing on a proposed overhaul of the Yorktown's weapon systems."

"Have either of you been here before?" Rick asked Admiral Fletcher and General Monroe.

Both officers shook their heads. "Only Fleet Command and senior Confederation officials were ever allowed through the gates," General Monroe commented. "I've escorted VIPs here from the spaceport, but the Marines were always ordered to remain outside the main gates."

The motorcade passed through the next two security gates before pulling up to the tower that housed the Division's administrative offices. Rick saw O'Connor waiting for them at the building's huge doors. Once the motorcade stopped, the Fleet Marine escorts exited their vehicles and formed a perimeter around the building entrance. After receiving the "all clear" signal, the Fleet officers exited the transport, followed by Rick.

"Good day, Mr. President," O'Connor said stiffly as Rick approached. "Welcome to the Advanced Weapons Division."

"Thank you, Director O'Connor," Rick replied, shaking the man's hand as he entered the tower lobby.

O'Connor greeted the three Fleet officers and escorted everyone to the elevators behind the receptionist's desk in the center of the lobby. Once the elevator started moving, O'Connor said, "Several of my senior engineers are waiting for us in the conference room, Mr. President. I'm sure they'll be able to answer your questions and give you an idea of what we have available and what we can provide for the defense of the planet."

Rick nodded silently. *I hope so. Our survival depends on whatever you have ready and whatever you can build quickly.*

One of the Senior Engineers looked over at the security monitor. "They're in the elevator, George," he said to Buchannan. "What are you going to do?"

Buchannan shook his head and stared out the window of the conference room. "Apart from showing them what's in the warehouses, I have no idea." He turned toward other engineers waiting with him. "We've never been asked to collaborate with the military to design weapons before. We deal with what's possible, not what's practical. We leave practical to the military and the government. Under normal circumstances, I'd tell them what we've been working on and let them tell us what they want. But today they're going to tell us what they want, and we're going to have to figure out what we can give them to do the job."

The other senior engineers nodded hesitatingly. This was not what engineers were used to doing, and Buchannan sensed that his colleagues were uncomfortable.

He was about to say something else when the conference room doors opened and the President and Fleet commanders entered the room.

CHAPTER 10

Bret devoured the first Travel Meal quickly and started on the second one. It had been several days since he and Corporal Burgess had eaten, and both were enjoying the food they had salvaged from the ruins of the Fire Moon Resort.

The food pouches were unlike anything Bret had seen before. The outer compartment contained the utensils, seasonings, cleaning wipes, water, and a chem-match. The inner compartment contained the food. Pinching the sides of the inner compartment near the top released two chemicals inside the walls of the inner compartment, which heated the food in seconds. Once eaten, the used items from the outer compartment were put back into the pouch, and the chem-match was used to ignite the pouch, leaving no trash behind.

Bret was enjoying a piping-hot beef stew when Corporal Burgess spoke. "We need to talk about what we're going to do."

Bret put the pouch down and looked at Burgess. "I've been thinking about that, too. What do you suggest?"

Burgess activated the chem-match, and the two empty pouches of food that he had finished burst into flames and quickly disintegrated. "From what I remember of this area, there are three resorts that share the local spaceport. Starliners, cargo ships, even some military ships land there. I'm sure most of the spaceport was destroyed during the attack, but it's possible that one of the smaller ships might have survived – or at least sustained minimal damage that I can repair enough to get us off this planet."

"So you think we should head for the spaceport?" Bret asked.

Burgess nodded. "If we can find a ship there that can still fly, we can escape. If anyone else from the resorts survived, they'll probably head there as well, and we can work together to escape. And if any of the other Confederation planets survived the attack, rescue ships will head for the spaceports first. It's our best option."

Bret finished his stew and put the used utensils and other trash in the empty pouches. "How long will it take us to get there?"

"On foot? Probably a couple of days. If we can find a working transport vehicle, then it will only take a couple of hours."

"When do we start?"

"At first light," Burgess replied. "Get some sleep. It'll be a long day tomorrow."

Bret nodded as the light from his burning pouches went out, leaving Bret and the corporal in darkness.

The senior engineers all stood when Rick entered the conference room, followed by his Fleet commanders.

O'Connor entered the conference room last and closed the doors behind him. "Good morning, ladies and gentlemen. Let me make the introductions."

After Rick exchanged a few pleasantries with the engineers around the table, O'Connor gestured for everyone to be seated.

"Director O'Connor," Rick began, "Am I correct in assuming that you've notified your staff that the Advanced Weapons Division now falls under the Fleet Command?"

"Yes, Mr. President," O'Connor replied.

"And that we're changing your research and development procedures and expenditures to focus more on collaborating with the military to define what weapons the Fleet needs, rather than coming up with what's possible and hoping someone can find a practical application for it?"

Rick noticed that the senior engineers looked uncomfortable.

"Yes, Mr. President," O'Connor said, looking around the room.

"Good. First of all, I need to know how many ships you have that are being fitted with updated weapon systems."

O'Connor glanced at his net-dev for a moment and typed a few commands. "We have twenty warships docked at our orbiting facility, and another fifteen smaller ships at our facilities here on the planet. I've just forwarded the list and classifications to Admiral Longstreet."

Turning to Admiral Longstreet, Rick asked, "How many Fleet ships does that give us altogether?"

Longstreet looked at the information O'Connor had just sent to him. "Seventy-eight, Mr. President. There were eight ships protecting Bacchus 12 when the attacks began. There were thirty-five ships being worked on by the Advanced Weapons Division, and another thirty-five ships survived the attacks."

"How many of each class of ship do we still have?" Rick asked.

"Most of the ships are medium and small classes," Longstreet said after checking his net-dev. "We have two Carriers: the *Yorktown* and the *Hercules*. We also have three Battleships including the *Waterloo*, twelve Heavy Cruisers, eighteen Cruisers, nineteen Destroyers, twelve Frigates, and twelve Fast Attack/Scouts. We also have nearly four hundred short and medium range Fighters, and a hundred short and medium range Bombers between the two Carriers. The *Hercules* is docked at the Advanced Weapons Division's orbiting facility. About twenty of the surviving ships haven't reached the Bacchus system yet. They were damaged and are still making repairs. Their captains also want to make sure that they don't accidently lead the enemy here."

Rick nodded. *We have more ships than I was expecting.* "What about civilian transports?"

"We're not completely certain about that yet, Mr. President," Longstreet replied. "It's possible there are civilian transports that survived the attacks, but we won't know for certain until we go to the other planets and find out. Between the ones that were here or diverted here when the attacks started, and the ones that were found by the surviving Fleet ships after the attacks, I'd estimate that we have about forty freighters and ten starliners either on Bacchus 12 or making their way here."

Rick nodded. "Thank you, Admiral." Turning toward O'Connor, he asked, "Director O'Connor, what weapon system upgrades are being done to the thirty-five ships you have at your facilities?"

"The primary upgrade is replacing their main guns with the Model 29 Plasma Cannons," O'Connor replied. "They have greater range and deliver much more destructive energy to the target. We're also upgrading their torpedo launchers to handle the Comet 32 torpedo, which carries a much larger warhead than the old Pulsar 26 torpedoes."

"Have any of these upgrades been done on the other surviving Fleet ships?" Rick asked.

"Very few, Mr. President," O'Connor answered. "This is only the third wave of the upgrades we've scheduled."

"Do you have enough of the new cannons and torpedo launchers to upgrade the rest of the Fleet?"

O'Connor looked over to Buchannan, who nodded. "Yes, Mr. President."

"How long will it take to finish the upgrades?" Rick asked.

"At least a month," Buchannan replied. "It's tricky work and we have limited resources to help with the installation."

Rick looked at Longstreet and then back to Buchannan. "What if you used Fleet personnel to help you?"

Buchannan looked shocked at the suggestion. "We've never used a ship's crew to help us with upgrades before."

Rick pressed the Senior Engineer. "Is there any reason why you can't?"

"It's a security issue, Mr. President," Buchannan sputtered. "Fleet personnel are not cleared on the weapon systems."

Rick was both annoyed and amused by the Senior Engineer's response. "Are you telling me that the people who use the weapon systems don't have the security clearance to know how the weapons were installed on their ships? You do know that the Advanced Weapons Division now falls under the military, right?"

"Yes, Mr. President."

"And if I give the military the clearance to know how their weapons systems are installed, is there any reason why the crews cannot help you install the upgrades?" Rick asked.

Buchannan fell silent. He looked at the other engineers in the room, who just shrugged. Buchannan looked at O'Connor with a pleading look on his face, but O'Connor didn't speak. Finally, Buchannan looked back at Rick. "No, Mr. President."

Rick looked over to Admiral Longstreet. "Do you have any objections to allowing your crews to help with the upgrades, Admiral?"

"None, Mr. President. Incidentally, the *Yorktown* and *Waterloo* have already received the upgrades."

"Excellent," Rick said. "The military is hereby granted the security clearance necessary to help in the installation of weapon system upgrades on all Fleet ships."

Rick turned to O'Connor. "Coordinate with Admiral Longstreet and the ship captains to begin using Fleet crewmembers for the weapon systems upgrades."

"Yes, Mr. President," O'Connor replied.

"Good. Now I'd like to talk about what you have that we can use to defend ourselves against an attack."

Buchannan picked up his net-dev and cleared his throat. "Mr. President, we were getting ready to begin upgrading the defenses on the space docks at Trinity 7 and here with the new Model 60 Plasma Cannons. None of them had been installed before the attacks, so they're all sitting in Warehouse 19. We also have a number of proximity nuclear mines for the minefields along the Confederation shipping routes. They get deployed when an old mine detonates or needs replacing. They're sitting in Warehouses 6 and 7. Apart from the Model 29 Plasma Cannons and the launchers for the Comet 32 torpedoes to be installed throughout the Fleet, we have no other weapons currently in stock. We do have a number of prototype weapons, but nothing in production."

Rick nodded. "Tell me about the Model 60 Plasma Cannons."

"It's our most powerful weapon in production," Buchannan said – the pride evident in his voice. "It's designed to fire energy plasma in either short bursts or continuous streams to breach a vessel's hull plating and penetrate deep into the interior of the ship. Depending on the vessel's armor plating, it could destroy an enemy ship with one shot."

"And they were supposed to be mounted on the space docks?" Rick asked.

Buchannan nodded. "Yes, Mr. President. The Fleet Command considered the docks a primary target and in need of greater defenses."

"Can they be mounted on a freestanding orbital platform or some other floating object, or can they be mounted only on the space docks?"

Buchannan looked confused. "I don't understand the question, Mr. President."

Rick shook his head and sighed. "I want to know if they can be adapted to protect this planet. Can you mount them on freestanding orbital platforms hidden in the planetary rings? Can you mount them on asteroids or on our moons? Can you mount them on derelict military or commercial ships in orbit around the planet?"

Buchannan looked at the other engineers, who nodded. "Yes, Mr. President. I believe that they can be adapted as you've described."

"Thank you," Rick said. "Now, what about the nebulas?"

"What *about* the nebulas, Mr. President?" Buchannan asked.

"Do you have any weapons that can keep the enemy from approaching the planet through the nebulas?"

Buchannan slowly shook his head. "No, Mr. President..."

"But we'll brainstorm some ideas and get back to you," O'Connor interjected. "I'm confident that we'll be able to develop something that will work for you."

Buchannan and the other engineers looked doubtful, but said nothing.

The meeting continued for another twenty minutes, and then Rick stood. "Director O'Connor, thank you and your senior engineers for taking the time to meet with us today."

"It was our pleasure, Mr. President," O'Connor said smoothly. "But don't you wish to tour the facility?"

"Another time perhaps," Rick replied. "I need to be getting back to the capital."

"Very well, Mr. President. I'll walk you out." O'Connor led Rick and the military leaders to the elevators.

Once O'Connor, the President, and the Fleet Commanders had left the conference room, Buchannan looked at the other senior engineers. "I'm glad that's over! I can't believe how demanding he was."

"Just how are we going to mount the Model 60 Plasma Cannons on a freestanding platform or create a weapon to prevent ships from navigating through the nebulas, George?" one of the senior engineers asked.

"I have no idea, but we'd better figure it out quickly."

As the President's motorcade headed back to the capital, Rick looked at Admiral Longstreet and General Monroe. "How do you think that went?"

"I've been trying to get clearance for my crews to help install the weapon systems for years," Longstreet replied. "We use the weapons, and we have to fix them if they break down on patrol, but we can't see how they're installed? It's the stupidest security rule I've ever heard of. I had planned on telling O'Connor to abolish that rule. I'm glad you did it for me, Mr. President."

"I'm just glad there are weapons in the warehouses that we can use," Monroe added. "The Plasma Cannons and the mines will come in handy."

"Do you think they'll figure out a way to protect us from ships traveling through the nebulas?" Rick asked.

Longstreet and Monroe shook their heads.

"That's what I was afraid of."

When O'Connor returned to his office, he dialed a number in his com-dev.

"Natalia? It's me. They just left, and they're on their way back. Find out how your boss thought the meeting went, and get the latest on the agricultural, industrial, and rescue initiatives. I'll meet you at your place at 9:30 tonight. Don't bother wearing much."

CHAPTER 11

Bret was exhausted by the time they stopped to rest for the night. He and Corporal Burgess had been walking since shortly after sunrise, and now the sun was below the horizon. The clouds of dust and smoke from the alien attack hung in the atmosphere and glowed in the fading light, giving the shy an ominous look. *I wonder how far we walked today.*

Bret and the corporal passed the ruins of two resorts on their way to the spaceport. Both had been leveled just like the Fire Moon Resort. The debris from the first resort still burned as Bret and the corporal walked past. As the sun sank lower on the horizon, they reached the second resort and discovered that it was in better shape. The main building had been destroyed, but some of the outlying buildings appeared intact.

With the sunlight fading rapidly, they made a quick search of the surviving buildings to find anything worth salvaging. The stables were empty and looked like they hadn't been used in some time. There was a garage near the stables, and cursory an inspection revealed several vehicles with the resort's logo on the hoods and doors.

There was no power in the garage, and it was too dark to make a thorough check of the vehicles to see if any of them still worked. Burgess suggested that they stop for the night. "We'll check the vehicles at first light. If any of them are working, we'll reach the spaceport before noon."

"I noticed a couple of cots in the stables," Bret said. "Why don't we stay there for the night?"

"Sounds good," Burgess agreed.

Burgess activated his emergency light and led the way to the stables. Once inside, Bret showed him the room where the cots were set up. Like the rest of the stables, the cots looked like they hadn't been used in a long time.

"What is this room?" Bret asked as he sat down on one of the cots.

"It looks like where the stable workers slept when the resort still had horses," Burgess replied. He shone his emergency light around the room and noticed a lantern hanging on the wall next to the door. He walked over to it and took it off its peg. He turned it over, found the power switch, and turned it on. The room filled with light. Burgess turned off his emergency light and walked over to the cot next to Bret, placing the lantern between him and Bret.

While the corporal checked each of the windows and doors in the room, Bret started going through the Travel Meals that they had rescued from the Fire Moon Resort. Burgess noticed a metal bucket against the far wall and retrieved it. He put it on the floor next to the lantern and sat down on his cot.

"What's that for?" Bret asked.

"The floor is made of wood," Burgess replied. "I don't want to burn the Travel Meals bags on something that could catch fire."

Bret nodded and handed several Travel Meals bags to the corporal to choose from. They ate in silence, and soon the Travel Meal bags were burning in the bucket.

Burgess drew his sidearm and placed it next to him on the cot as he stretched out.

"Are you married, Corporal Burgess?" Bret asked. "I just realized that I don't really know that much about you."

"No, sir," Burgess replied. "The Marines are my family. I haven't had time to even think about a relationship since I joined."

"What about before you joined the Marines?"

Burgess was silent. Bret quickly added, "If I'm getting too personal, let me know."

Burgess shook his head. "It's not that. I just haven't thought about her for a long time."

"Her?" Bret asked, curious to know more.

Burgess propped himself up on his elbow and looked at Bret. "The girl I was engaged to before I joined the Marines. She's

93

actually the reason I joined up. I found out that she was cheating on me with my best friend. I called off the wedding and joined the Marines the next day. I haven't spoken to her or been back to Felis 8 since then, although my mom told me that they got married a few months after I left."

"I didn't know you were from Felis 8," Bret said. "What was it like when you lived there?"

"It was nice. Lots of forests and mountains. But there was nothing much to do. Some people liked that. I didn't."

"Did you always want to join the Marines?" Bret asked.

Burgess smiled. "Yes, I did. My grandfather had been a Marine. My dad was a geologist; I barely remember him, though. He died when I was five – killed in a landslide while exploring caves on the southern continent. My grandfather raised me, and he loved the Marines. So, it seemed right for me to join up as soon as I became eligible."

Bret sat silently for a while.

"What about you, sir?" Burgess asked. "I'm guessing that you're not married, but do you have someone waiting for you on Bacchus 12?"

"Just my family," Bret replied.

Burgess looked at him. "No one else?"

Bret smiled. "I don't know if she's waiting for me, but there's someone I do hope is still there when and if we make it back."

"Who?"

"Her name's Jen. She's my dad's Communications Specialist. I've been crazy about her ever since Dad hired her two years ago. She's six years older than I am, but I don't care. If we survive, I'm going to tell her how I feel. What do I have to lose?"

"Good for you," Burgess said. "Take a risk; you'll never know unless you try."

"Exactly!" Bret agreed.

Bret fell silent. After a few minutes, he asked, "What do you think our chances are of getting off Manis 2 and back to Bacchus 12?"

"I don't deal in chances, sir," Burgess replied. "I focus on what needs to be done and what can be done. Regardless of the likelihood of success, we're going to try. If we succeed, then we succeed. If we fail, then at least we failed while trying. And I don't stop trying until I either succeed or die."

"I wish I could look at life like that," Bret commented.

"What's stopping you?" Burgess asked. "When you have nothing to lose, it's easy to try anything that might work. But when you have *everything* to lose, you should still try anything that might work. If you fail, then learn from it and try something else. If you succeed, let that give you confidence for the next time. It's really that simple."

"Is that a Marine way of looking at things, or your way?" Bret asked.

"Both, I suppose," Burgess said. "It's how my grandfather raised me to think, and it's how the Maries train you to look at a situation. Since he was a Marine, I guess he was preparing me for service all my life."

Burgess picked up the lantern and turned it off. "We should get some rest now, sir. It's going to be another long day tomorrow."

Natalia reached across O'Connor for the bottle of wine that sat on the night table next to his pillow. She usually liked the feel of his chest hair on her forearm, but this time she was more interested in the wine. She filled her glass and put the bottle back where it had been.

As she drank, O'Connor looked at her with a curious expression on his face. "What's wrong, my dear? You seem distracted tonight."

Natalia peered at him over her glass and smiled seductively. "Nothing's wrong, darling. I'm just thirsty, that's all."

O'Connor's expression changed slightly as his piercing gaze locked onto her eyes. "That's not what I'm talking about. You haven't seemed yourself since I got here. Why?"

Natalia put her glass down on her nightstand and turned back to face O'Connor. "I'm uncomfortable with what seems to be happening between us," she confessed. "At first, it was all about the sex, which is great, by the way. But now, it seems like it's all about the information that you want from me, and the sex is just how you pay me for betraying my boss."

"Betraying your boss?" O'Connor asked smoothly, rolling onto his side to face her. "Hardly. I'm a member of the Cabinet. I need to know what plans he's pursuing so I can make certain that my Division is ready to help in any way necessary. I can't anticipate his demands if I don't have a heads-up about what he's working on. We live in unusual times, my dear. I have to stay two steps ahead of what's going on if I'm going to put my resources in the right place to help the Confederation survive this crisis. You understand that, don't you?"

Natalia shifted position, causing the sheet to drop, exposing her breasts. "I understand what you're saying, but I don't like spying on my boss and the members of the Cabinet to get you the information that you want. What if I get caught?"

"You have something far more troubling to consider than getting caught," O'Connor said coldly.

"What?" Natalia asked.

O'Connor reached for her hand as if about to reassure her. He stroked it gently, and then he moved his hand up her arm toward her elbow. When he reached her forearm, though, his grip tightened. Natalia struggled, but his grip grew tighter.

"What if I were to expose your treachery to the president?" O'Connor asked. "I have vids of us together, you know. And I have copies of what you've been giving me. If I were to share those with him, anonymously of course, how do you think he'd react? What do you think would happen to you then?"

O'Connor released his grip, and Natalia pulled her arm free. "You wouldn't!"

"I never said that I would. I simply asked 'what if.' But it's something that you should think about before doing anything to betray *me*. Understood?"

Natalia nodded.

O'Connor's expression changed back to that of the appreciative lover. "Good. Let's not talk about it anymore."

He pulled her closer and kissed her. Even though his kiss was passionate, Natalia felt a coldness that she had never noticed before. Even when O'Connor moved on top of her, she felt like she was making love to a total stranger.

I've never seen this side of him before. I thought he loved me. I used to think that I'd do anything for him, but now I'm not so sure. I don't want to spy for him anymore, but if I stop, he'll expose me as a spy, and I'll be arrested for espionage or treason.

O'Connor reached his climax. Natalia pretended to enjoy herself and complimented him on his skills as a lover.

What have I gotten myself into?

Bret awoke from a deep sleep and heard a high-pitched whine. The room was dark, and he heard Corporal Burgess getting out of bed.

"What's going on?" he whispered loudly as he sat up and reached for his shoes.

"I don't know," Burgess replied softly. "It sounds like something flying overhead, but it's not a sound I've ever heard before."

Bret immediately felt fear. "Could it be the attackers?"

"Possibly. I'm going outside to look around. Stay here."

"Like hell!" Bret hissed. He finished putting on his shoes and stood. "I'm staying with you."

"Fine. Stay behind me, and don't make a sound."

Burgess opened the door, and they entered the main part of the stables. They crossed the floor to the main entrance, and Bret followed Burgess outside. The sky was getting lighter, but the sun had not yet appeared on the horizon.

Bret looked up, searching for whatever had made the strange sound. A minute later, he saw movement in the sky. The sunlight hitting its hull made it glow against the darkness. Bret nudged Burgess and pointed.

"What is that?"

Burgess stared at the craft as it slowly flew over the ruins of the nearby resort. It was larger than a Scout-class ship, but smaller than a Cruiser. "It's not a Confederation ship," he whispered.

"Do you think whoever's on board knows that we're here?" Bret asked.

Burgess watched the craft fly off to the north. "If they do, then they must not care about us. Let's go get the food and our gear. I want to see if any of those vehicles are still working and then get as far away from here as possible."

Five minutes later, they were in the garage. Bret held the lantern as Burgess checked each of the vehicles.

"Damn!" Burgess exclaimed after checking the fourth vehicle.

"What is it?" Bret asked.

"This is where they fix the broken vehicles. None of these work, and we don't have time to figure out what's wrong with them and finish the repairs."

Bret looked across the garage. "What about that one over there?" he asked, pointing to a vehicle in the far corner that was half covered with a large tarp.

Burgess walked across the garage floor and pulled the tarp off. "No way!"

"What is it?" Bret asked.

Burgess walked around the vehicle with a huge smile on his face. He kept repeating "No way!" as he inspected the vehicle.

Bret had never seen anything like it before. It sat low to the ground, and rather than a roof, it had an open top with a windscreen that wrapped around the front and sides. It offered little protection from the elements, but Bret thought that it looked very fast.

"Do you know what this is?" Burgess asked when he had finished walking around the vehicle.

"No."

"It's an old Galaxy M-33. They were military field transports about fifty years ago. They can go anywhere, they're the fastest things you've ever seen, and they're virtually silent. We still use them, but they've been replaced by the M-72. We used to take them apart and rebuild them in boot camp. This looks like a civilian version; not many of them were ever made."

"Does it still work?" Bret asked.

"Let's find out."

Burgess opened the door and sat down. He pushed the starter, and the engine hummed to life. Burgess smiled as he checked each of the gauges and readouts. Then he put it in gear and pulled forward. "It's drivable! And it has more than enough fuel to get to the spaceport."

He turned off the engine and stood up. "Okay, breakfast first, and then we're out of here."

Bret nodded and started bringing the bags of food over to be loaded into the back of the M-33.

After breakfast, Bret burned the Travel Meals bags and loaded the food and their gear into the back of the M-33 while Burgess went outside to look around.

"I don't see anything else flying around out there," he said when he returned a few minutes later.

"Should we chance the main road to the spaceport?"

"No, we should stay off-road." Burgess replied. "It'll take longer, but we won't be as exposed as we would be on the main road."

Bret looked at the vehicle, confused. "Isn't the M-33 too low to the ground for off-road driving?"

Burgess smiled. "The M-33 is terrain-adjustable. It rides low when you're on paved roads, and it can be raised up when you're driving off-road."

Bret nodded. "Perfect!"

O'Connor kissed Natalia goodbye as she held the door open for him. "Remember what I said, my dear." He patted her rear. "And remember to get me a copy of the latest intelligence reports. Shall I be here tomorrow night at 9:30?"

Natalia nodded.

O'Connor left her apartment and strode down the hallway toward the elevators. Natalia closed the door and looked at the bruise forming on her forearm.

I've got to tell Rick what's going on. But what will he do to me when he finds out? I wish there were someone who could help me figure out what to do.

Beth had showered and dressed by the time Rick came out of the bathroom. She gave him a kiss and sat with him at the table to eat breakfast. Rick had spent years trying not to bring work home with him, and when he did, he never brought it to the dining table. For him, the dining table was family space, and he didn't want his family to think that work was more important than they were.

But in the emergency quarters underneath the Planetary Administration building, Rick and Beth's work was spread everywhere – including on the dining table. Their quarters had become an extension of their offices.

Rick moved a stack of reports aside and flashed Beth a tired smile as she brought him a plate of food. "Where's Cindy?" he asked.

"Believe it or not, she left about an hour ago for work."

Rick was shocked. "Cindy? Work? What's going on?"

"Cindy has started working with me on the Agricultural project," Cindy explained. "She's helping to recruit volunteers to get things started until we can bring experienced survivors from the agricultural planets to help."

"Cindy? *Our* Cindy?"

"Yes, our Cindy. She's growing up quickly. It's amazing to watch. I just wish it hadn't taken an emergency like this one to bring her around."

Rick shook his head and took a bite of food. It was delicious. Despite everything going on around them, Beth insisted on cooking as often as possible. *She's a great cook, and I love her food, but I wish she'd let the staff help her. She's doing too much, and I don't want her to burn out.*

Beth watched Rick take another bite. "May I ask you a question?"

"Yes, the food is great," Rick said, putting his fork down. "Yes, I love your cooking. Yes, I think you're too busy to be doing all of the cooking. Yes, you may let the staff take the burden off of you. I'm proud of you for finally realizing that you can't do it all around here."

"Thanks, but that's not what I was going to ask," Beth said, smiling.

"Okay, what do want to know?"

"Did you notice something a bit odd in the Cabinet meeting yesterday?"

"Like what?" Rick asked.

"Like the way Natalia fawns over Director O'Connor."

"What?"

"You haven't noticed?" Beth asked. "There's definitely something going on between them. Every time he opens his mouth, she practically swoons. When she looks at him, I don't think she realizes that anyone else is in the room. I noticed it several times during the meeting. And judging from the way he looks at her, it's been going on for a long time."

"Natalia and O'Connor?" Rick tried to wrap his brain around the idea. "I thought she had better taste than that."

"He's a powerful man," Beth pointed out. "Some women are attracted to power. It's not that uncommon."

"Do you think it's serious or just a sexual thing" Rick asked.

"I think it depends on which one you ask," Beth replied.

"Should I do anything about it?"

Beth shook her head. "No, but I'd watch them closely. If O'Connor wields any influence over her, there's no telling what she might do to please him."

Bret and Corporal Burgess sat in the Galaxy M-33, looking down from the top of a hill at what was left of the spaceport. It had taken nearly five hours to reach it. They had stayed underneath the trees as much as possible to avoid being spotted from the air, stopping frequently to listen for alien ships overhead.

"Look at that!" Bret exclaimed.

Below them, at the base of the hill, were seven alien ships. Hundreds of human survivors had been rounded up and were being held prisoner by dozens of tall, thin figures dressed in what looked like crimson pressure suits. Bret was grateful that Burgess had insisted on traveling off-road. If they taken the main road, they might have been captured or killed by the alien invaders below.

The pressure suits and the matching helmets obscured the aliens' features. The aliens appeared to have two arms and two legs like humans, but they were much taller and thinner than average humans.

Burgess scanned the spaceport with a monocular that he found in the back of the M-33. The wreckage of several freighters and starliners were plainly visible. A handful of smaller ships were parked away from the wreckage – some appeared to be damaged, but others looked unharmed.

"We need to go around the spaceport and approach it from the other side," Burgess said. "I want to check out some of the small ships over there, and I don't want those aliens to see us."

"What about their prisoners?" Bret asked.

"I'm sorry for them, but they're not my responsibility," Burgess answered. "You are. My job is to get you to safety."

101

Bret watched as one of the aliens fired a weapon at one of the human survivors. The plasma from the weapon ripped through the woman, and she fell dead at the alien's feet. Another alien grabbed the woman by the leg, dragged her off toward a ravine, and tossed her in. Bret thought he saw other bodies in the ravine.

"We can't just leave them," Bret insisted.

Burgess turned the wheel of the M-33 and drove down the hill away from the spaceport.

"What are you doing?" Bret demanded.

"I'm going around the spaceport so we can approach it from the other side. Then I'm going to try to get one of those smaller ships ready to launch so I can get you off of this planet."

"And what if one of those alien ships comes after us?"

Burgess said nothing as he kept driving, but his expression showed that he was worried about the same thing.

CHAPTER 12

Cindy walked up the driveway to her school for the first time since the Code Black had been declared. Her two military escorts, Fleet Marine Corporals Ben Simmons and Angela Martinez, walked beside her as she headed toward a group of her friends who were standing next to a large fountain. She started to wave, but then she let her fall to her side. She stopped and looked around, as if uncertain of her surroundings.

"What is it, Miss?" Corporal Simmons asked.

Cindy hesitated. "It's strange. Every other time I've approached this school, I've always been excited to see my friends and catch up with them about what clothes they bought or what vids they watched or what music they downloaded… I know that's what they're talking about right now. But I don't care about any of that. I feel like I don't fit in with them anymore. It's weird."

"You don't have to do this." Corporal Martinez shifted the rifle slung over her shoulder. "We can take you back to the Administration Building if you'd like."

Cindy shook her head. "No, Mom needs volunteers." She started walking again. "If I can change the way I look at things, maybe I can get them to change, too."

Cindy approached her friends. It took a moment for them to recognize her. "Cindy!" the girls squealed as they ran toward her.

Corporals Simmons and Martinez stepped forward and unslung their rifles. Cindy's friends hesitated when they saw the Marines in the way. They stopped, looking at Cindy – confused.

"*Excuse* me," Tiffany said rudely to the Marines. "*That's* my friend. Move."

The Marines didn't budge. Corporal Martinez looked back at Cindy, who nodded. Martinez cleared her throat, and she and Simmons stepped back to stand on either side of Cindy.

"What's up, Cindy?" Tiffany asked, sounding put out.

Monica nodded. "Yes, where have you been?"

Jolene pouted. "You haven't returned any of my messages. What gives?"

The rest of the girls started talking at the same time, demanding to know why Cindy had disappeared, why she had missed several important parties, and why she wasn't dressed like she typically dressed.

Cindy held up her hand. "Now that my Dad is President, I've been living in the emergency quarters under the Planetary Administration Building. They moved us there when the other planets were attacked."

Tiffany looked bored. "Attack, attack, attack. All anyone talks about anymore is the attack on the Confederation. That's *so* yesterday."

"*Really?*" Cindy demanded, feeling genuine anger toward her friend. "Most of the people on the other Confederation planets are dead, and you don't want to hear about it anymore? What's so important to *you* that talking about the survival of mankind is such an inconvenience?"

Cindy's friends looked at her with shocked expressions. They had never heard her talk like that before. Tiffany looked like she'd been hit in the face.

Cindy didn't wait for Tiffany to respond. "You want to know where I've been and what I've been doing? I've been helping my mom. She's trying to find food for us to eat, and she's looking for sites around the planet where we can start growing our own. I've been helping her. But we need more people to help us. It's a big job, and we're stretched thin. That's why I'm here. I need volunteers to help."

"Why bother?" Jolene asked. "There's plenty of food. We were at the market yesterday, and the shelves were full."

Cindy stared at her friend with a cold gaze. "Where do you think the food comes from?"

"From the market," Jolene replied. "Duh!"

"And where did it come from before it got to the market?" Cindy pressed.

Jolene stared at her with a blank expression on her face.

"It came from the agricultural planets!" Cindy said, raising her voice. "The planets that were attacked. The planets that had most of their populations killed. There's almost no one left on those planets to grow or raise the food we eat, and we don't produce *any* food on Bacchus 12. Whatever food there is at the markets is all we have to live on until we can find more and start growing our own food. That's why we have to 'bother'!"

Monica's eyes opened wide. "There's no more food?"

Cindy shook her head. "The last food shipment before the attack brought us all of the food that we have, and it has to keep everyone on this planet alive. If we can't find more, and if we can't start growing and raising our own, then it'll run out, and we'll all starve. If that happens, it's game-over for the human race."

"And you're helping your mom find places on Bacchus 12 to start making our own food?" Monica asked.

Cindy nodded. "Last night, ships were sent to the agricultural planets to look for any food that's already been harvested and processed. They're also looking for farming equipment that can be salvaged, survivors who can work the equipment, and any seeds, seedlings, and cattle that can be brought back here to start our own food production. But if we don't have places selected and ready for food production, then it won't matter what those ships find and bring back with them."

Cindy looked at her friends, and her expression softened. "The world has changed on us. Going to the mall or going to parties is no longer important. Neither is hanging out with friends, no matter how much you want to. Helping to save everyone on this planet is all that's important now. That's what I'm doing. I want all of you to help me, and I want you to get others to help me."

"How?" Tiffany asked.

"Talk to every friend you have and get them to volunteer to help," Cindy answered. "And I'm going to talk to the entire school this morning. I want you standing with me so the school will see that you volunteered. You're the most popular kids in school. People will follow your lead."

"That's all?" Jolene asked.

Cindy shook her head and smiled. "No. You'll also have to work. We have to find locations to build farms and ranches, prepare the ground for planting seeds and seedlings, and learn how to farm and raise cattle from any survivors who are rescued from the agricultural planets. This won't be like volunteering to clean up a park or plant flowers around the school. This is taking responsibility for keeping the people on this planet from starving to death."

Jolene shook her head. "There's really no more food?"

"There's really no more food," Cindy assured her.

Cindy's friends were silent. Then Jolene said, "I'll volunteer."

Monica volunteered next. Soon, all of Cindy's friends had volunteered except for Tiffany.

"Come on, Tiff," Cindy said. "Join us. Show everyone else around here what the *new* meaning of cool and popular is."

Tiffany nodded slowly.

"Great, you guys!" Cindy said. "Now let's go talk to the rest of the school and see if we can find some more volunteers."

The brainstorming session at the Advanced Weapons Division's headquarters had been going on for hours, but the engineers sitting around the large conference table weren't anywhere close to a solution for the first item on the agenda. No one could figure out how to protect the planet from an enemy entering the star system through either of the two nebulas.

Jason Dorr, one of the Junior Engineers in the room, who was also part of the design team for the newest models of the Proximity Nuclear Mines, watched as Buchannan and the Senior Engineers stumbled repeatedly around the problem without coming up with a single new idea. Dorr reached for his net-dev and pulled up the schematics for the mines that his team had produced.

In the top corner of the schematic, Dorr saw the words, "Tactical Nuclear Fusion Proximity Mine Model 12" written in bold letters. As he stared at the net-dev, he focused on the word "Fusion."

Fusion occurs when two elements are forced together at high speeds. The nuclei of the two elements bind together, forming a new nucleus. The resulting energy release is like a small sun igniting. The explosion and heat make it ideal for the mines operating in the vacuum of space. But because of the vacuum, the detonation has to occur very close to the object to be destroyed. Otherwise, the destructive energy dissipates rapidly, and the damage to the object is reduced. If we put mines in the nebulas, they'd have to come into contact with the alien ships to be effective, and there's no way to make that happen because proximity detectors don't work in the nebulas. This is hopeless!

Dorr looked at the hyperlinks along the right column of the schematic. As he scrolled through the list, he saw a link titled, "Early Prototypes Using Alternative Nuclear Principles." Curious, he selected that link.

The link opened, and Dorr scanned the menu of documents. Near the bottom of the list, he saw one titled, "Nuclear Fission and the Pointlessness of Creating Shockwaves in a Vacuum." *Shockwaves?* Dorr selected that link and read the summary.

"Nuclear Fission occurs when atoms are split into atomic fragments. While the sudden release of energy creates a massive explosion and release of radiation, the true destructive power from a fission reaction is the shockwave that is released. The shockwave's destructive force has a diameter many times that of the explosion's diameter, making it an effective, if not extremely hazardous, destructive device. However, in the vacuum of space, the value of the shockwave is completely lost, and the destructive energy of the fission reaction is overshadowed by the instability of the nuclear material. Shockwaves require an atmosphere to travel through, and the radioactivity and instability of fissionable material makes this type of weapon undesirable when compared to nuclear fusion devices that have been tested."

Dorr scanned the rest of the article. He checked the date. It had been written more than a century earlier. He looked at the section headings and found one titled "Fissionable Materials."

"While Earth had natural occurring elements that were ideal for nuclear fission (uranium being the most common), the Confederation's planets have no such equivalent elements. The most effective solution tested is irradiated Olympium, which reaches a level of instability and destructive energy unmatched by any naturally occurring radioactive element found within the Confederation or on Earth."

Dorr looked up from his net-dev periodically to listen in on the discussion of the other engineers. They were still making no progress. He kept reading the document. An idea was forming in his mind, but he wasn't sure that he was ready to mention it to the other engineers in the room.

After a several minutes, George Buchannan stood. "We're getting nowhere. We haven't solved the problem with the nebulas, and we still have to figure out how to mount plasma cannons and torpedo launchers in a fixed orbit around the planet. Perhaps we should stop for the day and try again tomorrow."

There were nods around the room.

"No," Dorr said, louder than he intended.

All eyes turned toward him.

Buchannan looked surprised and slightly annoyed. "You have something you want to say, Jason?"

Jason looked around the room and nodded. "I've been scanning some of the old links about the early prototypes of the proximity mines, and I found an article on a nuclear fission device that used irradiated Olympium as its nuclear fuel…"

Buchannan interrupted him. "Fission devices are useless in space. There's no atmosphere to carry and amplify the shockwave. If there are no other suggestions, let's wrap up for the day."

"What is atmosphere?" Dorr asked, wanting to finish presenting his idea. "It's just a gas cloud that's held against a planet's surface by gravity, right?"

"Of course," Buchannan said, dismissively.

"Well isn't a nebula just a hydrogen gas cloud that's formed by the remnants of an exploding star? Can't a shockwave form and travel through that gas cloud in the same way that it does though the atmosphere of a planet? Wouldn't that shockwave destroy any nearby ship without having to put the mine right next to the hull of the ship like we do with the fusion mines?"

The room was silent. The other engineers looked at each other like they were trying to mentally work out what Dorr was suggesting.

"It's possible," Buchannan said slowly.

"But wouldn't an explosion of that magnitude inside the nebula ignite the hydrogen?" one of the other engineers asked.

Dorr shook his head. "Hydrogen needs to mix with oxygen to ignite, and no oxygen gets released from a fission reaction using irradiated Olympium."

"What about the star remnants in the nebulas?" another engineer asked. "Could a nuclear explosion near one of them start a chain reaction that would ignite the stars? Wouldn't that incinerate the entire star system?"

Buchannan answered, sounding excited. "No, there's not enough mass or density within the remnants to reach nuclear ignition. The worst that could happen is that the star remnants might break apart even more."

Looking at Dorr, Buchannan said, "Ok, let's assume for a minute that your idea will work. How would you trigger a fission device in the nebulas? Proximity detectors would be useless."

"I'm not sure about that," Dorr admitted. "I was trying to figure out how to create minefields inside the nebulas. I want the new mines to have the same destructive power as our current mines do when they explode next to a ship's hull."

"I think you've done that." Buchannan smiled. Looking around the room, he added, "Shockwaves in space! We've been trying to find something new that would work, and young Dorr here found something old to do the job. Good work, Jason! Now we just have to figure out the triggering mechanism, and we'll have a proposal to submit to the Director and the President."

There was renewed energy in the room as Buchannan sat down. "Someone order up some food," he said. "We've got a lot of work to do before we break for the day."

Bret sat in the corner of the *Pascal*, one of the Confederation Scout class ships on the far side of the spaceport, trying to stay out of Corporal Burgess' way. This was the sixth ship that they'd inspected, and so far, not one of the ships was in any condition to fly, let alone escape from the Manis star system.

They had arrived on the far side of the spaceport just before sundown, and they began inspecting the ships once darkness covered the area, so the aliens on the far side of the spaceport wouldn't see them. Bret offered to help Burgess with the inspections, but Burgess indicated that he could work faster without the assistance. Bret learned that Burgess used to repair ships before he joined the Fleet Marines, and as Bret had no experience with shipbuilding or maintenance, he did his best to stay out of the corporal's way. He hoped that the aliens were too busy interrogating their prisoners to notice the presence of two more humans just across the spaceport.

Burgess flipped a series of switches, and the readouts on the Engineer's panel in the cockpit lit up. "That's a good sign."

"What is?" Bret asked.

"There's still power in the engineering systems," Burgess replied. "The internal diagnostics will tell me what's wrong much faster than crawling around the ship looking for problems."

Burgess entered a series of commands into the engineering computer. He read the diagnostic reports as they displayed on the center screen. "Fuel levels are good. Fuel lines and fuel systems are good. Maneuvering thrusters are good. No weapon systems; that's a problem. Navigation and computer systems are functioning. Hull integrity is good. It looks like the starboard stabilizer suffered some damage; that should be easy to fix."

Burgess kept reading the diagnostic reports while Bret listened and tried to learn about the ship. *I was supposed to learn about propulsion and weapons systems as part of my advanced education in Theoretical and Applied Physics. I doubt that's going to happen now, but at least I can learn more about this ship by watching the corporal.*

Once the diagnostics were completed, Burgess smiled. "This ship will get us off this planet," he announced. "All I have to do is repair the starboard stabilizer, and that'll only take a couple of hours."

"What about those alien ships?" Bret asked. "They'll see us take off and come after us. If this ship doesn't have any weapons, we'll never make it out of the atmosphere."

"I know," Burgess confessed. "We'll have to disable or destroy their ships before we try to take off."

"How?"

"I'm open to suggestions," Burgess said.

Bret thought about the other ships they had inspected. "One of the ships we looked at had plasma cannons mounted on it. Could we mount them on this ship?"

"It would take too long to mount them and reprogram the targeting system," Burgess answered.

"What about mounting them on a stand and using them to manually fire at the alien ships?" Bret asked.

"You mean like a field cannon?"

Bret nodded. "All we'd need is a power source to run the targeting controls."

Burgess scratched the beard that had been growing on his face ever since the Fire Moon Resort had been attacked. "I've never done that before, but it might work. It'd take time, though. Any other ideas?"

Bret sat quietly for a minute. "Didn't the first two ships that we looked at have removable fuel cells?"

"Yes, it makes refueling quicker and safer. Pop an old cell out and replace it with a new one."

"Could we remove the cells and use them as bombs?" Bret asked. "If we could rig a detonator and place them next to the alien ships, it might damage them enough so that they couldn't come after us."

Burgess nodded. "That will work, but I don't think there's anything around that could be used as a detonator. And we'd have to get the fuel cells across the spaceport to the alien ships without being noticed."

"What about the plasma cannons from the other ship? If we mount one of them on the M-33 and use the vehicle to transport the fuel cells to the alien ships, we could plant the fuel cells near the engines of the alien ships, and then one of us could drive back here while the other one fires the cannon at the fuel cells to ignite them."

"I like that plan!" Burgess nodded enthusiastically. "I'll show you how to remove the fuel cells and unmount one of the plasma cannons. While you're doing that, I'll repair the stabilizer. Then we can both work on making the cannon work on the M-33."

Bret smiled, but then he thought about something else. "What if there are alien ships orbiting the planet?"

"One thing at a time, sir," Burgess said, turning off the Engineer's panel in the cockpit. "We'll deal with that when we come to it."

CHAPTER 13

Rick, Beth, Admiral Longstreet, and several other people sat in the Situation Room of the Bacchus 12 Administration Building, watching the holographic star chart of the Confederation. The first search-and-rescue missions to the agricultural planets had begun.

The projection highlighted the agricultural planets in different colors, depending on their purpose. The three ranching planets – Manis 5, Baris 8, and Equus 4 – were highlighted in purple. The four farming planets – Felis 2, Canis 4, Piris 3, and Trinity 6 – were highlighted in green. And the two planets that produced mostly plant-based fabrics and timber products – Felis 5 and Darius 13 – were highlighted in blue. Trinity 6 was represented by a black orb, signifying that the planet was dead, as were all of the planets in the Trinity system after the attack. The projection also showed groups of ships moving toward four of the highlighted planets.

"When will the Freighter *Beauregard* and the Battleship *Waterloo's* escort ships arrive at Manis 5?" Rick asked.

Admiral Longstreet checked his net-dev. "The *Waterloo* is already in orbit above Manis 5, Mr. President, and the *Beauregard* will land within the hour along with its escort ships."

"Any signs of an alien presence in the Manis system?" Rick asked.

"Not yet, Mr. President," Longstreet replied. "But we've only scanned Manis 5, not the rest of the star system. We don't want to give away *our* presence by performing long-range scans."

Beth shot a look at Rick, and Rick knew exactly what she was thinking. *They're so close to Manis 2. I know Beth wants me to send a Scout ship to look for Bret, but I can't. If the Scout ship is spotted by the aliens, they could also discover the Beauregard and the Waterloo. We'd lose both ships and put the rescue missions in jeopardy. I want to find Bret as much as she does, but the risk is too great.*

"What about the Freighter *Horatio* and the Destroyer *St. Petersburg*?" Rick asked, wishing that he could console Beth about their son. "Have they reached Felis 2 yet?"

Longstreet checked his net-dev. "The *Horatio* and its escort ships landed twenty minutes ago. The *St. Petersburg* is in a low orbit above the planet."

"Is there any word yet on the condition of the Travel Meals facility?" Beth asked.

"No, ma'am," Longstreet replied. "The landing area is still being secured. We should know within the hour."

Rick nodded. *We need those Travel Meals to keep us fed until we can start producing our own food. If the factory and its warehouses are destroyed, or if the food is contaminated, then there's no hope of having enough food to last us until Beth's project starts showing results. What will we do then?*

Admiral Longstreet gave an update on the other two freighters. The *Armstrong*, protected by the Cruiser *Montreal* and three escort ships, was approaching Canis 4. The Freighter *Ericsson*, protected by the Heavy Cruiser *Edinburgh* and two escort ships, had already landed on Piris 3 and was conducting searches of the grain warehouses around the landing site.

"All of the freighters and Fleet ships that are part of the search-and-rescue missions are on high alert in case they meet with any resistance," Longstreet said at the end of the update. "So far, there's no sign of alien ships on any of the four planets."

"Thank you, Admiral," Rick said.

There was nothing to do but wait for updates from the four planets.

Beth leaned in and whispered, "I haven't told you about Cindy yet."

"What about Cindy?" Rick asked.

"Oh, not much. Only that she recruited fourteen hundred volunteers to help with the agricultural initiative."

"What?!" Rick exclaimed softly.

Beth nodded. "She started with her friends. They helped her recruit most of the people from her school. And then she went to the other schools around the planet and did the same thing. Almost every young person between the ages of sixteen and eighteen has volunteered. She's organizing them into teams, and I've already started sending them out to the southern continent to search for farm and ranch sites."

"That's incredible!" Rick said. "What's gotten into her?"

"I don't know," Beth replied. "But I'm loving it. She's really grown up in the past couple of weeks. I always knew that she had it in her, but now she's discovering it for herself. I think we can expect great things from her in the future."

Longstreet cleared his throat. "Forgive me for interrupting, Mr. President. I've just received a message from Director O'Connor. His engineers have solved the problem of preventing the aliens from approaching Bacchus 12 through the nebulas. They'd like to present their solution to us in the morning."

Rick smiled. *Finally! I was beginning to wonder if any of those engineers actually knew how to solve a problem.* "Have Natalia schedule the meeting, Admiral. I want to see what they've come up with and get it deployed as quickly as possible."

"Yes, Mr. President."

Bret dragged the last of the fuel cells from the damaged ships over to the *Pascal*, the ship that he and Corporal Burgess would be using to escape from Manis 2.

"Here's the last of them," he said after he had placed the fuel cell with the ones that he had already removed.

"Good." Burgess said. "Get some rest. I won't need your help for a few more hours."

Bret sat down and watched Burgess working. For two nights, they had been preparing for their escape. Burgess showed Bret how to remove the fuel cells from the two damaged ships, and then the corporal started repairing the damaged stabilizer. It took Burgess only three hours to finish the repairs. While Bret continued removing the fuel cells, Burgess started unmounting the plasma cannon from one of the other damaged ships.

They stopped working at dawn so the aliens across the spaceport wouldn't see them. Bret hoped that the aliens couldn't detect their presence in the ship, but that was a risk he and Burgess had to take.

Burgess finished unmounting the plasma cannon around midnight on the second night, and it took the rest of the night to remove the firing control panel, used to control the cannon, from the cockpit of the damaged ship.

While Bret finished retrieving the fuel cells, Burgess managed to load the M-33 into the ship's small cargo bay so he could work on it without being seen. There wasn't much room to move around in the cramped space, but Burgess was making progress mounting the plasma cannon onto the back of the vehicle.

Shortly after noon, Burgess stepped back and looked at the cannon mount he had rigged for the M-33. "Look at this," he said to Bret.

Bret stood and walked over to the M-33. The plasma cannon had been mounted on a platform at the rear of the vehicle. It was elevated high enough that it could easily rotate 360 degrees to fire without hitting Bret or Corporal Burgess. It also looked like it could pivot upward to fire at a target in the air or on higher ground.

"It looks great!" Bret complimented. "Does it work?"

Burgess reached over to the control panel on the floor. He activated the controls, and the cannon swiveled and pivoted smoothly.

"What's left to do?" Bret asked once Burgess turned off the controls.

"I still have to mount the control panel inside the vehicle, and then we have to load the fuel cells. If we work together, we should be ready an hour or two after nightfall."

"Who's going to operate the cannon, and who's going to drive the vehicle?" Bret asked.

Burgess motioned for Bret to help pick up the control panel. "I'm more experienced with the cannon controls, so you'll have to drive while I detonate the fuel cells. You do know how to drive, don't you?"

Bret nodded. "I've been driving for three years. I've never driven a vehicle like this, but I should do okay."

As they mounted the control panel to the M-33's dashboard, Bret asked, "What do you want me to do while you're placing the fuel cells?"

"Stay with the vehicle and watch for aliens," Burgess replied.

Bret held the panel while Burgess attached it to the mounting bracket he had salvaged from one of the damaged ships. Finally, Bret said, "I want to see what's being done to the prisoners. I know we can't rescue them, but they're being executed for a reason. If they're being interrogated, I might be able to learn why the aliens attacked us and what they want. That's valuable intelligence that the Fleet will need, assuming that there still is a Fleet."

Burgess stopped working and stared at Bret. "I'm not supposed to let you out of my sight. Getting separated in the dark so close to seven alien ships is risky and is a violation of my orders."

"And if we miss this opportunity to gather intelligence about our enemy, we could be risking even more deaths," Bret stated. "I think you need to weigh the difference between simply obeying an order and the benefits of discovering what's going on."

Burgess nodded slowly. "Okay. But I want you to be armed. We found several small arms and rifles in the same ship that had this plasma cannon. We'll grab them before we head to the other side of the spaceport."

"Deal!" Bret smiled.

Admiral Longstreet checked his net-dev for an update from Felis 2. "Mr. President, the Travel Meals factory was damaged, but the warehouses are largely intact. The search parties report that there are thousands of pallets of Travel Meals ready for shipment. They've begun loading them onto the freighter."

Rick nodded. "That's great news, Admiral. If they can get those Travel Meals back here, they'll have guaranteed our survival for several months. Did they find any survivors?"

Longstreet shook his head. "No, Mr. President. There's no sign of survivors at this time."

The news from the other search-and-rescue missions was also promising. Little harvested or butchered food had been found, but farming equipment, seedlings, seeds, and flocks had survived the attacks and were being loaded onto the freighters and escort ships. But more importantly, survivors who understood farming and ranching had been found and were being evacuated. Beth would have something to work with as she attempted to make Bacchus 12 self-sufficient.

Rick put his hand on Beth's and smiled at his wife. "This is good. We're finding what we need."

Beth nodded. "We just have to get it all back here safely."

The last fuel cell had been loaded into the cargo trunk of the M-33. The rear seat of the vehicle was filled with small arms. Burgess sat in the passenger seat so he could operate the plasma cannon controls, and Bret was in the driver's seat.

"I wish we had time to test the plasma cannon," Burgess said. "But there's no way it would go unnoticed by the enemy. We'll just have to hope that it works."

Turning to Bret, the corporal asked, "Are you ready, sir?"

"Yes," Bret replied.

"Then let's go."

Bret turned on the engine. It barely made a sound. The gauges and readouts lit up, and Bret adjusted them so that they gave off as little light as possible. Bret moved the accelerator forward and drove down the ramp from the ship's cargo bay. Once clear of the ship, he adjusted the ride setting so the vehicle was as low to the ground as possible, making it harder to see. Then he turned the vehicle toward the alien ships, which were still on the opposite side of the spaceport.

Bret wore special goggles that Burgess found in the M-33's storage locker. They allowed him to operate the vehicle at night without the need for running lights. Burgess used the targeting controls to watch for any movement around the alien ships. Bret hoped that none of the alien ships had proximity detectors or sensors that would detect the M-33 as it approached their position. *If they catch us coming toward them, I hope the plasma cannon works and can disable their ships long enough for us to escape.*

As they approached the alien ships, neither Bret nor Burgess noticed any increase in activity. "So far, so good," Burgess whispered.

Bret approached the farthest alien ship slowly. *No alarms. No patrols. They must either be confident that there's no one left to offer any resistance, or they're inside their ship, monitoring our approach and getting ready to blow us out of existence.*

A few minutes later, they reached the far alien ship. Bret stopped and pulled the accelerator all the way back. He and Burgess got out and grabbed their weapons from the back seat. Bret slung two rifles over his shoulder and tucked three sidearms into his belt. Burgess put on a pair of the same kind of goggles that Bret had. Bret gave Burgess a thumbs-up, and the corporal returned the sign. Burgess then reached for the first fuel cell while Bret moved off to spy on the aliens.

Bret slowly walked past each of the alien ships. There were no patrols to be seen. He paused each time he crossed the gap between the ships, looking to see where the prisoners were being held. When he reached the gap between the fourth and fifth alien ships, he found what he had been looking for.

Bret stood at the rear of the fourth alien ship, just below the main engine ports. On the opposite side of ship, there were dozens of human prisoners being kept together in a group by several aliens wearing crimson pressure suits and helmets. Bret looked at the size of the group of prisoners. There appeared to be only about half the number of prisoners that he'd seen when he and Burgess first approached the spaceport. He inched his way closer, trying to keep from being seen or heard as he moved.

When Bret reached the front end of the alien ship, he watched as two aliens dragged a prisoner forward by his arms and forced him onto his knees. Another alien with stripes on the arms of his pressure suit stood in front of the prisoner. The alien held out his hand, and a holographic image appeared above it.

Bret looked at the image. *That doesn't look like a star chart, but there's something familiar about it.*

The prisoner shook his head with a panicked look on his face. The alien moved the image closer to the prisoner's face, but the prisoner kept shaking his head. The alien closed his hand, and the image disappeared. Then the alien drew a weapon and fired. The plasma tore through the prisoner, and he fell – dead. His body was dragged away to the ravine where Bret had seen the bodies of other prisoners.

Bret felt like throwing up, but he dared not make a sound. *Whatever that image is, the aliens seem to want it badly. I know I've seen it before, but I can't remember where.*

Bret saw the aliens select another prisoner. He crept back toward the engines of the alien ship so he wouldn't have to watch another execution. When he reached the rear of the alien ship, he saw Burgess placing the fuel cells in the engine port of the third ship. He crept back to where Burgess was working, and together they finished placing the fuel cells.

Bret put one of his rifles back inside the vehicle and noticed two strange weapons sitting on the seat. "What are those?" he whispered.

"Two of their guns," Burgess replied. "I took them off a sentry near the second ship."

Another sentry was spotted as they loaded fuel cells on the fourth ship. Burgess used his knife to disable and disarm the sentry while Bret continued placing the fuel cells around the engine port.

Thirty minutes later, all of the fuel cells had been placed around the alien ships. Three alien weapons sat the back seat of the M-33.

"How far away should we be before opening fire?" Bret asked as he put the vehicle in gear.

"At least halfway back to our ship," Burgess replied. "The fuel cells are volatile enough on their own. I have no idea about the fuel in the alien ships."

Bret slowly drove away from the alien ships. He heard the servos operating in the plasma cannon's mount as Burgess worked the controls to aim the cannon at the first alien ship.

When they finally reached the halfway point, Burgess tapped Bret on his shoulder. "Get ready."

Bret nodded and gripped the steering controls. Burgess flipped up the thumb switch on the targeting control and pressed the button.

A brilliant blue light appeared just over Bret's shoulder. The plasma cannon fired an intense burst of energy toward the engine port of the first alien ship. Burgess didn't wait to see if it hit the fuel cells. He aimed and fired at the next alien ship.

Bret saw the flash of light before he felt the shockwave and heard the explosion behind him. He glanced back and saw the engine of the first alien ship vanish into a massive fireball. The second alien ship's engine port disappeared a few seconds later.

Burgess fired at each of the alien ships. The force of the explosions was tremendous. Bret had a hard time keeping control of the M-33. At one point, he thought that the shockwaves might flip the vehicle over.

Once Burgess had hit all of the alien ships and the fuel cells had exploded, he shouted, "Punch it! Get us back to our ship, and let's get off of this rock!"

Bret didn't need any encouragement. He pushed the accelerator all the way forward, and the M-33 raced across the spaceport while Burgess continued firing at the alien ships to disable them as much as possible.

When Bret reached the ship, he drove up the ramp into the cargo bay and shut down the engine. He raised the ramp while Burgess ran to the cockpit to prepare for liftoff.

Bret took his seat and fastened the safety harness. Burgess finished the pre-flight checklist. He activated the lifting engines, and the ship rose into the air. Burgess then activated the thrusters, and the ship steaked away from the spaceport.

Once they were in the upper atmosphere of Manis 2, Bret swiveled his chair to look at Burgess. "We did it!"

"Yes we did, sir," Burgess agreed. "It was a good plan."

Bret smiled. "I wonder what happened to the surviving prisoners."

"I don't know, sir. I saw figures scattering once the first ship exploded. Hopefully they got away."

"I can't believe how big the explosions were," Bret said.

"I know," Burgess agreed. "The fuel cells had refined Olympium in them, but I'd swear that the alien ships were using Olympium in their engine cores as well. The brilliant purple color of the flames gives it away, and the explosions were all the same color."

Olympium? The aliens use Olympium? Bret thought about the holographic image that the alien showed to the prisoner. *Now I know where I've seen that image before. It's the elemental structure of Olympium! That's what the aliens are after!*

Bret shared his revelation with Burgess.

"If that's true, sir, then Bacchus 12 is their real target."

Bret nodded. "And if they're interrogating prisoners about Olympium, it may be that they haven't found Bacchus 12 yet."

"But how would the aliens know to look for Olympium within the Confederation?" Burgess asked.

"Well, we use it in all of our ships and our weapons systems," Bret replied. "It leaves a particular molecular signature when it's used that can be detected. If they need Olympium and realized that our ships use it, that may be why they attacked us."

"We have to let somebody know about this," Burgess said. "But I don't dare use the Fleet communications channels in case they're being monitored by the aliens."

"Then it's imperative that we get home with this information as quickly as we can," Bret said.

"I agree. We'll be clear of Manis 2's gravity in a few minutes, and then I can activate the main engines and get us home."

Bret relaxed for the first time in days. *We're going home! I wasn't sure I'd ever see the rings of Bacchus 12 again.*

He was about to say something when an alarm began flashing overhead.

"What's that?" he cried.

"Proximity alert," Burgess shouted over the alarm. "We've just been scanned by a ship in this star system. If I activate the main engines for Bacchus 12, they'll know exactly where we've gone. We can't let that happen."

Bret began to panic. "What do we do?"

Burgess looked grim as he scanned his instruments to identify the source of the scans. "I have no idea, sir!"

CHAPTER 14

On board the Fleet Battleship *Waterloo*, the scanner technician watched her monitor closely for any enemy activity in the Manis star system. The *Waterloo* provided protection to the search-and-rescue operations down on Manis 5, and her job was to make certain that no aliens approached the system undetected.

Her short-range scanners were focused on the planet below, but she periodically activated the ship's long-range scanners to check for activity around the other two habitable planets in the system. She couldn't keep the long-range scanners on for long, or she risked having them detected by alien ships.

She finished scanning Manis 6. There was no alien activity detected. Then she turned the long-range scanners toward Manis 2. She had detected movement in Manis 2's lower atmosphere on one of her previous scans, but there had been no further contacts since then.

The scanners immediately picked up an explosion on the surface of Manis 2.

"Admiral Marshall! I'm picking up a disturbance on Manis 2."

Vice-Admiral Fletcher Marshall, head of Confederation Fleet Operations, looked up from the report he was reading. "Where?"

"Near Spaceport 4. It's a massive explosion."

"Any ships detected in that area?" the admiral asked.

The technician stared at her monitor intently. Then she saw something. "Yes, sir. One ship moving away from the surface into the upper atmosphere. It's small. Scout Class possibly. I'm scanning for a Fleet transponder signal."

Admiral Marshall turned to his communications technician. "Send a flash message to Fleet Command. Alert them to the explosion on the planet surface and the ship we've detected. Tell them that we're investigating."

"Yes, sir."

"And inform the *Beauregard* that we may need to leave this system with little advanced notice," Marshall added.

"Yes, sir."

Admiral Marshall put his hand on the scanner technician's shoulder. "Don't lose that ship. I want to know what it's doing and where it's going."

Admiral Longstreet heard a sound coming from his net-dev and knew that there was another update from one of the search-and-rescue missions. He picked up the net-dev and read the message.

"Mr. President, the *Waterloo* has detected an explosion on Manis 2. They're also tracking a ship leaving the atmosphere. They're investigating."

Rick looked at Beth. "Is there any more information, Admiral?"

"No, Mr. President," Longstreet replied. "This just happened. The *Waterloo* has informed the *Beauregard* to prepare to leave Manis 5 should the ship prove to be an enemy scout."

"Where was the explosion detected?" Beth asked.

"Near Spaceport 4, ma'am."

"That's where Bret's starliner landed," Beth said to Rick, her voice sounding panicked. "Are the aliens attacking the survivors on the planet?"

Rick grabbed her hand. "We don't know what the explosion is or what that ship is. It's too soon to start thinking the worst. Let the *Waterloo* investigate. We'll know more soon."

Beth nodded as tears filled her eyes.

Bret looked at Corporal Burgess. "Have you found the source of the scans yet?"

Burgess nodded. "Manis 5."

"Manis 5?" Bret asked. "Isn't that a cattle planet?"

123

"Yes, sir. There's a ship in orbit around the planet."

"Is it one of ours or one of theirs?"

Burgess entered a command into the command console. "I can't tell yet. I'm scanning for a Fleet transponder signal."

"Does this ship have a Fleet transponder?"

Burgess nodded. "It's a Fleet Scout Class ship, and all Fleet ships have transponders."

"Should we shut it down in case that's an alien ship out there?" Bret asked anxiously. "We don't want it identifying us as a Fleet ship, do we?"

Burgess reached for the transponder controls, but then he withdrew his hand. "If that's a Fleet ship, the transponder is all that will keep them from blowing us out of the sky. If it's an alien ship, they already know that we're not one of theirs, and they'll come after us whether or not the transponder is on."

"Admiral Marshall!" the scanner technician on board the *Waterloo* exclaimed. "I'm detecting a Fleet transponder from the ship leaving Manis 2. It's one of ours!"

"Hail that ship!" Marshall ordered his communications technician.

Bret heard a voice coming through the speakers in the ship's cockpit. "Unidentified Scout ship over Manis 2, this is the Confederation Battleship *Waterloo*. Identify yourself."

"It's one of our ships!" Burgess shouted.

Bret felt relieved. *Thank God! I thought we were done for.*

Burgess activated the transmitter controls. "Waterloo, this is the Fleet Scout Ship *Pascal*. It's good to hear from you."

"*Pascal*, this is *Waterloo*. What is your designator?"

"Designator?" Bret asked. "What's that?"

Burgess smiled. "They want to know why we were on Manis 2. If they know that the planet was attacked, they want to know why we survived and if we're in league with the attackers."

"Oh," Bret said, feeling anxious again.

"*Waterloo*, this is *Pascal*," Burgess responded. "I'm a Fleet Marine on Confederation escort duty. I have a diplomatic package on board. Refugee status. Repeat, refugee status."

"*Pascal*, this is *Waterloo*. State origin of diplomatic package."

"*Waterloo*, this is *Pascal*. Origin is Nebula." Burgess gave the code name for the Bacchus star system.

"*Pascal*, this is *Waterloo*. Stand by."

There was silence from the speakers. After almost a minute, Bret heard the voice again.

"*Pascal*, this is *Waterloo*. Change course and rendezvous with us immediately. *Waterloo* Actual wishes to meet the diplomatic package."

Burgess looked over at Bret. "The captain of the *Waterloo* wants to debrief you personally."

Bret smiled. He liked the idea of being under the protection of a Fleet Battleship.

Burgess typed a command into the navigation console. "*Waterloo*, this is *Pascal*. Changing course now."

Admiral Longstreet looked at his net-dev. He stared at the message, and then he smiled at Beth.

"What is it, Admiral?" she asked.

"It's a message from the *Waterloo*, ma'am. The ship leaving Manis 2 is a Fleet Scout Class ship. It's carrying a Fleet Marine escort and a VIP. They claim that the VIP is from Bacchus 12."

"Bret!" Beth cried.

Longstreet nodded. "Unless there's another VIP from here with a Fleet Marine escort on Manis 2, then it should be your son."

Rick noticed Jen smiling for the first time in more than a week. "Are they on their way here?" he asked Longstreet.

"No, Mr. President. Vice-Admiral Marshall ordered them to proceed to Manis 5. He'll debrief them and then bring them home once his search-and-rescue mission is concluded."

"Why not just let them come straight home?" Beth asked.

"Your son has been on a planet that was attacked by aliens, and he survived, ma'am," Longstreet replied. "If he witnessed the attack, or if he had contact with the aliens, he has valuable intel that's time-sensitive. We have a mission going on within the same star system, and if there's an active alien presence, the *Waterloo* has to know that immediately. Plus, the navigation beacons in the

Bacchus system have been deactivated. His ship would never be able to navigate through the debris fields to reach the planet without a Fleet escort. I know that you're anxious to see your son, but this is the best course of action."

"May we at least speak to him?" Beth asked.

"No ma'am. I'm sorry, but mission protocol only allows for short burst transmissions so any enemy ships won't be able to pinpoint the location of our ships or of Fleet Command. Admiral Marshall will send an update of your son's condition once he's aboard the *Waterloo*."

Rick put his hand on Beth's arm. "You're right Admiral. At least we know that he's alive."

Bret was awestruck when the *Waterloo* came into view. He had never seen a Fleet Battleship before, and he found its size and armaments impressive. Much of the surface of the dreadnaught bristled with gun emplacements so that the ship could fire in all directions.

Fleet fighters formed up around the *Pascal* and escorted it to the *Waterloo*'s main landing bay. Once the outer doors of the landing bay had closed and the bay had re-pressurized, Bret looked through the forward view ports and saw a company of Fleet Marines approach the ship and form two columns. Several officers then approached the ship.

"They're welcoming you aboard with full military honors," Burgess noted.

"Why?" Bret asked.

Burgess shrugged. "I don't know, but we shouldn't keep them waiting."

He led Bret to the main hatch. "I'll exit first," Burgess said. "Wait until I tell you that it's safe to disembark."

"But we're on a Fleet ship," Bret protested.

"And I'm your Fleet Marine escort," Burgess countered. "It's protocol."

Bret nodded. Burgess opened the hatch and stepped out.

Bret watched the corporal approach the officers and snap to attention.

"Corporal Jameson Burgess serving as Fleet Marine escort for Bret Douglas, son of the Bacchus 12 Planetary Administrator."

Admiral Marshall returned Burgess' salute. "Things have changed since the destruction of the Confederation, Corporal. Your package is now the son of the new Confederation President."

"Yes, sir," Burgess acknowledged.

"Please retrieve the package, Corporal," Marshall instructed.

"Yes, sir."

Burgess returned to the *Pascal*'s main hatch. "It's safe, sir. Follow me."

Bret followed Burgess onto the deck of the landing bay.

When they reached the officers, Admiral Marshall and the others snapped to attention. "Mr. Douglas, I'm Vice-Admiral Fletcher Marshall, head of Fleet Operations and commander of the Fleet Battleship *Waterloo*. It's a pleasure to have you aboard."

Bret nodded. "Thank you, Admiral."

"I'm grateful to find you alive and well, sir," Marshall continued. "The President has been notified that you're alive, and he and your mother are anxious for us to return you to Bacchus 12."

Bret shook his head. "I'm sorry, Admiral. Did you say 'the President'? What about my father?"

Admiral Marshall smiled. "You don't know. There have been a lot of changes since the destruction of the Confederation. Allow me to fill you in of what's going on, and then you can tell us what happened on Manis 2 and how you escaped. We detected a large explosion on the planet just before your ship appeared on our scanners. I imagine you have quite a story to share."

"Excuse me, Admiral," Burgess interrupted. "We have three weapons on the *Pascal* that were taken from the aliens on Manis 2, and we have a knife with the alien's blood in it. They should be inspected as soon as possible."

Admiral Marshall signaled to one of his officers to retrieve the weapons. He and Burgess disappeared into the *Pascal* and returned a few minutes later.

"This is fantastic!" Admiral Marshall exclaimed when Burgess presented the weapons and the knife. "These are the first artifacts recovered from the aliens. Now I really want to hear about what happened on Manis 2!"

Admiral Marshall led Bret, Burgess, and the officers out of the landing bay.

The debrief lasted for almost two hours. Admiral Marshall explained what happened to the Fleet and the Confederation as a result of the alien attack. Burgess provided the details of how he and Bret survived on Manis 2 and how they escaped.

An inspection of the alien weapons confirmed that they had Olympium cores, just like Confederation weapons. When Bret relayed his discovery about the aliens wanting to find Olympium, Admiral Marshall immediately ordered that information to be sent in a flash communication to Fleet Command.

Once the debrief was over, the *Waterloo*'s medical staff examined Bret and Corporal Burgess thoroughly. When that was finished, they were escorted to VIP quarters near the Admiral's cabin, where they each had the chance to shower and shave for the first time since the attack on Manis 2. Fresh clothes were brought to them, and their old clothes were taken by the science department to be examined for alien residue. Food was then brought up from the galley.

After they had eaten, Bret and Burgess were alone in the VIP quarters onboard the *Waterloo*. It was Bret's first chance to process everything that he had learned from Admiral Marshall and his officers.

Only one planet survived the alien attack, and it's my home. Most of the Fleet was destroyed. Dad is now the President of the Confederation, and Mom is a member of the Cabinet and in charge of operations to relocate food production to Bacchus 12.

It was a lot for Bret to process.

"Do you want to talk about anything, sir?" Burgess asked.

Bret shook his head. "How long before we head for home?"

"I don't know, sir," Burgess replied. "They're still finishing up the mission on the planet. I'm guessing that we'll be home in a couple of days."

Bret nodded. *All I want to do is hug my family. And I want to apologize to my dad for the way I acted the last time I saw him. It seems like a lifetime ago, and the argument seems silly in light of what has happened.*

Bret leaned back on the bed and fell asleep almost immediately.

With the exception of Archbishop Canterbury and Admiral Fletcher on the *Waterloo*, the entire Cabinet was in Rick's office.

"Based on the last flash message received from the *Waterloo*," Admiral Longstreet began, "the aliens are searching for Olympium. Their weapon cores use Olympium, just like ours do, and their fuel source is refined Olympium."

"Mr. President," O'Connor interrupted, "we must protect the Olympium at all costs! It's the source of our energy, it flies our ships, and it powers our weapons. We cannot survive without it!"

"I know, Director O'Connor," Rick said. "Your engineers have solved the problem of protecting us against any aliens approaching Bacchus 12 through the nebulas. The test detonation of the fission mine was very convincing, and I know your people are working hard to build and deploy as many mines as possible. They're also deploying the plasma cannons and torpedo launchers around the planet, and they're finishing the upgrades on the surviving Fleet ships. I can't think of anything else we can be doing to protect the planet. Can you?"

O'Conner looked annoyed and shook his head. "I'm not talking about protecting the *planet*, Mr. President. I'm talking about protecting the Olympium!"

"Isn't that the same thing?" Enrique Fuentes asked.

"No, Mr. Vice President, it isn't. If the aliens get through our defenses, what are we going to do to protect the Olympium?"

Rick interjected. "If the aliens get through our defenses, Director, then protecting the Olympium won't matter. There will be no one left on Bacchus 12 to stop them.

O'Conner lowered his eyes. *I don't give a damn about Bacchus 12 or your precious people, Mr. President. MY Olympium isn't going to fall into enemy hands. If you won't help me protect it, then I'll do it myself. I'll see it destroyed before I let an alien race take it away from me.*

CHAPTER 15

In orbit around Felis 2, Captain Ryan of the Fleet Destroyer *St. Petersburg* spoke to Lt. Commander Thorson of the Freighter *Horatio* via a vid-com link.

"We've finished loading all of the Travel Meals into the cargo holds," Thorson reported. "We've also salvaged two medium-sized freighters: the *Tokyo* and the *Melbourne*. They had only minor damage. We've repaired them both. Their cargo holds were already filled with Travel Meals ready for shipping, so we're bringing back a lot of food that's ready to eat."

"I'll alert Fleet Command," Ryan said. "When will you be ready to leave the surface?"

"We're conducting one last walkthrough of the factory," Thorson replied. "We'll be taking off in about twenty minutes."

"Good. I want to get this cargo back to Bacchus 12 as soon as possible."

Admiral Longstreet looked at his net-dev and saw the update from the *St. Petersburg*. He shared the update with Rick. At the end of the update, he added, "Commander Thorson estimates that we'll have enough food for eight to ten months, depending on the number of refugees added to the population."

Rick nodded. "Thank you, Admiral."

The Situation Room was more empty than usual. Beth had left the capital and gone to the southern continent to inspect the initial sites selected for farming and ranching. She also planned to meet with Cindy and the other volunteers working on the agricultural projects. Director O'Connor had returned to the

Advanced Weapons Division offices to oversee the work on the planetary defenses. Archbishop Canterbury stayed inside his church. He rarely attended the status meetings anymore, and Rick was getting worried about the elder theologian.

Karl Pitowski, the new Director of Planetary Services, stood up. "Mr. President, I want to renew my objections about bringing refugees to Bacchus 12. Even though Beth has set up temporary facilities near the new farms and ranches on the southern continent, they won't hold many people and aren't durable enough to last long. We have no places to put the refugees that the search-and-rescue missions will find and bring back here. We have no building supplies to set up permanent housing options. Where are we going to put these people, and how are we going to clothe and house them?"

Michael Thatcher, Director of Refugee Services, spoke up. "Mr. President, unfortunately, I have to agree with Karl. We are not prepared to clothe and house refugees at this time. I know that we had to secure farmers and ranchers so we can start growing our own food and prevent us all from starving, but we don't have adequate housing for them, and we have no room for any other refugees."

"What do you suggest that we do?" Rick asked. "You know my position on the matter. We cannot abandon the survivors on the other Confederation planets. We have to bring them here."

Thatcher nodded. "I know that, and I agree with you. But before we bring too many more refugees here, we'd better do something about the housing problem first. We should send a search-and-rescue mission to Felis 5 and Darius 8. Felis 5 has the timber and fabric industries, and we have to have both of those if we're going to house and clothe refugees and our own people. Darius 8 has the heavy construction industries including pressed stone and other building supplies. If we can start bringing the raw materials from those planets here, along with refugees who know how to use them, we can be solving the housing and clothing issues before too many more refugees arrive."

"I agree with Michael, Mr. President," Enrique said. "We need supplies so we can prepare for bringing the refugees here. We need to finish planning for where the new housing will go and how it'll be connected to utility services so we don't put too much overload on the existing facilities."

Karl nodded. "That's all I'm asking for, Mr. President. Let's go get the supplies we need before we add too many more people to our population. We need permanent farming and ranching facilities, and then we need more housing and more clothing ready for new refugees."

Rick looked around the room and saw several people nodding. "What do you think, Admiral?"

Admiral Longstreet reached for his net-dev and looked up some information. "We originally limited our search-and-rescue missions to four at a time, each with one Capital Fleet ship, two escort ships, and a single freighter. We didn't want to commit too many of our Fleet resources or freighters in case of alien contact. Now that we know there are aliens in the Manis system, our focus should be on getting the supplies we need as quickly as possible, rather than being cautious. I've been holding our two Carriers and two of our Battleships back to protect Bacchus 12, but if we send out the *Hercules* for search-and-rescue duty, and we increase the number of freighters per Capital Ship to five or six, we can operate five concurrent search-and-rescue missions and bring back much more cattle, food, and supplies per mission. It'll deplete our planetary defenses, but it'll allow us to move faster to get the things we need. It's your call, Mr. President."

Rick thought about what Longstreet had presented. "I don't like reducing the number of Fleet ships protecting Bacchus 12, Admiral. It's a huge risk. But if we *were* to increase our missions as you described, what would be the next five missions that we should undertake?"

Longstreet entered some information into his net-dev and a holographic projection of the Confederation star chart appeared in the center of the room. Five planets were illuminated in green.

"I'd recommend the following. Send the *Waterloo* and seven freighters to Equus 4 to continue their efforts to secure ranchers, cattle, and ranching equipment, and send the *St. Petersburg* and five freighters to Baris 8 for the same reason. Send the *Edinburgh* and four freighters to Darius 13 to secure farmers, plants that can be used for fabrics and any pre-made fabrics and clothing that may be warehoused there. Send the *Montreal* and four freighters to Felis 5 for the same reason, and to secure timber for building materials. And send the *Hercules* and seven freighters to Darius 8 to secure building materials and construction workers. However, that would put a lot of our Fleet resources in the Darius system, and it could be a tempting target for any aliens in that sector."

Rick shook his head. "I don't still don't like it."

"Why not go ahead and send the *Hercules* now?" Thatcher asked. "If we have enough freighters and escort ships available, it could be on its mission while the rest of the Fleet is here at Bacchus 12. It would prevent us from having too many of our ships away from the planet in case of attack."

Longstreet nodded in agreement. "Mr. President?"

Rick leaned back in his chair. *I wish Beth were here. I'd like her input on the farming and ranching missions. But she's not here, so it's up to me.*

"Have the weapon system upgrades been completed on the *Hercules*?" Rick asked.

"Yes, Mr. President. It was the first ship completed."

Rick nodded reluctantly. "Do it. Send out the *Hercules* as soon as its escorts and freighters are ready."

"Yes, Mr. President. And I'll start making preparations to send the other ships back out as soon as they've arrived and unloaded their cargo."

The *Horatio*, along with its three Fleet escort ships and the salvaged freighters *Tokyo* and *Melbourne*, left the surface of Felis 2 and jointed the Fleet Destroyer *St. Petersburg* in orbit.

"All ships ready to get underway," the *St. Petersburg*'s executive officer reported.

Captain Ryan was about to order all ships to leave orbit when the scanner technician interrupted. "Captain, I'm picking up unidentified contacts entering the Felis system!"

"How many?" Ryan asked.

"Nine. They appear to be medium sized ships. Possibly Troop Transports."

"Are there any other Confederation ships operating in this area?" Captain Ryan asked.

"No, sir," the executive officer responded.

"Can you tell if the ships have spotted us?" Ryan asked.

The scanner technician shook his head. "They're not approaching us, Captain. They appear to be heading for Felis 8."

"Good," Ryan said. Turning to his communications technician, he ordered, "Signal the escort ships and the freighters. Tell them the following: Alien ships entering Felis system; break orbit immediately and head for Bacchus 12."

"Alien ships have been spotted entering the Felis system, Mr. President," Longstreet said.

"Do they pose any danger to the Fleet ships or the freighters?" Rick asked.

"No, Mr. President. The nine alien ships are approaching Felis 8. The *St. Petersburg* and her escorts and freighters got away without being spotted. They're on their way back with their cargo."

Rick nodded slowly. *Felis 8. That's mostly residential and small manufacturing. I don't like leaving its survivors stranded in the face of an enemy force, but I can't send a military strike force against the aliens without risking our own safety and the safety of the search-and-rescue missions.*

Rick watched the holographic star chart floating in the center of the room. *Some days I just hate this job.*

Bret heard a knock on the door. Burgess got up and checked to see who it was. Admiral Marshall stood in the corridor outside of the *Waterloo*'s VIP quarters.

"Mr. Douglas, Corporal Burgess, I thought you'd want to know that the freighter *Beauregard* and her escort ships have left the surface and will be joining us shortly. We'll break orbit and head for Bacchus 12 within the hour. You'll be home late tomorrow."

"Thanks you, Admiral," Bret said, smiling.

"Not at all, Mr. Douglas." With that, Admiral Marshall turned and walked away. Corporal Burgess closed the door.

"Are you looking forward to being home?" Burgess asked.

Bret nodded. "Will you still be on my protection detail once we get back?"

Burgess shrugged. "I don't know, sir. It's possible."

"If I request you, will they assign you to me?" Bret asked.

Burgess thought about this. "Under the circumstances, I think that if you made the request, they'd approve it."

"Are you okay if I make the request?"

Burgess smiled. "Yes, sir. But why?"

"Because I know that you have my back. I want someone with me that I trust. I trust you."

"Thank you, sir,' Burgess said with a nod. "To be honest, I'd like to remain on your detail. And it's not because you're the President's son."

"Oh? Why then?"

"It's like you said… trust," Burgess replied. "You had my back on Manis 2, and I had your back. You had great ideas, but you also listened to me about the prisoners even when you didn't want to. You let me do my job. I can't stand trying to protect people who don't let me do my job."

"Thank you, Corporal Burgess," Bret said.

"You're welcome, sir," Burgess replied.

"Mr. President, all of the initial search-and-rescue missions have broken orbit and are heading back to Bacchus 12. There's no sign of alien pursuit. The *Hercules* and her escorts and freighters will be leaving in six hours."

"Thank you, Admiral," Rick said. "Are the probes we sent out to look for survivors able to spot any alien ships?"

"Let me check on that, Mr. President." Longstreet reviewed the data on his net-dev for several minutes. Finally, he said, "Yes, they are, Mr. President. In fact, alien ships have been spotted in the Felis system, the Manis system, the Equus system, and the Piris system. There have also been intermittent contacts in the Trinity system, but it's hard to get any readings from there due to unexpected interference."

"What's the source of the interference?" Rick asked.

"Unknown, Mr. President. We're looking into it, but we have to be careful not to alert the aliens to what we're doing."

O'Connor stood at the windows of his office, overlooking the campus of the Advanced Weapons Division. When he heard a knock on the door, he hit a button on the credenza next to him, and the door opened. Peter Fleming, O'Connor's Director of Mining Operations, entered.

"You wished to see me, Director O'Connor?" Fleming asked.

O'Connor turned around and faced his subordinate. "Yes, Peter." He gestured to a cluster of chairs near the windows. "Have a seat."

"Thank you."

Once they were seated, O'Connor got right to the point. "You've probably heard the reports that the aliens who attacked the Confederation are looking for Olympium."

Fleming nodded.

"The military is doing all that it can to protect the planet from attack, but should they fail and the planet is invaded by these aliens, I don't want them to triumph over us by also getting the Olympium."

"What can we do to stop them?" Fleming asked.

"If the planet is overrun, and there's no way to keep them away from the Olympium, I want it destroyed," O'Connor replied.

Fleming was shocked. "Destroyed? How?"

"That's what I want you to help me figure out. I want a device, or multiple devices, that can be triggered in case of planetary defeat. I want to start a chain reaction in the Olympium refineries and in the mines that will destroy all of the Olympium in the planet."

"You realize that starting a chain reaction in the Olympium will destroy the planet?" Fleming asked. "The explosions from the bombs going off around the Olympium will spectacular to see, and once all of the Olympium is ignited, Bacchus 12 will explode like a supernova, killing everyone on the planet and destroying everything in orbit around us."

"Trust me," O'Connor said smoothly. "If this device were ever triggered, there would be no human life left on the planet or in orbit. If the aliens kill us all, I see no reason why they should get to take the prize that they seem to covet so dearly."

Fleming nodded. "I understand. Let me start working on some ideas, and then I can show them to you for approval."

O'Connor stood. "Thank you, Peter. Let me know when you have something for me to look at."

"Yes, Director, O'Connor." Fleming stood and walked to the door.

"Oh, Peter. One more thing."

"Yes, Director?"

"You have three days."

The door opened, and Fleming left the office. "Yes, Director," he said as the door closed behind him.

The bruises on Natalia's arm had all healed, but she hadn't forgotten how they got there. No matter how many times she had made love to O'Connor since that night, she didn't feel any warmth or tenderness coming from him. He took pleasure from her but gave little in return.

When he finally rolled off of her and held up his wine glass for her to refill, she knew she needed to talk to someone about what was going on. *I wonder if I should talk to Beth again?*

Beth had confronted Natalia about O'Connor shortly before she left for the southern continent. It was late in the afternoon. Natalia had excused herself from one of the search-and-rescue status meetings to go to the restroom, and Beth followed her.

"How are things between you and Director O'Connor?" Beth had asked.

Natalia was shocked that Beth knew about the affair. "How did you…"

"It's obvious," Beth had said. "The way the two of you look at each other during meetings… it's clear that you two have been together for a long time."

"I don't see how that's any of your business…"

"Who you sleep with *is* none of my business, Natalia." Best began tersely, "But you work for my husband, and he's O'Connor's biggest rival. If O'Connor is using you to spy on Rick or report on what Rick is doing, then that's my business, and it's Rick's business."

"He's never asked me to…"

Beth held had held up her hand. "I don't care to know what he has or hasn't done. But you should talk to Rick and let him know about the affair. He needs to know whether or not he can trust you. If you don't talk to him on your own, I'll have to tell him, and you don't want him finding out that way."

137

Natalia thought about what Beth had said to her as she refilled O'Connor's wine glass. *She'd tell me to talk to Rick. I guess I should do that. But what if he can't trust me anymore?*

Natalie looked at O'Connor as he drank the wine. *How much less would Rick trust me if he found out from someone else?*

"Is something bothering you darling?" O'Connor asked. "You seem far away."

Natalia smiled and shook her head. "I'm just happy, that's all. All the endless meetings about planetary defense make me look forward to our time together even more."

"I know what you mean," O'Connor said, putting his wine glass on the table next to the bed. "I've been dealing with how to protect the Olympium from alien attack."

"Protect the Olympium? How could you do that?"

"By destroying it should the aliens reach the planet surface," O'Connor replied. "The only defense left to us in case of attack is to deny the aliens what they want the most. My engineers are working on a way to set off a chain reaction that will destroy the Olympium all over the planet. No prize, no victory. It's perfect, don't you think?"

Natalia nodded, but inside she wanted to scream. *You'll destroy the planet and everyone who survives the alien attack! That's your idea of protecting the Olympium?*

O'Connor leaned over and started nuzzling Natalia's neck. His hand moved to caress her cheek, but then his hand was around her throat. "I'm sure you understand that you're never to repeat anything I tell you, don't you, darling?"

Natalia nodded. O'Connor's grip lessened, and then he rolled onto his back with a look of smug satisfaction on his face.

Natalia knew right then what she had to do. *I have to talk to Rick in the morning. He has to know about this. No matter what Rick might do to me, he has to know.*

CHAPTER 16

Rick rode the elevator in the Planetary Administration Building from the emergency quarters to his office. Four Fleet Marines rode at his side. As the President of the Confederation, he was never without a Marine escort. More Marines patrolled the hallways of the Administration Building constantly, searching rooms for any monitoring or explosive devices, and checking everyone who entered any areas frequented by Rick and members of his Cabinet.

Rick glanced at his escorts and hid a smile. *These Marines are so serious about their duties. I appreciate their dedication to my safety, but is it really necessary? Apart from aliens, who wants ME dead? And what good would four Marines do when most of our Fleet couldn't stop the attacks on the other Confederation worlds? I didn't spend much time with military personnel in the past. I wonder if they're all this focused. If only one of them would crack a smile once in a while.*

The elevator stopped on the floor for Rick's office. Two Marines stepped out, checked the hallway, and then signaled for Rick and the others to exit. As Rick walked to his office, the Marines surrounded him in close formation. The other Marines patrolling the hallways snapped to attention as he passed. *I'll never get used to that. But if they need military protocols like this to help them process what's going on, I guess I can play along.* He returned their salutes and continued toward his office.

When he reached his office, the two Marines guarding his door snapped to attention. Natalia, who was already at her desk, stood. Rick returned the Marines' salutes and motioned for Natalia to follow him. The two Marines opened the doors to his office.

Rick and Natalia entered while Rick's escorts took their posts around the reception area outside Rick's office.

"What's first on my agenda today, Natalia?" Rick asked, putting his briefcase on his desk.

Natalia hesitated, prompting Rick to turn and face her. He gave her a questioning look, and she stared at her net-dev, clearing her throat.

"What is it, Natalia?" he asked.

"Nothing, Mr. President," she replied nervously.

Bull shit! "Look at me Natalia," Rick said gently.

Natalia looked up.

"I know when something's wrong. What is it?"

Natalia looked down. Rick came around his desk and stood next to her. He took her net-dev and turned it around so he could see what was on it. It showed his calendar and highlighted the first meeting of the day… with Natalia.

"I don't understand," Rick said. "You and I have a meeting this morning?"

Natalia nodded.

Rick gestured toward the two couches nearby and told her to sit down. He sat across from her and said, "What's on your mind?"

Natalia didn't answer at first, but Rick continued pressing her. Finally, he said, "You put the meeting on my calendar. Whatever you want to talk to me about, it must be important enough for you to schedule a formal meeting to discuss it. I'm not a mind reader. Whatever it is, you're going to have to tell me."

Natalia looked up. Her eyes brimmed with tears. Rick watched silently, wondering what could be so bad that Natalia had to work up this much courage to tell him.

Rick was about to stand and get ready for his next meeting when Natalia finally blurted, "I've been sleeping with Director O'Connor."

Rick leaned back on the couch. "And that required a meeting to tell me?"

Natalia stared at Rick, obviously expecting a different response. "Beth told you?"

"No, but she mentioned a while back that she thought there was something going on between you two. You both give off strong signals when you're together in meetings or in the hallways. She noticed it, and she pointed it out to me. I've noticed it, too, but I didn't see a reason to say anything to you. Director O'Connor may have tried to become President of the Confederation, but it's not like he's the enemy, is it?"

Natalie shuddered. "He might be."

"What are you talking about?" Rick demanded, leaning forward.

Natalia swallowed hard. "He's a snake, he's abusive, he's self-absorbed, and those are just his good qualities. He's dangerous, Mr. President. And I think he's losing touch with reality."

"In what way?"

"He ordered the Director of Mining Operations to rig the Olympium refineries, mines, and ore deposits to self-destruct. He's going to destroy the Olympium if the aliens breach the Bacchus system. He wants to deny them their victory and their prize, as he put it. You know as well as I do that destroying the Olympium deposits around Bacchus 12 will destroy the planet and everyone still alive on it."

"How do you know this?"

"He told me when we were... together... last night, Mr. President," Natalia replied, looking down again.

Rick didn't need to ask what "together" meant. He stared at her for a minute. Then he asked, "What else has he told you when you're alone?"

Natalia folded and unfolded her hands. "He asked me to give him copies of reports related to discussions on planetary defense and the search-and-rescue missions. He said that he needed to be kept up-to-date if he were to focus the Advanced Weapons Division on the initiatives that would best support your plans."

"And did you give him those reports?"

Natalia nodded.

"What else did you give him?" Rick asked, hiding his anger.

"He asked me to keep him informed about what you're working on."

Rick shook his head. "And it never occurred to you to tell me this? You didn't think I'd want to know that he asked you to spy on me?"

Natalia's head snapped up. She pulled up her sleeve and moved her scarf aside. Rick could just make out the bruising on her arm, but the bruises around her neck were still plainly visible. "Do you see these, Mr. President? He hurts me. I'm afraid of him. At first, he was loving, polite… a perfect gentleman. Now, he likes doing this and threatening me. I wanted to tell you a long time ago, but he made it clear what he'd do to me if he ever found out that I told anyone about us or what he's been asking me to do. I believe him. But I couldn't keep silent about him planning to destroy the planet. I had to tell you. He's insane. He doesn't care if he kills us all as long as the aliens don't get the Olympium. He must be stopped."

Rick nodded silently. Natalia covered her bruises and looked down again, like a prisoner waiting for the judgment of the court. Rick stared at her, trying to figure out what he should do. After a couple of minutes, an idea came to him.

"Does he know that you're telling me this?"

Natalia looked up with a surprised expression on her face. "No, sir."

"Good. Don't tell him. I want you to pretend like this conversation never took place. But instead of giving him information about me, I want you to give me information about him. I can't move against him unless I know how he plans to trigger the Olympium to self-destruct. I can't risk him destroying the planet just to avoid being arrested on espionage charges. Understand?"

Natalia nodded.

"I want you to give me a list of everything that you've provided to him and everything you've told him. I need to know how much damage you've done. Then I'll decide what to do about your participation in his plans. I've never had a better assistant, and I don't want to lose you. If you stop spying on me for him and start spying on him for me, it might be enough to save you from espionage and conspiracy charges."

"I'm so sorry, Rick," Natalia said. Tears streamed down her face.

"So am I. But you came to me on your own, and that means a lot to me. For now, we'll both act like nothing has happened. There's no telling if he has anyone else watching me, so you can't act sad or worried when you leave this office It's business as usual until I tell you otherwise."

Rick stood. Natalia hesitated; then she rose and gave him a hug. He hugged her back.

"Thank you for being honest with me," Rick said.

"Thank you for being understanding," Natalia sobbed. "I know I was stupid. I should have told you sooner, but I loved him, and I thought that he loved me. It turns out that I'm just his plaything, and I'm tired of being used for his pleasure."

Rick held her until the sobbing stopped. By the time she left his office, she had regained her composure.

As Rick watched her leave, he frowned. *What's O'Connor's game? I know that he's power-hungry, but to seduce my assistant and get her to spy on me is going too far. I'm going to have to watch him closely. I need someone at the Advanced Weapons Division to spy on him for me. Natalia's only going to find out what he tells her. I need someone who can find out what he's not telling her.*

Rick reached for his com-dev and sent Admiral Longstreet a message outlining what Natalia had told him

Rick sat down, waiting for Longstreet to answer. *Some days I really hate this job.*

The Confederation Carrier *Hercules*, her eight escort ships, and the seven freighters that she was protecting arrived at Darius 8 and assumed a low orbit around the planet. Rear-Admiral Michelle Flynt, commanding the *Hercules*, looked over the shoulder of her chief scanner technician, checking for any alien presence in the Darius system.

"I don't detect any alien ships on the planet, Admiral," the chief scanner technician reported.

"I know they're in the system somewhere," Admiral Flynt noted. "See if you can access the probes that we sent to all of the planets after the attacks. If they can pick up survivors, they may be able to pick up aliens."

"Yes, Admiral."

Flynt turned to her communications technician. "Inform the escort ships and the freighters that they're cleared for landing operations."

"Yes, Admiral."

Thirty minutes later, the freighters had landed, and the escort ships were deploying to protect the freighters in case of attack. Admiral Flynt listened to the reports coming in from the surface, but she kept her eyes on the scanners. *I know you're out there. You're not going to catch me off-guard like you did with the rest of the Fleet.*

"Order all squadrons to alert status," she instructed her executive officer. "And I want all gun and torpedo emplacements manned and ready. If we see an alien ship anywhere near us, I want the plasma cannons to blow it out of existence before it can tell anyone else that we're here."

Her officers scrambled to obey her orders. She continued watching the scanners. *I know you're out there.*

The Council Chamber was filled to capacity when Rick stepped up to the podium to present an overview of the planetary defense plans. He gave his introduction and then asked Admiral Longstreet to provide the details.

Longstreet presented the plans for redeploying the Confederation proximity detectors around the Bacchus system, and redeploying the fusion mines from the shipping lanes and placing them along the two safe passages leading to Bacchus' planets. He then discussed the placement of the Fleet ships within the Bacchus system, the orbital defenses around the planet, and the fission mines being deployed within the two nebulas. No mention was made about defenses around the Advanced Weapons Division itself or the Olympium refineries, mines, or ore deposits. Neither Rick nor Longstreet wanted to give O'Connor the impression that they knew about his plans, nor did they want O'Connor speaking to the Confederation Council.

Over the next hour, the Council members asked numerous questions about the deployment of planetary defenses, and in the end, they approved the plans.

Once the Council meeting was over, Rick and Admiral Longstreet headed for Rick's office. "I didn't see Archbishop

Canterbury sitting with the rest of the Cabinet members," the Admiral noted as they walked.

"He's been missing a lot of meetings lately," Rick said. "I should go see him and make sure that he's okay."

"Is your wife still on the southern continent?" Longstreet asked.

Rick nodded. "She finished selecting the initial farming sites this afternoon, and the ranch sites should be finalized tomorrow morning. It's a good thing, too, since the freighters sent on the search-and-rescue missions arrive tomorrow afternoon."

"Are the temporary shelters completed for the refugees?"

"Not yet," Rick replied. "But there are teams working on that, and they'll keep working until the shelters are finished."

Once they were inside Rick's office, he asked, "Have you thought of anyone inside O'Connor's organization that we can use who is more loyal to the Confederation than to O'Connor? We need a mole in the Advanced Weapons Division to keep us informed about what's going on over there."

Longstreet shook his head. "Not yet, Mr. President. They're all loyal to the Division, and by extension, its director. It'll take a while to find someone that we can trust."

"We don't have a while," Rick reminded him. "We must know how his engineers are rigging the Olympium to self-destruct, and we have to find what the triggering mechanism is. We can't stop him otherwise."

"I know, Mr. President. I'll keep working on it and report back to you."

"Thank you, Admiral."

The communications technician on board the *Hercules* looked up from his console. "Excuse me, Admiral Flynt, but I've just received reports from the *Tokyo* and the *Melbourne*. They've found the construction supplies that we're looking for, and they've found survivors who are experienced construction workers. They report that they'll be fully-loaded and ready to leave the planet surface in two days."

Admiral Flynt nodded. The seven freighters that landed on Darius 8 had been divided into two groups – one under command of Lt. Ezra Hague of the Freighter *Tokyo*, and the other under the command of Lt. Jerome Newman of the Freighter *Melbourne*. The two groups landed near manufacturing centers on separate continents to look for supplies and survivors.

"Pass along my congratulations, and tell them to work quickly. If we detect aliens in this system, we'll have to leave orbit with little warning."

"Yes, Admiral," acknowledged the communications technician.

Flynt looked around the bridge of her ship. *That's good news. We need those supplies and resources.*

She looked at the chart of the Darius system being projected next to the navigator's console. *We're too exposed here. Tactically, this is not an optimal deployment. It will take our escort ships too long to reach us from the planet surface if the aliens find us. I hope we can make it back to Bacchus 12 undetected, but I doubt that's going to happen.*

"Any report on re-tasking the probes to search for alien life on Darius 8 and Darius 13?" she asked.

"Yes, Admiral," Flynt's executive officer said. "Fleet Command is already working on that. They'll be sending us the software patch within the hour."

"Let me know when it's ready to test," Flynt instructed.

"Yes, Admiral."

Bret stood on the bridge of the *Waterloo*, watching the ship navigate one of the two safe passages through the debris field around the outer rim of the Bacchus system. *I can't believe I'm almost home again. I've been gone only a few weeks, but it seems like years.*

The Fleet Battleship made its next turn, and Bret felt his anticipation building. He glanced at Corporal Burgess, who stood at his side, and was amused to see a blank expression on the Fleet Marine's face.

I wonder if he's excited that we're almost home, or if he's just relieved that we'll be safe for the first time since Manis 2 was attacked.

The *Waterloo* turned again, and cleared the debris field. In front of them were the planets of the Bacchus system, nestled between the two nebulas. The ship passed Bacchus 14 shortly after clearing the debris field. Bacchus 13 was visible off the port side of the ship as the *Waterloo* continued moving toward the interior of the planetary system. A short while later, the rings of Bacchus 12 came into view.

"I've never seen a more beautiful sight," Bret said softly.

"We're approaching from the night side of the planet," Admiral Marshall said. "It's just before dawn at the capital. Once we're in orbit, we'll shuttle you down to the surface ahead of the freighters."

"Will my family be at the spaceport?" Bret asked.

Admiral Marshall shook his head. "A company of Fleet Marines will meet you and escort you to your father's office. I've been informed that your mother and sister are on the southern continent, waiting to meet the other search-and-rescue mission freighters when they land."

Bret nodded, feeling slightly disappointed that no one would be at the spaceport to meet him. Then he thought about his sister. *Cindy's on the southern continent helping Mom? I can't wait to find out what that's all about.*

Twenty minutes later, the *Waterloo* was in orbit above Bacchus 12. Bret and Corporal Burgess were escorted from the bridge to the shuttle that would take them down to the planet. Bret thanked Admiral Marshall for getting him home, and then he boarded the shuttle.

Less than thirty minutes later, the shuttle landed at the spaceport. One of the shuttle crewmembers opened the hatch, and Bret smelled the scents of home rushing in. Looking through the open hatch, he saw a company of Fleet Marines approaching the shuttle in two columns, just like they did on the *Waterloo*. He followed Burgess through the hatch and stood next to the shuttle as the Marine Company Commander greeted them.

The Marines positioned themselves around Bret and escorted him to the ground transportation that would take him to the city. As he approached the vehicle he'd be riding in, he recognized the person getting out of the rear compartment – Jen!

Bret hesitated for a moment, but Jen didn't. She rushed forward and hugged Bret.

"What are you doing here?" Bret asked, feeling his heart racing as he hugged his father's Communications Director. She was warm and her scent intoxicating. He felt flushed, excited, and nervous all at the same time.

"I knew that your father was tied up in meetings this morning, and I asked him if I could come greet you instead." Jen replied, sounding happy. "I wanted you to see a friendly face waiting for you when you landed."

Bret couldn't bring himself to let go of her, and she evidently felt the same way because her arms didn't release him either.

Finally, Corporal Burgess cleared his throat. "Forgive me, sir, but these Marines have orders to get you to your father."

Bret let go and glanced at Burgess. The corporal winked at him, but said nothing. He held the door while Jen and Bret entered the passenger compartment, and then he joined the driver in the front seat. The other Marines got into their escort vehicles, and soon the motorcade headed for the Planetary Administration building.

Bret and Jen were alone in the back of the vehicle. Before Bret could say anything, Jen said, "I'm so happy that you're home. When we heard about Manis 2, I feared the worst. Your parents never lost hope, but I didn't think I was going to ever see you again."

"I didn't think I was going to see you again, either," Bret said. "And I promised myself that I'd say something to you if I did…"

Before Bret could finish, Jen leaned over and kissed him. Not the kind of kiss that you give to a relative or a friend. This kiss had passion; the same kind of passion that Bret felt for her. He pulled her closer, losing himself in the moment.

When Jen finally pulled away, he said, "I was going to tell you that I'm in love with you, but I like what you said better."

Jen giggled. "I promised myself that I'd do that if you ever came home. I'm in love with you, too."

'You are? Why didn't you ever say anything?"

"Why didn't you?" Jen asked with a smile.

"Probably for the same reason that you didn't," Bret replied. "I thought we had plenty of time."

"And do you still think we have plenty of time?" Jen asked.

Bret looked into her eyes. "I don't know how much time we have or don't have, but I don't see any reason to wait until some far off 'perfect time'. The only perfect time is now. I don't plan to let a single moment slip by again. If I feel something, I'm going say so. If I want something, I'm going to ask for it."

"What do you want?" Jen asked.

"You," Bret replied leaning in. "I've always wanted you."

Jen put her arms around his neck. This time, Bret kissed first. Even though the motorcade raced toward the city, time stood still for both of them.

Twenty minutes, later, the motorcade pulled into the lower level of the Planetary Administration building. The company of Marines left their escort vehicles and formed two columns leading from the door of Bret's vehicle to the building entrance.

Burgess stepped out and opened the door to the passenger compartment. His face was expressionless when Jen exited the vehicle, but he grinned as Bret got out behind her. Bret grinned back.

"Oh," Jen began once Bret was out of the vehicle, "I forgot to tell you. Your father has been meeting with his Cabinet this morning. That's why he couldn't be at the spaceport to greet you. They're all waiting for you and your Marine escort in your father's office to meet you and to hear about what happened on Manis 2."

"Do I have to meet with them now?" Bret asked. "I just got home."

Jen smiled. "I'm afraid so. That's the life of the President's son. Besides, I want to hear about what happened, too. You can pretend you're just telling me."

"Okay." Bret felt better about having to meet with his father's advisors so soon.

Burgess and the driver of Bret's vehicle, Corporal Conrad Nesbit, stayed close to Bret as he and Jen were escorted upstairs to the President's office by the company of Marines. When they reached the top floor of the building, Bret saw his father coming toward him as he stepped out of the elevator.

"Bret!" Rick said, rushing forward.

"Dad!" Bret hugged his father.

"Thank God you're all right, Son."

"I missed you, Dad. And I'm so sorry about the way I acted before I left. I…"

"Don't worry about it," Rick said, cutting him off. "You're safe, and you're home. Nothing else matters."

Rick looked at Corporate Burgess. "Thank you for bringing my son home, Corporal."

Burgess nodded. "Neither of us would have made it home if it weren't for him, Mr. President."

Rick nodded. "I want to hear all about it from both of you. My Cabinet wants to hear about it, too. Come with me. I'll introduce you to them."

Rick put his arm around Bret's shoulder and walked toward his office. Burgess, Nesbit, and Jen followed them. The Marine escort returned to their vehicles.

"Thanks for sending Jen to greet me, Dad," Bret whispered when they reached Rick's office.

Rick grinned. "Something told me that you'd be happy to see her."

Bret wanted to ask his dad what he meant by that, but the Marine guards had already opened the door to Rick's office. Bret saw several people inside. They all stood and applauded as Bret entered behind his father. On the vid-monitor near Rick's desk, Bret saw the two faces that he'd been waiting all morning to see again.

Beth and Cindy were smiling at him over the vid-com link. "Welcome home, Bret," they both cried out.

CHAPTER 17

The executive officer of the *Hercules* entered the Senior Officer's Wardroom and walked to the admiral's table. Admiral Flynt was eating a light lunch while reading reports from the freighters on the planet below.

"Excuse me, Admiral," the executive officer said, standing a short distance away from the admiral's table.

Flynt looked up. "Yes?"

"You wanted to be notified when the technicians had finished applying the software patch that will task the planetary probes to search for alien life. It's ready for testing."

Flynt nodded. "Run the tests. I'll join you on the bridge shortly."

The executive officer nodded. "Yes, Admiral."

The executive officer left the wardroom to carry out his orders. Admiral Flynt finished her lunch, put her net-dev in the oversized pocket on the left leg of her trousers, and took her food tray to the counter marked "Dirty Dishes." Manpower on a Fleet Carrier was not wasted on menial kitchen duty. Officers cleared their own tables, and dishes were cleaned by machines located one deck below the Wardroom.

Admiral Flynt headed for the bridge. When she arrived, the executive officer stood next to the scanner console along with three other officers.

"Admiral on the bridge!" the Fleet Marine guard announced when she entered the command center.

"As you were," she said automatically. She hated it when her bridge staff jumped to attention every time she showed up on the bridge.

She crossed the room and stood next to the executive officer.

"The first test worked, Admiral," the executive officer said. "The probes in the Manis system show alien life on Manis 2. We're expanding the search."

"Check this system and all of the systems closest to our position," Flynt ordered. "If there are aliens nearby, I want to know about it."

"Yes, Admiral," the scanner technician acknowledged.

The scanner technician entered a series of commands into the console. Less than a minute later, the scanner console began displaying data from the Darius, Equus, and Piris systems.

"There's an alien presence on Equus 6 and Piris 9, Admiral. The scanners don't show any alien presence on the planets in the Darius system."

"Continue testing the other planetary probes, but monitor the Darius system continuously," Flynt ordered.

"Yes, Admiral," the scanner technician acknowledged."

Turning to the communications technician, Flynt said, "Send a burst transmission to Fleet Command. Tell them that the software patch worked, and alert them to the alien presence on Equus 6 and Piris 9."

"Yes, Admiral."

Flynt continued watching the scanner. *How long will it take them to reach the Darius system, and will we have enough warning before they get here in order to escape without a fight? If they detect us, they'll know that part of the Fleet survived, and then they'll start looking for our base of operations. I don't want my lack of vigilance to cause them to find out that Bacchus 12 exists.*

Bret and Corporal Burgess sat down next to Rick's desk. Bret watched Jen cross the room and take her seat next to Natalia. She flashed a quick smile at him but then put on a serious face.

Rick asked the members of his Cabinet to introduce themselves to Bret. Once that was done, he stood.

"Many of you have heard me talk about my son, Bret, who was trapped on Manis 2 when the attacks began. He, along with his Fleet Marine escort, Corporal Jim Burgess, survived the attack and managed to escape from Manis 2. The Fleet Battleship *Waterloo* intercepted them and brought them home. I thought it would be beneficial for everyone to hear their story at the same time."

As Rick sat down, Bret turned to Corporal Burgess. "I think Corporal Burgess, here, can give you a better idea of what happened and what we went through. Most of what I did happened just before we escaped from Manis 2."

Corporal Burgess stood and began telling the story. He started with how he discovered that aliens were attacking the resort and the steps he took to protect Bret before the resort was destroyed. Next, he told about their search for food and the plan they made for finding a way off the planet.

Bret observed the expressions on the faces of Cindy and his mother on the vid-monitor, but it was Jen's face across the room that he watched closely. He didn't want them to be alarmed about the dangers he and Burgess faced, and he didn't want them to worry about what might have happened. He was home and safe. That's all they needed to be thinking about.

When Burgess reached the part of the story about reaching the spaceport and sabotaging the alien ships, Bret spoke up. "While Corporal Burgess placed the fuel cells around the engines of the alien ships, I crept up on the aliens who were interrogating survivors. They couldn't communicate with humans, so they had a holographic projection of an Olympium element. I didn't recognize it at first. The prisoners who couldn't identify the projection were shot and killed. When Corporal Burgess and I were heading back to our ship and the corporal opened fire on the alien ships, he could tell from the purple fire that the aliens were using Olympium fuel in their engines. That's when I recognized the projection and realized that the aliens must be looking for Olympium."

Burgess picked back up with the story. "We disarmed two aliens and brought their weapons back with us. They're on the *Waterloo*. From what Admiral Marshall told us, they use Olympium cores just like our weapons."

Director O'Connor squirmed in his seat, and Bret noticed that he looked particularly agitated. *I have to remember to ask Dad about him.*

Once Burgess finished telling the story of their escape and rescue, the Cabinet members asked him and Bret lots of questions. Bret and Burgess did their best to answer them. Finally, Rick stood up and the Cabinet members fell silent.

"I think we've interrogated these two enough for one day," Rick said, smiling. "We'll reconvene at the search-and-rescue mission briefing this afternoon."

Karl and Enrique shook Bret's hand as they left Rick's office. Admiral Longstreet introduced himself and General Monroe, whom Bret already knew.

Bret shook the admiral's hand. As he shook the general's hand, he said. "General Monroe, may I ask you a favor?"

"Certainly," Monroe replied.

"I don't know what the protocol is, but I'd like for Corporal Burgess to be permanently assigned to my protection detail."

Monroe smiled. "Done. I'm also assigning Corporal Nesbit to your detail. He was your driver from the spaceport this morning. They'll be with you during the day and whenever you leave this building. There are more than enough Marine guards in this building to keep you safe when Burgess and Nesbit aren't with you."

"Thank you, General."

Monroe smiled and then hurried out of Rick's office to get to his next meeting.

O'Connor walked up to Bret. "Congratulations on your escape and safe return home," he said smoothly. "I'm Director O'Connor of the Advanced Weapons Division. Tell me, what are your plans now that you're home?"

Bret hesitated for a moment. "I don't know, sir. I've been so focused on getting back home that I haven't really had time to consider what happens next. I was supposed to be attending advanced training for Theoretical and Applied Physics in the next school term, but I don't know if the Advanced Training Center still exists."

"It doesn't," O'Connor informed him. "The Advanced Weapons Division has taken over the duties of the destroyed Fleet shipyards on Trinity 7, so we handle propulsion systems as well as weapon systems now. If you received the aptitude scores for Theoretical and Applied Physics, then you should come work for me. I can set you up with an internship, and my engineers can teach you all about weapon and propulsion systems. Our training programs are far superior to the introductory-level knowledge you'd gain from the Advanced Training Center. My engineers can instruct you in the real world applications of physics. What do you think about that?"

"I'm flattered, Director O'Connor," Bret said. "May I discuss it with my family first?"

O'Connor flashed his snake-like smile. "Of course you may. Get settled in, and give your family time to welcome you home. Let me know in two or three days."

O'Connor shook his hand again and then left Rick's office.

Jen was the next to greet him. Before he could say anything, she hugged him. Bret felt her trembling slightly. They held each other for a moment, and then she gave him a quick kiss. She let go of him and walked toward the door. She turned around, smiled, and gave Bret a small wave. Bret waved back, and then she was gone.

Rick walked over to Bret. "What did O'Connor want?"

"He offered me a job with the Advanced Weapons Division, since the Advanced Training Center was destroyed."

"He did?" Rick asked. "Excuse me for a moment."

Rick walked over to the vid-monitor. "Beth, I need to put you and Cindy on hold for a few minutes. Bret and I will be back soon."

Before they could say anything, Rick hit a button on the vid-com console and the screen went blank.

"Admiral Longstreet, I need to speak with you," Rick said. Turning to the rest of the people in the room, Rick added, "I need the room for a few minutes."

The remaining Cabinet members left Rick's office. Corporal Burgess said, "Corporal Nesbit and I will be just outside when you're ready, sir."

"No," Rick said, walking over to Bret. "Corporal Burgess, I want you and Corporal Nesbit to stay. This concerns you as well."

155

Natalia was the last member of Rick's staff to leave, and she closed the door behind her. Only Rick, Longstreet, Bret, and his two Marine escorts were left in Rick's office.

Rick looked at Admiral Longstreet. "Admiral, O'Connor offered Bret a job with the Advanced Weapons Division."

Longstreet smiled and looked at Bret. "Did he, now?"

"I'm starting to think that something's going on here," Bret said. "I'm a little out of the loop, so could someone fill me in?"

Rick motioned for everyone to sit down. Then he said, "What I'm about to say cannot be discussed with anyone outside of this room. You'll understand why in a moment."

Rick gestured toward Corporals Burgess and Nesbit. "What I'm about to ask of you is far beyond the typical duties of the protective service. If you're uncomfortable with this assignment, let me know. You'll be reassigned to another protective detail, and this will never be discussed again. Your careers will be unharmed."

Burgess looked at Nesbit and then back to Rick. "Whatever it is, Mr. President, we're in."

Rick nodded. "Thank you, but let's wait until you hear what we have to say. Admiral Longstreet and I have been watching Director O'Connor very closely. We're concerned that he's becoming unstable. We've learned that he's having the Olympium deposits rigged to blow up. He's said that he'll destroy the Olympium if the aliens breach the Bacchus system. He thinks that the Olympium is his, and he won't let the aliens take it."

"Won't that destroy the planet?" Bret asked, shocked at the implication.

Rick nodded.

"Then why haven't you arrested him?" Bret demanded.

"It's not that simple," Longstreet interjected. "We don't know how he has the Olympium rigged, and we don't know how he plans to trigger the detonations. If we move against him without that knowledge, he could destroy the Olympium, and all of us on Bacchus 12, just to avoid capture."

Bret nodded. "Then I guess you don't want me to go work there."

Rick shook his head. "On the contrary. There's nothing we want more than for you to go work there."

"I don't understand," Bret said, confused.

"We need someone on the inside the Advanced Weapons Division to watch O'Connor and find out how the Olympium is rigged and how he plans to trigger its destruction," Rick explained. "We need a mole who's working for us. You can refuse, of course, but I hope you'll help us. There's a lot riding on this."

"Won't he be watching me while I'm watching him?" Bret asked.

Rick nodded. "I'm sure of it. And he'll have to watch your two Marine escorts, who will be with you every minute that you're at work."

"As the new kid," Longstreet interjected, "it will be normal for you to ask lots of questions and look around the facilities in your spare time. It gives you the perfect excuse to observe O'Connor and the head of Mining Operations, who has been tasked with rigging the Olympium."

Bret thought about what his Dad and Admiral Longstreet had just told him. *I wanted to help Dad protect us against alien invaders. I didn't know that we face serious danger from one of our own. I do want to help. I guess spying on O'Conner while I'm learning about Theoretical and Applied Physics won't be so bad.*

"I'll do it."

Rick smiled. "Excellent, Son!"

Turning to the two Fleet Marines, Rick said, "I'm counting on the two of you to keep him safe. If O'Connor suspects Bret of spying, there's no telling what he might do. The two of you will also be in a position to watch what's going on. I hope you'll help us with that in addition to your protection duties. But as I said before, you don't have to do this."

"We're still in, Mr. President," Burgess confirmed.

Rick nodded.

Longstreet stood and motioned for the two Marines to stand. "We'll leave you now, Mr. President. I know Bret wants to talk to his mother and sister."

"We'll be right outside," Burgess said as he and Nesbit followed Longstreet out of Rick's office.

Rick walked over to the vid-com console and hit a button. Beth and Cindy's faces appeared on the vid-monitor again.

Bret grinned. "Hi, Mom! Hi, Cindy!

157

The Fleet Minesetter *Trafalgar* approached the minefield near the Baris system. Eight other Minesetters accompanied the *Trafalgar* as part of its task force.

The Captain of the *Trafalgar*, Commander Anthony Chandler, entered the deactivation code into his console. The monitor displayed a warning message that the minefield was about to be deactivated. Chandler re-entered the deactivation code, and the monitor confirmed that the minefield was now deactivated. This was a required step before the mines could be retrieved and relocated to the Bacchus system.

"*Trafalgar* to Task Force," he said into his communications console. "Minefield is deactivated. Begin retrieval."

The Minesetters, which were mostly used to lay mines in new minefields and replace old or detonated mines in existing minefields, moved forward and began retrieving all of the mines. Magnetic grapples pulled the mines into the ships' storage bays.

After six hours, all of the mines had been collected. Chandler smiled. *It's always easier to remove a minefield in space than it is to deploy a new one.*

"*Trafalgar* to Task Force," Chandler said into his communications console. "Set course for Nebula. We have new minefields to deploy."

The *Trafalgar* activated its main engines, and the ship headed for Bacchus 12. Admiral Longstreet had ordered all of the minefields around the Confederation to be moved. The mines were being relocated to the two approaches that safely led to the Bacchus system. This was one part of the overall planetary defense strategy that the Confederation Council had approved.

Chandler watched his monitors to make sure that the Task Force was following him. He also checked for any alien ships that might be following. There weren't any. *This would be a lousy time for an alien attack. I'd hate to lose all of these mines.*

Chandler leaned back in his chair. *Two minefields retrieved, eight more to go. With any luck, we'll have all of the mines relocated to Bacchus and deployed in under two weeks.*

CHAPTER 18

Beth watched the freighter *Armstrong* land at the temporary spaceport near the initial farming sites on the southern continent. The ship touched down and slowly settled on its landing struts. Cargo ramps opened along the port and starboard sides, and the first men, women, and children rescued from Canis 4 exited the freighter and stepped onto the ground of their new home.

Volunteers directed the refugees to a large shelter built on the eastern edge of the spaceport. More volunteers waited inside to record the names and skillsets of each of the refugees before assigning them to temporary housing.

Looking around, Beth finally caught sight of Cindy, who was coordinating the thousands of volunteers helping out. Cindy had recruited most of them, and when Beth had asked her to help with the volunteer assignments, Cindy had taken over the project as her own, leaving Beth's team free to focus on testing the soil and designing irrigation systems for the new farms.

I can't believe how my daughter has grown up over the past weeks. We'd never be ready for today if she hadn't stepped in and organized everything. She has volunteers helping the refugees, unloading the salvaged farming equipment, unloading and inventorying the seeds and seedlings, and getting the freighters prepared for their next search-and-rescue mission. I'm so proud of her.

Everywhere that Cindy went, her two military escorts were never more than a few feet away. Even though there were Fleet Marines posted around the temporary spaceport, Corporals Ben

Simmons and Angela Martinez were there to keep the President's daughter safe.

Beth checked her net-dev and saw the reports from Cindy's volunteers already coming in. She scanned the list of farming equipment that had been salvaged and the inventory of seeds and seedlings. Then she looked at the list of refugees. Almost all of the rescued men and women had critical skills that would be necessary to set up the new food production systems on the planet. *It's a good start, but we need more experienced farmworkers if we're going to make this work.*

Beth walked toward the large shelter. Once Cindy's volunteers were finished assigning the refugees to temporary housing, Beth would address the farmers and give them a better sense of what would be happening over the coming weeks and months.

Beth looked up and saw the second freighter approaching the spaceport – the *Ericsson* from Piris 3. *This is no longer a research project. This is happening for real. There's no Plan B if this fails, so we can't fail.*

Beth saw Cindy and a large group of volunteers heading for the second freighter. *Thank God for my daughter.*

Cindy and her volunteers worked tirelessly to unload the two freighters and help the refugees get settled. It was dark by the time the *Armstrong* and *Ericsson* had left the spaceport and were heading back into orbit for their next search-and-rescue missions.

Cindy sat on the ground, leaning against a tractor and eating from a Travel Meals pouch. Her two Fleet Marine escorts were sitting next to her. They seemed happy to be off their feet for a little while.

Cindy was exhausted but delighted with how smoothly the day had gone. Her volunteers had assisted almost a thousand refugees and unloaded two freighters. *I've never worked so hard in my life. I'll bet my friends haven't either.* She smiled as she thought about Tiffany, Jolene, and Monica helping to process the refugees from Canis 4 and Piris 3. *It's a good thing I didn't have them unloading the freighters. Jolene would have wrecked the tractors, and Tiffany would have broken the freighter. I love them, but they should never be allowed around any machinery larger than a com-dev.*

"Excuse me, ma'am," Corporal Martinez said. "What time do you want to head over to the other spaceport?"

A second temporary spaceport had been built fifty miles away where the ranches were being set up. The freighter *Beauregard* was scheduled to land shortly after dawn, and Cindy and half of her volunteers needed to be there to unload the freighter and assist the refugees. Cindy heard several transports lifting off to carry volunteers to the other spaceport.

Cindy tossed the chem-match into her Travel Meals pouch. "I guess we should go now. I don't know how late the transports will be flying tonight, and I don't want to risk getting there after the *Beauregard* lands in the morning."

Corporal Martinez stood and helped Cindy to her feet. Corporal Simmons led them through the maze of farm equipment toward a group of volunteers waiting to board the next transport.

Once Cindy and her escorts were seated on the transport, she heard the engines revving up. They were airborne a moment later, streaking over the grasslands toward the other spaceport.

I'm looking forward to tomorrow. I've been around plants all of my life, but I've never actually seen cattle before. According to the inventory, the Beauregard is bringing back cattle, sheep, pigs, chickens, and goats. They're also bringing back horses for the ranchers to use. I'd love to learn how to ride a horse.

Twenty minutes later, the transport landed at the other spaceport, and Cindy and her Marine escorts headed for the large shelter with the rest of the volunteers. They found three cots and lay down to get some rest. There were more than enough Fleet Marines patrolling the spaceport, so Cindy's protection detail was able to lie down for a few hours. Cindy was still thinking about horses when she fell asleep.

Cindy woke the next morning just before sunrise. Many of the volunteers were already folding the cots and setting up the tables for collecting information from the refugees and making their temporary housing assignments. Cindy looked around, but her Marine escorts were not there. She folded her cot and stacked it with the others. She was about to get something to eat when

Corporal Martinez and Corporal Simmons approached her carrying breakfast.

"You're up," Martinez said. "We were hoping to be back before you knew we were gone."

Simmons offered Cindy a Travel Meals pouch, and Cindy took it gratefully. They sat down against the wall and ate. Cindy finished her pouch faster than she'd ever eaten a meal before. "I guess I'm hungrier than I thought."

"I'm always that way after a long day," Simmons said.

"Me, too," Martinez said.

"I've never worked this hard before," Cindy admitted, "so I'm not used to this yet."

Martinez smiled. "Don't worry. You'll get the hang of it soon enough."

Cindy nodded. Simmons took their empty pouches and disposed of them in a bin by the main entrance. Cindy and Martinez joined him and walked out of the shelter to make sure that the volunteers were ready for the *Beauregard*.

Cindy had just finished checking in with the volunteer team leaders when she heard the freighter approaching.

Unlike the previous day, the volunteers wouldn't be unloading the freighter while the refugees were being assigned their temporary housing. Unloading live animals was different from unloading farm equipment and plants. It took training to handle livestock, and the volunteers weren't trained. Instead, most of the volunteers would be setting up cattle pens to hold the animals until the ranchers could set up permanent barriers to keep the various types of animals separated from each other.

I'm glad we have only one freighter to unload today. It's going to take a while to learn how to handle the animals. By the time the next cattle freighter arrives, we'll know more about what to do and how to do it.

The *Beauregard* landed smoothly. Cindy was shocked by its size. It was nearly three times the size of the freighter they had loaded the day before. *I've never seen a ship that big before.*

The freighter's passenger ramps lowered, and the men, women, and children rescued from Manis 5 disembarked. The ramps leading to the cargo holds remained closed so the animals couldn't escape.

Cindy and her volunteers directed the refugees to the large shelter, where their information would be collected and their temporary housing assignments made. Unlike the refugees from the farming planets, the ranchers had a more rugged look, and Cindy thought that the men were very handsome.

One in particular.

She saw him as he came down the ramp and walked toward the large shelter. He was tall, tanned, and muscular. The three men he was with looked like him, and Cindy assumed that they were his older brothers and his father. The young rancher approached her.

"Where do we need to go, miss?" he asked politely.

Cindy's heart skipped a beat.

She pointed to the large shelter. "That way," she replied, recovering her composure. "We'll get your housing assigned and then bring you back here to help unload the animals. Which animals are your specialty?"

"Cattle," he answered.

"They're being unloaded first," Cindy said after checking her net-dev. "Come back here once you have your housing assignment."

The young rancher nodded. "Thank you, miss," he said. Then he and the three men with him melted into the group of refugees heading for the large shelter.

"Wow," Cindy said as she lost sight of him.

An hour later, the refugees who were cattle ranchers met back where Cindy waited for them. Cindy looked around and finally saw the young rancher standing with the three other men that she had seen him with earlier.

"Good morning," she shouted over the whine of the freighter engines. "My name is Cindy Douglas, and on behalf of the President of the Confederation and all of us working to set up a self-sustaining agricultural system here, I want to welcome you to Bacchus 12."

Cindy pointed to several metal holding pens in the distance. "The cattle will be the first animals unloaded from the freighter, and they'll be taken to those holding pens until we can get more

163

permanent structures built. Are any of you experienced ranch foremen?"

Eight refugees held up their hands.

"Fantastic! Will you be willing to oversee the unloading? We have volunteers here to help, but we need your experience to show us how to get the cattle off the freighter and over to the pens safely."

The eight refugees nodded.

"Great! What do you need us to do first?"

The older man who had been with the young rancher spoke to the other foremen for a moment, and then he stepped forward. "We'll get the cattle off the freighter. Have your volunteers waiting at the bottom of the ramp to help get the cattle to the pens."

Cindy appreciated the calm authority in the man's voice. Turning to her volunteers, she shouted, "You heard the man. Follow his instructions."

The ramps to the cattle cargo holds lowered, and the foremen led the rest of the experienced cattle ranchers back on board. A few minutes later, the first cow was led down the ramp.

"This is a dairy cow," the foreman said. "All of the dairy cows need to be put in the same pen. Don't mix cow breeds in the same pen."

He showed the volunteers how to lead the cow. More dairy cows came down the ramp. Soon, the volunteers were leading the cattle to their pens.

Cindy stayed for several minutes to make sure that the cattle unloading was going well. Then she walked over to another group of refugees and volunteers who were waiting to start unloading the sheep.

Within two hours, teams were unloading all of the animals and leading them to their pens. Cindy walked around to each of the teams to make sure that everything was going smoothly.

When she reached the ramps leading to the cargo holds for the cattle, she didn't see any of the ranchers or the volunteers nearby.

Did they finish the cattle already? I hope not. I'd like to see that young rancher again.

She heard a banging sound coming from the far cargo hold. She walked up the ramp, looking for the source of the sound. When she reached the top of the ramp, she heard the banging again. She followed it to one of the cargo holds.

She saw ten of the ranchers in the middle of the cargo hold. They were trying to get a rope around the neck of the largest cow Cindy had ever seen. The way it pawed the deck and snorted made it seem dangerous, and its pointed horns made it look deadly.

Cindy stayed back along the wall of the cargo hold so she could watch the ranchers without getting in their way. But as she moved to one side to get a better view, the animal saw her. It lowered its head and pawed at the deck angrily. Then it charged.

It broke through the ring of ranchers and ran straight at Cindy.

Cindy froze. She couldn't move. All she could see was the great black beast charging her and the grey horns on its head pointing at her chest.

Corporals Martinez and Simmons, who had come up the ramp behind Cindy, unslung their rifles and prepared to shoot the animal.

Before they could fire, one of the ranchers managed to toss a rope around the beast's neck. He snaked the other end of the rope through one of the tie-down rings on the cargo hold deck, knotting it as quickly as he could.

The beast ran the slack out of the rope, and its head jerked as the rope held. But the rear of the beast swung around from its forward momentum, and before Cindy could move out of the way, she was pinned against the wall of the cargo hold.

The beast thrashed about, trying to get loose from the rope. Every time it moved, Cindy felt crushed. She cried out in pain.

The ranchers pulled on the rope, but they weren't strong enough to drag the beast forward away from Cindy. Corporals Martinez and Simmons joined the ranchers and pulled on the rope, but Cindy was still trapped, and each time the beast moved, it forced the air out of her lungs. She was having trouble breathing, and she was getting dizzy. She couldn't even scream.

Her vision blurred, but she saw a shadow jump on the back of the beast. Terrified and furious, the beast started trying to buck off whatever was on its back. The shadow rolled off and ran for

Cindy, who had fallen to the floor when the beast lurched forward. It picked her up and carried her out of the cargo hold.

"Are you all right, Miss?" a familiar voice asked.

Cindy's vision began clearing, and she saw the face of the person who had rescued her. It was the young rancher that she had seen earlier. She nodded. "I think so, but my ribs hurt."

Corporal Martinez ran up to check on Cindy. Hearing Cindy complain about her ribs, the Marine reached for her comdev. "I need a medical team in cargo bay nine of the *Beauregard*. Little package is down!"

The Fleet medical team arrived five minutes later. Cindy was poked, prodded, and scanned by several people as the team assessed her injuries. Finding nothing broken or seriously hurt, they bandaged her up to provide padding for the bruises forming on her chest and abdomen.

Once they left, Cindy looked at the young rancher, who had remained by her side the whole time. "Thank you for saving me back there. What was that?"

"That was a bull," he replied. "It's a male cow, and they're used for breeding. They don't like being handled, and they hate being moved. We save them for last. It had broken loose just before you showed up, and we were trying to get a stronger rope around it so we could lead it to its pen."

"Do they charge like that all the time?"

The young rancher nodded. "That's why we keep them separate from the other animals. They're violent and wild. But they're necessary if you want cows to be born."

"Remind me to never go near one again," Cindy said.

There was a shout from the cargo hold.

"We'd better get out of here," the young rancher said. "They're bringing the bull out."

He helped Cindy to her feet, and he led her and Corporal Martinez down the ramp and away from the freighter. A minute later, the ranchers, holding the ends of several ropes that went around the bull's neck and torso, brought the bull down the ramp and led it away to the special pen set up to hold it.

Corporal Simmons came down the ramp and walked over Cindy. "Are you all right, ma'am?" he asked.

"Yes, thank you," Cindy replied.

"I notified your mother, ma'am," Martinez said. "She'll be here within the hour."

Cindy nodded. Looking at the young rancher, she held out her hand. "My name is Cindy. Cindy Douglas. What's yours?"

"Colten McNabb."

Cindy leaned forward and gave Colten a kiss on his cheek. "I have to go now, Colten. But I hope I get to see you again."

Colten blushed and smiled. "I hope so, too, Cindy."

Cindy walked away, followed by Martinez and Simmons. She glanced back, but Colten had left the area around the freighter to join the others leading the bull to its pen.

"Colten McNabb," she said to herself. "Talk about someone who could make you want to take up ranching."

"Your son is here to see you, Mr. President," Natalia informed Rick.

"Send him in."

The Marine guards opened the doors to Rick's office.

"Come in, Bret," Rick said when Bret stepped in.

"I know you're busy, but do you have a minute?" Bret asked when the doors closed behind him.

"Sure, Son. Sit down."

Bret sat down across from Rick.

"What's on your mind?" Rick asked.

"I just notified Director O'Connor that I'm accepting his job offer. He wants me to start tomorrow. Is that all right with you?"

Rick leaned back in his chair and smiled. "It's great! Are you okay with it?"

Bret nodded. "I want to help you in any way I can. Cindy's with Mom setting up farms and ranches. This is what I want to do."

"I appreciate that," Rick said. Changing the subject, Rick asked. "There's something I've been wanting to ask you, but I haven't had the chance. What happened to the artwork that you took with you to Manis 2?"

Bret looked sad. "The roof of the exhibition hall fell and crushed everything."

"I'm sorry, Son. Your pieces were beautiful. It's a shame that no one got to see them."

Bret nodded.

"Well, I'm just grateful that you came back to me," Rick said.

Natalia stuck her head in the office. "I'm ordering dinner to be sent up, Mr. President. Is Bret joining you?"

Rick looked at his son. "Have dinner with me? It'll give us more time to catch up on what's been going on."

Bret smiled and nodded. "Sure."

Rick looked at Natalia and nodded.

"I'm surprised you're keeping her around after what you told me about her and O'Connor," Bret commented after Natalia closed the door.

"She's spying on him for me now."

"Do you trust her?"

Rick shrugged. "I won't know until you start work. Natalia won't know what you're doing for me. I can compare what she reports to what you report. If they contradict each other, then I know that I can't trust her."

"What will you do then?" Bret asked.

"I don't know. No one's been charged with treason or espionage for as long as I can remember. I'd hate for her to be the first."

Admiral Longstreet's shuttle touched down in the landing bay of the Fleet Battleship *Ticonderoga*. As soon as he was on board, Captain Seamus Reagan greeted him.

"Welcome aboard, Admiral," Reagan said. He escorted Longstreet to the bridge.

"Admiral on deck!" the Fleet Marine guard announced when Longstreet arrived.

"As you were," Longstreet said.

"Prepare to get underway," Reagan said to his navigator.

"Yes, Captain," the navigator replied.

The *Ticonderoga* had been tasked with moving the proximity detectors from the edge of Confederation space and placing them around the Bacchus system. Working with the Advanced Weapons Division, the engineers aboard the

Ticonderoga had relocated more than a thousand proximity detectors so far. The detectors were being disguised to look like normal space debris, rather than part of a detection grid, before being redeployed.

Longstreet was on board to inspect the *Ticonderoga's* progress and to assess the amount of time needed to complete the deployment.

The *Ticonderoga* navigated through one of the safe passages out of the Bacchus system. Longstreet saw Minesetters laying new minefields along the passage.

"Which proximity detectors have you been redeploying?" Longstreet asked.

"We've been redeploying detectors from sectors R-J, P-L, Z-F, G-W, and K-M," Captain Reagan replied. "We've also cleared the detectors from sectors A-X and B-D, but we don't dare approach the detectors in Sector A-B due to communications interference around the Trinity system."

"And how close are you to completing the deployment?"

"Sixty percent," Reagan said. "We'll have that up to eighty percent in a week."

"Why is it taking so long?" Longstreet asked. "The Minesetters are moving the minefields at ten times that speed."

"That's because the Minesetters aren't disguising the mines when they redeploy them. We're making the proximity detectors look like asteroids, rocks, and rogue comet remnants. That takes time."

Longstreet nodded.

The *Ticonderoga* exited the passage and changed course. Reagan showed Longstreet a holographic projection of the new proximity detector deployment and ordered the navigator to bring the ship close to the detectors that were deployed the previous day.

"What do you see, Admiral?" Regan asked as the ship reached the new detectors.

"Nothing. I don't see anything that looks like a proximity detector."

Reagan smiled and pointed to the holographic projection. Two of the detectors were indicating the presence of a ship nearby.

"That's the *Ticonderoga*, Admiral. The detectors are working perfectly."

"What do you need to help you finish deploying the detector net faster?"

Without hesitating, Reagan said, "The Battleship *Normandy*. If I had her out here, we could finish the net in three days."

Longstreet thought about it for a moment. "Done."

"Thank you, Admiral," Reagan said.

"Three days, Captain. You have three days."

"Yes, Admiral."

"Good. Have my shuttle take me back to Bacchus 12."

CHAPTER 19

Rick and his Cabinet members sat in the Situation Room to hear Admiral Longstreet's report on the planetary defenses and the search-and-rescue missions. The first rays of the morning sun streamed through the windows as Longstreet began speaking.

"Thank you for agreeing to meet so early." Longstreet activated holographic projections of the Confederation, the Bacchus system, and of Bacchus 12. "First of all, the initial search-and-rescue missions have been successfully concluded. The freighters have all been unloaded and are heading back out as follows: the *Waterloo* and seven freighters to Equus 4, the *St. Petersburg* and five freighters to Baris 8, the *Edinburgh* and four freighters to Darius 13, and the *Montreal* and four freighters to Felis 5."

"What about the *Hercules* and its mission to Darius 8?" Rick asked.

"The *Hercules* reports that the mission is going well, and they should be ready to leave the planet sometime tomorrow. The cargo holds of the seven freighters will be filled with construction supplies and equipment, and several hundred construction workers and their families have been rescued."

Rick nodded.

Longstreet continued. "As for the planetary defenses, the bulk of the proximity detectors from the Confederation shipping lanes have been relocated to the Bacchus system. They're being deployed like a net around the system, and they're being disguised as rocks and space debris so the aliens won't detect them so easily. Deployment of the proximity detectors should be completed in three days. The minefields from the Confederation shipping lanes have been relocated to the two safe approaches through the outer debris field of the Bacchus system. In addition, the replacement mines warehoused at the Advanced Weapons Division facilities are being deployed inside the debris field and around the Bacchus system. It will take at least a week to complete setting up the new minefields."

Longstreet entered a command into his net-dev, and the location of the proximity detectors and the minefields appeared on the holographic projection.

"As for the planetary defenses," Longstreet said, gesturing to the holographic projection of Bacchus 12, "Plasma cannons are being mounted on the larger asteroids within the planetary rings and on the four largest of Bacchus 12's moons. The remaining plasma cannons and torpedo launchers are being placed on orbital satellites. Many of these are being hidden behind Bacchus 12's five smaller moons so that no approaching ships will see them. All of the plasma cannons and torpedo launchers can be controlled from a central command center, or they can be set to automatically fire on any ship without a Fleet transponder."

"When will the deployment of the plasma cannons and torpedo launchers be completed?" Rick asked.

"Hopefully within the next two weeks, Mr. President. The delay is with the orbital satellites. They're having to be fabricated from scratch, and it's slow going. Director O'Connor's people are working as fast as they can."

"Mounting the plasma cannons on the moons and asteroids is already completed?"

"Yes, Mr. President," Longstreet replied. "They were placed first."

"Why weren't the torpedo launchers placed on the moons and asteroids as well?" Enrique asked.

"Because of the gravity, Mr. Vice President. It slows down the torpedo's acceleration and throws off the targeting controls. Director O'Connor's people recommended, and I agreed, that the torpedo launchers needed to be mounted on orbital satellites."

"What about the deployment of the Fleet?" Rick asked.

Longstreet entered another command into his net-dev and the holographic projection of the Bacchus system updated to show

Fleet deployment. "Our outer defenses will be comprised of two battle groups under the Battleships *Ticonderoga* and *Normandy*. They will take position halfway between Bacchus 12 and the safe passages leading through the outer debris field. They'll hit any ship that survives the minefields. The Battleship *Waterloo* will be held in reserve just behind Bacchus 11. It can be deployed against any enemy ships entering the Bacchus system through the debris field or the nebulas. Our inner defenses will be comprised of two more battle groups under the command of the Carriers *Yorktown* and *Hercules*. They'll take positions behind our largest four moons. The plasma cannons and torpedo launchers constitute our last line of defense."

"What about the nebulas?" Enrique asked.

Longstreet updated the holographic projection of the Bacchus system again. "The fission mines are being placed throughout both nebulas. They're the largest nuclear devices ever constructed, and the shockwaves they'll create should be strong enough to destroy any ships in their vicinity."

"When will the nebula minefields be completed?" Rick asked.

"Two weeks minimum. Irradiated Olympium is tricky to work with, and the nuclear devices have to be assembled carefully. Then programming the detonators and placing the mines takes time."

"What if we don't have two weeks?" Enrique asked.

"Then we'll have to make do with what we have," Longstreet replied.

Admiral Flynt was reading the reports from the *Tokyo* and the *Melbourne* when the *Hercules'* scanner technician interrupted her.

"Excuse me, Admiral Flynt, but scanners are picking up the *Edinburgh* and her four freighters approaching Darius 13. They'll be in orbit in thirty minutes."

"Very well. Continue scanning the system for alien ships."

"Yes, Admiral."

This is too many Fleet ships in one place. If the aliens hit us here, we could lose ships that are needed to protect Bacchus 12.

Bret arrived at the Advanced Weapons Division campus twenty minutes before he was supposed to start his first day of work. The guards at the main gate didn't want to let Bret's security detail onto the campus, but after the guards placed a call to Director O'Connor, who was still in the Cabinet meeting, Corporals Burgess and Nesbit were allowed to remain with Bret.

Jason Dorr waited for Bret near the main entrance when he arrived at the Advanced Weapons Division's central office. "Good morning, Bret," he said, holding out his hand. "I'm Jason Dorr. I'm one of the junior engineers here, and I'm overseeing the nebula minefield project. You've been assigned to my team, so you and I will be working closely together."

"Pleased to meet you, Jason," Bret said. He then introduced his Marine escorts.

Jason motioned for Bret and the Marines to follow him as he crossed the lobby and headed for the escalators that led underground. "I understand that your aptitude scores earned you a spot in the Theoretical and Applied Physics program."

"That's right," Bret acknowledged.

They rode the escalator down to the underground complex that linked all of the surface buildings, laboratories, manufacturing facilities, and warehouses together.

"Well, you're going to be getting a crash course in applied physics with my team," Dorr said, turning right at the bottom of the escalator. "We're irradiating Olympium as fuel for nuclear fission devices that will be deployed inside the two nebulas. They'll create shockwaves within the hydrogen gas clouds. Any ship within a hundred mile radius of the mine will be destroyed."

"That's impressive," Bret commented.

Dorr nodded and led them down a wide hallway with adjacent corridors branching off at regular intervals. It reminded Bret of a tree with the branches spreading out.

"It's taking so long to create and deploy the mines," Dorr continued, "that we're going to try to build a higher yield device that will create a shockwave large enough to destroy a ship within two hundred miles or more of the mine. That's what the team is working on today. You'll be part of the team."

"Sounds exciting," Bret said, happy to be working on something so important.

"It is," Dorr stated, taking a left at the corridor marked "Nuclear Mine Development Complex."

Signs along the corridor gave continuous updates about radiation protocols and the status of the radiation shielding around the fusion and fission fuel facilities. Dorr led them to a large set of doors marked "Fission Development."

The Fission Development facility was completely underground. The equipment for irradiating the Olympium was kept on the lowest level. Fuel ready for weaponization was stored on the next level up. Fission core and mine assembly was just above that, and the warehouse for completed mines and the team workspaces were on the uppermost level, where they had just entered. Protective clothing was required on the bottom three levels and in the warehouse, but not in the offices, workspaces, or meeting rooms. The facility was constantly monitored for radiation leaks and contamination that could put the workers in danger.

Dorr gave Bret and his Marine escorts a quick tour and introduced them to the team. Bret was assigned to a workstation, and then Dorr led them to a meeting room. Burgess and Nesbit waited just outside, and Bret followed Dorr into the room and took a seat at the circular table. Once the rest of the team had arrived, Dorr stood up.

"We need to build a bigger bomb with a much larger yield. How can we increase the yield without using so much irradiated Olympium that we accidently reach critical mass prior to detonation?"

Bret looked down at the net-dev built into the table in front of his seat. He clicked on the link titled "Creating Fissionable Fuel" and scanned the summary while the engineers in the room discussed ways to increase yield without risking premature detonation.

Irradiated Olympium is created by taking Olympium ore and processing it into a powder to remove impurities. The powder is then bombarded with artificially created high-intensity radioactive waves. Once irradiated, the powdered ore is shaped into the nuclear core of a fission weapon. The shape is based on the mass and yield requirements of the device.

Bret was confused. *Why are they using raw Olympium ore to make their fissionable material?*

175

Bret cleared his throat, and Door looked at him sharply.

"You have something to add to the discussion, Mr. Douglas?" He sounded slightly annoyed.

Bret looked around the room at the engineers staring at him. "I just have a question. I'm not that familiar with nuclear fission. I noticed that you're using powdered Olympium ore to create your fissionable material, right?"

"Yes," Dorr replied.

"Well, Olympium's special property is that it's an energy amplifier. Wouldn't refined Olympium give you a greater yield?"

"Not without the risk of reaching critical mass during the irradiation process," Dorr replied dismissively.

"I understand that, but what about the Olympium gel that's used in fuel cells? Wouldn't Olympium in a gel form have a different critical mass? Couldn't it allow for a device with greater yield *and* minimal risk of premature detonation?"

"We've never tried that," one of the other engineers commented.

"A gel should be more stable than powdered ore," another engineer stated.

Dorr nodded, "We've never even considered that approach. Olympium gel has the highest energy amplification coefficient of any form of refined Olympium. If it can be irradiated safely, there's no telling how large the explosion and resulting shockwave might be."

Dorr immediately ordered his engineers to design a simulation to test Bret's theory.

Beth walked down the main hallway of the hut that her staff was using as temporary housing near the sites for the new ranches. She saw Corporal Martinez at her post in front of the door to Cindy's room.

"Good morning, ma'am," Martinez said as Beth approached.

"Good morning Corporal," Beth responded. "Is she up yet?"

"Yes, ma'am." Martinez stepped aside.

Beth knocked on the door. "Cindy? It's Mom."

"Come in," she heard Cindy say from inside the room.

Beth opened the door. "I wanted to check your bruises. How are you feeling?"

"Sore."

Cindy's ribs and abdomen were taped up with a reinforced bandage that kept her from bending or twisting comfortably until her bruises from the charging bull were fully healed. Cindy could barely bend over or get out of bed without loosening the bandages.

Beth sat on the bed next to Cindy and started carefully unwrapping the bandages. The bruises were a deep purple, but Beth saw yellow along the edges.

"They're starting to heal," Beth commented as she helped Cindy rewrap them.

"They hurt like hell," Cindy muttered.

"It could be worse," Beth said gently. "That bull could have killed you."

"It would've if it hadn't been for Colten," Cindy reminded her. "He's the one who saved me."

"I heard about him," Beth said. "His father is in charge of the cattle ranchers. He's found a better place to put the cow pastures, and he and his ranchers are putting up the fences this morning."

"Are you going to inspect their work?" Cindy asked with a hopeful look on her face.

"Why, so you can come along and see Colten again?" Beth chuckled.

"Maybe," Cindy replied, smiling.

Beth nodded. "As a matter of fact, I'm heading over there in about thirty minutes." Beth finished rewrapping the bandages and helped Cindy pull her shirt back down.

"You're welcome to come with me," Beth added.

Cindy threw her arms around her mother, and Beth heard Cindy gasp in pain.

"Are you sure you're up to it?" Beth asked.

"Yes, Mom!" Cindy sounded determined.

"Okay, but go easy with the hugging. I don't want you popping a rib just so you can grab onto your rancher friend."

Cindy rolled her eyes and laughed. "No promises, Mom."

Bret looked down at his com-dev. There was a message from Jen. "Dinner tonight?"

Bret smiled. "Yes," he typed. "When and where?"

Jen responded a moment later. "My place as soon as you get off work. I'm cooking."

"Perfect. See you there. What's the address?"

Jen replied with the address, and Bret put the com-dev back in his pocket.

Bret looked around the conference room. The engineers on Dorr's team had been running simulations for several hours to test the effects of radioactive waves on Olympium gel and the subsequent explosive yield of a device using irradiated Olympium gel as nuclear fuel. So far, the simulations looked positive. With a slight change to how the Olympium was irradiated, using Olympium gel yielded an explosion ten times more powerful than using the powdered Olympium ore, and the resulting shockwave had a destructive radius of nearly a thousand miles. Plus, the assembly of the mines would be much faster because of the stability of Olympium gel.

"It looks like your idea is going to work, Mr. Douglas," Dorr said at the end of the last simulation. "Now we need to build a prototype and test it in the nebula. We'll start on that in the morning. In the meantime, we need a supply of Olympium gel sent over from the fuel refinery."

The meeting ended an hour later. Bret left for the evening and made his way through the underground corridors to the central office. Burgess and Nesbit walked with him.

Once they were in their vehicle and through the main gates, Nesbit asked, "Are you heading back to the Planetary Administration Building, sir?"

"No." Bret gave Jen's address to Nesbit.

"I'll have to inform the Protective Services ops-center, sir," Burgess said. "We'll need additional resources if you're planning to be there overnight."

Bret blushed. "I don't know if I'm going to stay overnight."

"It doesn't matter, sir," Burgess said. "We have to be prepared for any contingency."

Bret glanced over at Burgess and saw that Burgess was grinning. "Do what you have to do, Corporal."

The vehicle pulled up to Jen's building thirty minutes later. Burgess and Nesbit got out of the vehicle and spoke to the Fleet Marines who were patrolling the perimeter. Then Burgess opened Bret's door.

"The additional resources are here already, sir. They'll keep you safe inside the building."

Bret nodded and got out of the vehicle. Burgess and Nesbit escorted him to the door of Jen's building, and then they returned to the vehicle to wait for him. One of the additional Fleet Marines escorted him to the elevator and rode up to the fifth floor with him. Another Fleet Marine met Bret at the elevator and escorted him to Jen's door.

Before he could knock, the door opened. "Hi, Bret!" Jen said with a big smile on her face. "Come in."

Bret walked in. As soon as the door closed, Jen had her arms around his neck. "I've been wanting to do this all day," she whispered as she leaned in for a kiss.

"Me, too."

Ten minutes later, Jen had her back against the door, running her fingers through Bret's hair as he kissed her neck. "Do you want to eat now or later?" she whispered huskily.

"I want whatever you want," he said, nuzzling her ear.

She grabbed his hand and led him across the living room. They passed the dining room and the kitchen on the way to Jen's bedroom.

Beth and Cindy disembarked from the transport that had brought them to the site of the new cattle ranch. The fields were thick with the sturdy grasses that grew all around the southern continent. Fencepost holes had been dug, and the posts were being set when Beth and Cindy arrived.

Tucker McNabb, Colten's father, walked over and greeted them. "Good morning. We're making good progress here. When we're done, this pasture will hold up to five hundred cows and ten bulls. The bulls will be in separate pens, of course."

Tucker looked at Cindy. "How are you feeling, miss?"

Cindy smiled. "I'm still sore, but I'm healing."

"That's good," Tucker said. "Bulls are a nasty business. I don't know too many people who've survived what you went through. You're either lucky or blessed."

"I'm grateful," Cindy said. "Colten saved my life."

"I've never seen him try what he did in that cargo hold," Tucker said. "I don't know what he was thinking, but it worked. It's a wonder he didn't land on his head when that bull started bucking, but he landed on his feet and got you out of there before the bull could turn around."

"Is Colten here?" Cindy asked. "I'd like to thank him again."

Tucker pointed to a group of ranchers setting one of the fence posts. "He's over there."

Cindy looked at Beth, who nodded. Cindy ran in the direction that Tucker pointed, holding her ribs to keep them from hurting.

Tucker looked at Beth. "My son hasn't stopped talking about that young woman since he met her."

"She hasn't stopped talking about him either," Beth said. "I think she'd like to give ranching a try."

Tucker smiled. "Well, if she can face a bull like that and walk away, she'd make a good little rancher."

Beth smiled, and Tucker led her over to the fence line to show her his plans for the first cattle ranch.

The scanner technician on the *Hercules* rechecked the data on his monitor.

"Admiral Flynt! Enemy contacts entering the Darius system!"

"How many?" Flynt demanded.

"Fifteen ships altogether. Mostly mid-sized. No Capital Ships."

"Where are they heading?"

"Here, Admiral. Darius 8."

"How long have we got?" Flynt asked.

"An hour at the most," the scanner technician replied.

"That's not enough time to recall the freighters and escort ships from the surface," Flynt stated. "They won't be ready to lift off for at least six more hours. And with the *Edinburgh* in orbit above Darius 13, and her escort ships and freighters on the planet, they won't have time to escape either. If we try to run, we'll lose the freighters for certain. If we fight, we'll let the aliens know that parts of the Fleet survived. They'll start looking for our base, and they could find Bacchus 12."

"What do we do, Admiral?" the *Hercules'* executive officer asked.

"We have no choice. We fight."

Flynt turned to face her bridge staff. "All hands to battle stations! Activate all plasma cannons and torpedo launchers. Communications, send a burst transmission to Fleet Command and let them know our situation. Notify the *Edinburgh* that she's to remain hidden if at all possible. Then notify the freighter and escort ships on Darius 8 to be prepared to leave the planet at a moment's notice. We'll try to hold the aliens off long enough for them to escape."

Alarms went off all over the ship, and the panels around each hatch changed color to red. The *Hercules*, one of the last two remaining Carriers in the Confederation Fleet, prepared for war.

CHAPTER 20

It was after midnight when Natalia stuck her head into Rick's office. "Mr. President? Admiral Longstreet needs you in the Situation Room. He says it's urgent."

Rick nodded. He followed Natalia out of his office and down the hall. *What is it now?*

When Rick entered the Situation Room, a large holographic projection of the Darius system floated over the center of the conference table, and Fleet officers and technicians were busy with their com-devs and net-devs. Everyone was talking at the same time, and Rick couldn't follow any of the conversations.

Admiral Longstreet noticed that Rick had entered the room. "Mr. President!"

Immediately, the conversations in the room stopped, and the Fleet personnel stood and snapped to attention.

"As you were," Rick said – a phrase that he had learned to say by watching Admiral Longstreet.

The Fleet personnel sat, and Longstreet walked over to Rick. "Fifteen enemy ships have been spotted entering the Darius system, Mr. President. There's no way that the ships on Darius 8 or Darius 13 can escape undetected. The *Hercules* is moving to engage the enemy to give the escort ships and freighters on Darius 8 a chance to escape. The *Edinburgh* has been ordered to remain hidden in Darius 13's upper atmosphere until there's an opportunity to escape or until they come under attack."

Damn! I hoped that the search-and-rescue missions wouldn't run into the enemy before the planetary defenses were in place. If the Hercules engages the enemy, they'll know that part of the Fleet still exists and is operating from a base that they haven't discovered yet. This is not good.

Rick looked at the holographic projection of the Darius system. The Fleet warships were shown in green, and the freighters were in blue. The alien ships, approaching Darius 8, were in red.

"Can the *Hercules* take on fifteen enemy ships?" Rick asked.

"Unknown, Mr. President," Longstreet replied. "Admiral Flynt reports that these are mid-sized ships only. If the *Hercules* has the element of surprise, her fighters and bombers could inflict serious damage on the enemy. The *Hercules* also has the new plasma cannons and torpedo launchers. It'll be the first time they've been tested in combat conditions, but they should give the *Hercules* the advantage in firepower."

"*If* they still have the element of surprise," Rick commented. "What about her escort ships?"

"They're on the planet protecting the freighters," Longstreet replied.

"Are there any other Fleet ships that can reach them in time?" Rick asked.

Longstreet shook his head. "No, Mr. President."

"So the *Hercules* is on its own?"

"Yes, Mr. President."

Rick stared at the holographic projection. "God help them!"

Admiral Flynt looked at the star chart displayed in front of her. *One Carrier against fifteen mid-sized alien ships with unknown weapons. How are we going to survive this?*

As she thought about the tactical situation, an idea came to her. "Prepare to activate the main engines," she ordered.

"We're leaving the Darius system, Admiral?" the executive officer asked. "Abandoning the escort ships and freighters on the planet?"

Flynt smiled and shook her head. "No. We're going to launch all of our squadrons, and then we're going to redeploy the ship behind the enemy. With the main engines, we might be able to get behind them before they know we're there. The fighters and bombers should keep them distracted, giving us time to take out their engines. That'll disable them, and if we can hit their fuel cells, we can destroy them."

The executive officer nodded. "A jump maneuver, Admiral? It's risky. It could damage the ship if we use it too many times."

"Do you see an alternative?" Flynt asked.

The executive officer shook his head. "No, Admiral. I think it's the best plan. I just wanted to point out the dangers to the ship."

"Understood," Flynt acknowledged. "Prepare to redeploy on my command."

The executive officer checked the battle console. "All squadrons ready to launch, Admiral. Plasma cannons manned and ready. Torpedo launchers manned and ready. Fusion torpedoes loaded and ready to fire."

"Main engines online and ready at your command," the navigator reported.

"Very well," Flynt acknowledged.

Flynt checked the star chart again. *The alien ships are still grouped together. We'd better attack before they redeploy around the planet.*

"Launch all squadrons."

The executive officer lit a button on the battle console to signal the squadrons to launch immediately. "All squadrons launching, Admiral."

Flynt nodded. "Navigator, once the squadrons are away, activate main engines and bring us to this position." She pointed to a position in space behind the approaching alien ships.

The navigator nodded and entered the coordinates in the navigation system. "Course plotted and ready, Admiral," he said.

"Very well."

The executive officer watched the readouts on the battle console. When the last fighters and bombers had launched, he said, "All ships are away, Admiral."

"Now, navigator!" Flynt ordered.

The navigator activated the main engines. "All hands, brace for rapid acceleration and deceleration!"

The main engines on Confederation ships were designed for travel over large distances at very high speeds. They were powerful enough to make it possible to travel between star systems in days, rather than the years it would take with the maneuvering engines used to lift off planets or change course during a flight. They were rarely used for short distances, because of the strain it placed on the ship to accelerate and then decelerate so quickly.

A moment later, the *Hercules* decelerated, and Flynt lurched forward in her chair. Checking the star chart, she saw the *Hercules'* new position. They were directly behind the alien warships – right where she wanted to be.

"Forward plasma cannons and torpedo launchers, open fire!"

The weapons fired. Blueish-white streams of plasma energy streaked toward the three closest alien ships, hitting their engines. Torpedo detonations were visible on the hulls of two enemy ships. One enemy ship began spinning out of control. It collided with another enemy ship, and both ships exploded.

"Fighters and bombers are engaging, Admiral," the executive officer reported.

"Continue firing forward plasma cannons and torpedoes," Flynt ordered.

"Yes, Admiral."

The alien ships began spreading out.

"All plasma cannons and torpedoes, fire as soon as enemy targets are in range!"

The executive officer relayed the orders to the firing crews.

Two alien ships turned, and their weapon emplacements now faced the *Hercules*. The battle console showed that the enemy weapons were targeting the Carrier.

"Enemy ships about to fire, Admiral," the executive officer shouted.

"All hands, brace for weapons impact!"

Rick watched the battle play out on the holographic projection. The fighters and bombers launched and headed toward the alien ships. Suddenly, the *Hercules* disappeared from the projection.

"What happened?" Rick cried out.

A moment later, the *Hercules* reappeared behind the Alien ships and opened fire.

After several minutes of fighting, two alien ships had collided and were destroyed. Two more were crippled and drifting out of control. Fighters and bombers from the *Hercules* were attacking several of the alien ships. Two alien ships were engaging the *Hercules*, and the rest of the nine alien ships were redeploying to attack the *Hercules* from different directions.

Rick watched the two alien ships attacking the Fleet Carrier. The projection showed the weapons systems on all three ships firing. One of the alien ships sustained heavy damage, but the other one gave the *Hercules* a pounding. *How much more can they take?*

The *Hercules* disappeared from the projection again.

"Where they destroyed?" Rick asked, leaning forward for a better view of the projection.

Before anyone could answer, the *Hercules* reappeared behind several of the alien ships that were redeploying to attack the Carrier. The *Hercules* fired at their engines. Three of the alien ships were disabled. The fighters and bombers targeted those three ships as the *Hercules* maneuvered to attack other alien ships.

"Admiral Flynt is using her main engines to jump the ship behind the enemy," Longstreet said with admiration. "It's a dangerous move, and it could severely damage her ship, but it's working."

Fire suppression and damage control teams were working furiously around the ship. The *Hercules'* hull plating was thick and strong, but the alien weapons had caused hull failures in six sections of the Carrier. She was still maneuverable, and her weapons systems were still operational, but Flynt knew that her ship couldn't take much more abuse.

Seven alien ships were destroyed or out of commission. Of the eight that remained, most had suffered damage, and three were heavily damaged.

Flynt had used the main engine jump maneuver three times, but she feared that the ship couldn't handle it a fourth time. It didn't matter. She had successfully herded the alien ships to the opposite side of the planet from the freighter and escort ships. They now had their escape window.

"Order the freighters and escort ships back to Bacchus 12," Flynt told her executive officer.

"Yes, Admiral."

The star chart showed that several alien ships were moving to surround the *Hercules*. Flynt knew that they couldn't survive a concentrated attack from so many ships. *I guess this is the end. She was a good ship and crew.*

Four new ships appeared on the star chart. *Did they call for reinforcements to help finish us off?*

The color of the new ships turned green. *Those ships have Confederation Fleet Transponders! They're ours!*

The executive officer shouted. "Admiral, the *Edinburgh* and her escort ships have arrived and are engaging the enemy."

"The *Edinburgh*? I ordered her to stay hidden around Darius 13."

"I guess they decided to disobey orders, Admiral."

I need to remember to thank them if we get out of here.

"Order all squadrons to concentrate on the alien ships closest to us. And fire every torpedo we have left. Target the engines of the alien ships. We have to disable them enough to escape from here."

"Yes, Admiral."

Longstreet pointed to the holographic projection. "The freighters and escort ships have safely left Darius 8 and are heading back here, Mr. President. Ten alien ships have been disabled or destroyed. Three of the *Edinburg's* four escort ships have been destroyed. The *Edinburgh* is reporting damage to its lower hull in two sections. The *Hercules* has damage in nine sections of its hull but is still maneuverable. Her squadron strength is down fifty percent."

"What about the freighters that were left on Darius 13?" Rick asked.

"They haven't been on the surface for long, but they found exactly what we're looking for – clothes, cloth, weaving and sewing equipment, plants for fabrics, and workers who know what to do. They need at least a day to finish loading."

Rick looked at the situation in the Darius system. "I don't think we're going to defeat the remaining alien ships without reinforcements, Admiral. The *Hercules* and the *Edinburgh* need to break off the attack."

"The Hercules needs to make temporary repairs before returning here, Mr. President. And we still have freighters on Darius 13. I advise redeploying the *Hercules* and the *Edinburgh* to Darius 13. They can make repairs and escort the remaining freighters home late tomorrow."

"Won't the aliens detect them and come after them?" Rick asked.

"We have to risk it, Mr. President. The *Hercules* can't make it home in its present condition, and it's in no position to protect and escort the freighters on its own."

Rick nodded. "Give the order."

"Yes, Mr. President."

Rick watched the projection. Alien ships were moving in to finish off the *Hercules*. The *Edinburgh* had engaged an alien ship, preventing the Heavy Cruiser from helping the *Hercules*.

Then the *Hercules* and the *Edinburgh* disappeared from the projection.

"Please tell me that they've redeployed to Darius 13," Rick said.

Longstreet nodded and pointed to the holographic projection. Two Fleet ships were now orbiting on the far side of Darius 13 from the surviving alien ships.

Rick relaxed. "Tell Director O'Connor to prepare the space dock to expedite repairs when the *Hercules* returns."

"Yes, Admiral."

As Rick watched the alien ships on the holographic projection, he was shocked to see some of them open fire on the other alien ships that had been disabled. The disabled ships disappeared from the projection. "What are they doing?"

"They're destroying their disabled ships," Longstreet said. "Rather than risk capture, they just killed their own people."

"They have enough resources and manpower to destroy their own ships," Rick said, stunned at the implication. "It's bad enough that they had enough ships to nearly wipe out the Confederation, but *this*? How do we fight an enemy this ruthless and determined?"

Longstreet looked directly at Rick. "We refuse to surrender, Mr. President. And if it's our time to die as a species, then we take as many of them with us as possible. We make them bleed for every inch of the Bacchus system that they take from us."

Rick watched the surviving alien ships redeploy around Darius 8, and he nodded. "What else can we do?"

Cindy and Colten sat on a hill overlooking the cattle pasture. The rings were glowing a brilliant red, and light from the four largest moons illuminated the pastures. The nebulas made it difficult to see starlight from other star systems, even when the moons weren't visible, but their glow filled the night sky with color.

"I've never seen a night sky like this before," Colten commented. "Manis 5 has only one moon, and it's rarely visible from the ranch. You have four moons, and they seem to be visible all the time."

"Nine moons," Cindy corrected him. "Four large ones, which you can see now, and five smaller ones that aren't visible yet. Plus there are thousands of asteroids in the planetary rings."

Does it ever get dark at night?" Colten asked.

Cindy shook her head. "When the moons aren't visible, it's not this bright, but the rings and the nebulas light up the sky every night. It's only really dark when there's a storm coming and the clouds cover the sky."

Below them, Cindy saw the cows grazing.

"I can't believe how quickly the fences were put up," Cindy said. "I thought it would take weeks to get the cattle in the new pastures."

"You have to be quick when working with animals," Colten said. "Besides, there are more freighters coming with more cows and bulls. We have to be ready for them, or we'll never get caught up. There's too much work to do to waste a minute."

Cindy nodded. She glanced down the hill and saw her two Marine escorts patrolling at a discreet distance. She smiled.

"Are you going to be here when the next freighters arrive?" Colten asked, ignoring Cindy's protection detail.

"Yes, but I'm not going to help unload the bulls."

Colten laughed, and Cindy felt her heart beating a little faster. "I think it's a good idea for you to leave the bulls for us to deal with," he said. "We don't need a repeat of last time."

"Hey, just because I got hurt once doesn't mean that I don't want to learn everything I can about ranching. It just means that I need to be more careful around the animals until I understand them better."

Colten nodded. "That's a sensible way to look at things. Animals respond to confidence, and confidence comes from understanding. The more you learn, the more they'll cooperate with you."

"Even the bulls?" Cindy asked.

"No, not the bulls. They do whatever the hell they want, and you have to learn how to get out of their way and just let them."

They both laughed.

"Will you teach me?" Cindy asked. "About the animals? About ranching?"

Colten looked at her in the moonlight. "I'll teach you anything I can."

They stared at each other, smiling. Cindy inched closer, and Colten leaned in. Below them, the cattle grazed, and the two Marines continued their patrols. Cindy and Colten didn't notice.

Their lips touched, and it was electric. Neither one pulled away. They just held each other in the moonlight.

Bret woke up and glanced at the clock next to the bed. It was just after 4:00. *I've been asleep for only two hours.* He looked over at the angelic face of the woman next to him. He propped himself up on an elbow and watched her sleep.

Bret had been in Jen's apartment for three hours before they finally stopped to eat dinner. Jen was a fantastic cook, and the meal was excellent. But once the dishes were cleaned and the food put away, they went back to the bedroom to pick up where they had left off.

I don't care if I fall asleep at work tomorrow. I wouldn't trade anything for the night I've had.

He reached over and gently brushed aside a lock of hair that had slipped down over her face.

Jen stirred and opened her eyes. She smiled. "Hi."

"I didn't mean to wake you," Bret said softly.

She wrapped her arms around him. "That's okay. I'd rather be awake if you're awake."

She kissed him, and he felt his face getting warm. Then she pulled back and moved her right hand down his chest. As it moved lower, he breathed deeply. He felt her hand connect, and he shuddered slightly.

Jen smiled. "I was hoping you'd feel that way."

"Really?" Bret asked.

"Really."

Bret pulled her close. "Whatever you want," he whispered.

Repairs were proceeding rapidly aboard the *Hercules* above Darius 13. Repairs to the hull breaches would require the space dock at Bacchus 12, but the repairs to the engines and weapons systems were proceeding well with the parts on hand.

Admiral Flynt sat in her command chair, reading the damage reports. The chief scanner technician approached her.

"Admiral, do you have a moment?"

Flynt looked up and nodded.

"Do you remember when we installed the software patch to allow us to use the planetary probes to look for aliens in addition to human survivors?"

"Yes."

"Well, the scanners have been repaired, and I wondered if I should check the probes around all of the Confederation planets, so we can get a sense of where the aliens are. If we can find where they've concentrated, we might be able to determine what they're doing."

"Check the Trinity system first," Flynt said. "I received a report from Fleet Command about interference coming from there that's blocking the signals of the probes around Trinity 5, 6, and 7. We're closer, so perhaps we can break through the interference."

"Yes, Admiral," the scanner technician acknowledged.

The scanner technician entered a series of commands into his console. Less than a minute later, the scanner console began displaying data from the Trinity system.

"There's a large alien presence on Trinity 5 and Trinity 7, Admiral."

"Can you tell where they are or what they're doing?" Admiral Flynt asked.

The scanner technician entered more commands into the console. A moment later, he said, "They seem to be concentrated around the underground archives on Trinity 5 and at the Fleet Headquarters on Trinity 7, Admiral."

"Why those two places?" the executive officer asked, coming over to look at the scanner data.

Flynt straightened up with a worried look on her face. "What's the one thing that both of those facilities have?"

The executive officer shrugged.

"Star charts," Flynt stated. "The Trinity 5 archives have all of the star charts of the planets that were first explored by Earth before the cataclysm, and both facilities have the detailed charts of the star cluster that makes up the Confederation."

"Star charts?" the executive officer asked, not appearing to understand the implication.

"What's the one planet that they haven't found yet?" Flynt asked.

"Bacchus 12," the executive officer replied. His eyes widened. "You mean…"

"Yes," Flynt interrupted. "They must know by now that part of the Fleet survived, but they don't know where our base of operations is. They must have realized that there's another planet out there, and they're looking for it."

Turning to the communications technician, Flynt said, "Send a burst transmission to Fleet Command. Alert them to what the aliens are doing on Trinity 5 and 7. Tell them that we'll continue to monitor the alien activity."

"Yes, Admiral."

Flynt continued watching the scanner. *How long will it take them to find Bacchus 12, and how long after that before they attack?*

CHAPTER 21

Director O'Connor sat in his office on the top floor of the Advanced Weapons Division's central office. It was more than an hour before dawn, but he enjoyed the quiet time that coming to work so early afforded him. The campus below was alive with activity. The Advanced Weapons Division's facilities worked around the clock, but the central office building was typically empty at that time of the day.

A knock at the door startled him. *Who the hell is knocking on my door at THIS hour?*

He pushed the button on his desk to open the door. "Come in," he barked irritably.

Peter Fleming, O'Connor's Director of Mining Operations, entered the office.

"Peter? What are you doing here at this hour?" O'Connor demanded.

Fleming held up a small black case. "It's done, sir. The nuclear devices are in place."

O'Connor gestured for Fleming to approach his desk. "What's that in your hand?"

Fleming opened the case. Inside was a pendant on a chain. Fleming removed the pendant and held it up. "This is the detonator transmitter."

With his thumb, he flipped up the covering on the bottom of the pendant, revealing a button. "Push this button, and the fusion devices that I placed at the refineries, the mines, and all major ore deposits around the planet will explode. It will be the most spectacular explosion anyone has ever seen."

Fleming closed the covering and handed the pendant to O'Connor.

"Is it activated now?" O'Connor asked.

Fleming nodded. "Yes, sir. The fusion devices are armed and ready. Just push the button, and it's goodbye Olympium."

"How long will it take for the Olympium to be destroyed once the bombs explode?"

"The ore near the bombs will be ignited almost immediately. It will take a day from the time that the bombs explode until the chain reaction in the ore causes the planet to disintegrate. Trust me, sir. The aliens won't get the Olympium once you push that button."

O'Connor flipped up the covering and looked at the button. He stared at it in silence for more than a minute. Then he closed the covering and put the chain around his neck. "I assume I'm supposed to wear this so it'll always be close to me?"

"Yes, sir," Fleming said.

"Excellent, Peter. There's just one more thing for you to do."

"What's that, sir?"

"Add one more fusion device – the largest one of all."

"Where do you want it planted?" Fleming asked.

"Here on this campus," O'Connor replied. "All of our military secrets are on this campus. I see no reason why the aliens should have a day to ransack our facilities before the planet is destroyed."

Fleming frowned. "How would I be able to plant a fusion device on this campus unnoticed? Planting the devices around the mines and ore deposits was easy, as was planting devices around the refineries. But there are thousands of people on this campus every minute of the day. Someone will see me."

"Then use one of the fusion mines in Warehouse 6 or 7," O'Connor said, irritated that Fleming didn't think of that himself. "There are still a few that haven't been deployed. Put a sign on one of the mines to indicate that it's not functioning properly, arm the fusion device, and hook it up to this detonator transmitter."

Fleming nodded. "Yes, sir. I'll take care of that right now."

"Thank you, Peter," O'Connor said, pushing the button on his desk that opened the office door.

Peter walked toward the door but then stopped and turned around. "Director O'Connor? I'm just curious. When are you planning to detonate the bombs?"

O'Connor stared at Fleming. *As soon as the aliens are within sight of Bacchus 12. I want them to see the Olympium destroyed right before their eyes and know that their mission to destroy us was for nothing.*

"If the aliens reach the planet," O'Connor replied. "It's just as a last resort."

"So you're not going to detonate the bombs *before* the aliens reach the surface of the planet?" Fleming asked.

Of course I am, you fool. If I'm killed in their initial bombardment of the planet, who will push the button? No, it has to be done before they can fire on us.

"Why would I do that?" O'Connor asked smoothly. "What if the Fleet and the planetary defenses should turn them away? I'd be destroying the planet for nothing."

Fleming nodded and left the office.

O'Conner watched him leave and then pushed the button to close the door. *Even if we do turn them away, they'll be back. Doesn't he understand that? As long as the Olympium is here, they'll be back. The Olympium is everything. It's all that matters. It must be destroyed, and they must know that it's destroyed. It doesn't matter if we live or die. All that matters is keeping the aliens away from the Olympium. I'll see this quadrant of space burn before I let them have even a speck of my Olympium.*

Admiral Longstreet and General Monroe waited in the situation room for Rick to arrive. Holographic projections of the Darius system, the Trinity system, and the Bacchus system were visible around the room.

The Fleet officers stood and snapped to attention as he entered the room. "Good morning, Mr. President," Longstreet said.

"Good morning," Rick responded. "Please – as you were."

As the Fleet officers retook their seats, Rick noticed the projection of the Darius system first. "Did something happen to the *Hercules* or the *Edinburgh*?"

Longstreet shook his head. "No, Mr. President. But Admiral Flynt on the *Hercules* did discover something unsettling."

Rick sat down, and Longstreet explained Flynt's discovery of the aliens on Trinity 5 and Trinity 7.

"You think they're looking for star charts that will lead them here?" Rick asked. *We're not ready for an attack yet.*

"It appears so, Mr. President. There's no telling how long it will take them to hack into our systems, find the charts, and then plot a course to Bacchus, but we need to be prepared for an attack to come any day."

"We need to recall the Fleet," Rick said. "We need those ships back here for the defense of the planet."

Longstreet nodded. "We're in contact with each of the search-and-rescue missions. The freighters and escort ships from Darius 8 arrived in orbit an hour ago, and the freighters will be landing just after dawn."

"Where?" Rick asked.

"We're having them land on the western continent, Mr. President. Wallace Myerson, your Director of Manufacturing and Fabrication, believes that region is best suited for heavy industries, including construction. We have a temporary spaceport set up there. We can use the transports to move construction equipment and personnel around the planet to build shelters, houses, and whatever other structures we need for the refugees."

"Even on the eve of an alien invasion, you're still worried about refugees and setting up new industries on the planet?" Rick asked.

"Of course, Mr. President. We can't stop everything else we're doing and wait for the aliens to attack. We need food, clothes, houses, manufacturing and fabrication facilities... this doesn't change just because the aliens may know where we are."

Rick smiled and nodded. "When will the rest of the search-and-rescue missions return?"

"They'll be leaving Darius 13, Equus 4, Baris 8, and Felis 5 tomorrow, Mr. President. The freighters should be landing the day after that. The space dock has been alerted to the *Hercules'* condition, and the Advanced Weapons Division is ready to make as many repairs to her as time allows before the aliens arrive here."

"What kind of advanced notice will we have that the aliens are coming?" Rick asked.

Longstreet entered a command on his net-dev and the three holographic projections were replaced with a projection of the entire Confederation. Several planets were highlighted in red. "The red planets are the ones that have an alien presence on them. We also know where many of their ships are located. We're assuming that they don't have another armada standing by to handle the invasion of Bacchus, so if we see their ships start redeploying and concentrating, we'll take that as the signal that they're heading this way."

"How much time will that give us before they arrive?"

"Perhaps a day, Mr. President."

"That's not a lot of time," Rick noted.

"No sir, it's not," Longstreet agreed. "But it'll have to do."

When Bret arrived at the meeting room on the upper level of the Fission Development facility, Jason Dorr and the other engineers stood and applauded.

"What's going on?" Bret asked, feeling confused.

"For an eighteen year-old who hasn't gone through the advanced training program in Theoretical and Applies Physics, your grasp on nuclear fission is impressive," Dorr said with a huge grin on his face.

"I don't understand..." Bret began.

"Your idea of using Olympium gel!" Dorr interrupted. "It was genius! Most of us stayed all night working on it. We had a supply of gel sent over, we irradiated it based on the simulation, constructed a fission prototype, and had the prototype loaded onto a Minesetter and sent to the far edge of one of the nebulas an hour ago."

Dorr activated the monitors around the room. "We were just waiting for you to arrive before we detonated the prototype."

"How much gel did you use in the prototype?" Bret asked, taking his seat.

"The maximum that the simulation indicated was safe," Dorr replied. "If we're going to test for an increased yield, we might as well see what the largest yield looks like."

Bret saw on the monitors that the Minesetter had placed the mine inside one of the nebulas and was evacuating the area quickly.

"The Minesetter is out of the estimated danger radius," Dorr said. "Activating the mine... now!"

Everyone in the room watched the monitors. At first, nothing happened. Then a brilliant flash light appeared – brighter than their sun. Bret looked intently at the monitor closest to him, and he saw the shockwave rippling through the hydrogen gas.

Analysis data appeared underneath the image of the shockwave, measuring intensity and distance. The distance measurement showed 1,000 miles, and the intensity measurement was still nearly at a hundred percent. At 1,500 miles, the intensity measurement had dropped only twenty-five percent. At 2,000 miles, the intensity measurement showed that the shockwave was no longer lethal to a Capital Ship but still enough to destroy smaller ships.

The room erupted with cheers and applause. "Ladies and gentlemen," Dorr shouted over the noise, "we have just created the largest man-made explosion and shockwave in recorded history! And with no time required to process the ore, and the gel able to irradiate much faster and still remain stable, the time to create the devices is reduced ninety percent!"

Dorr pointed to Bret. "And we have this young man to thank for it!"

The engineers in the room slapped Bret on the back and shook his hand.

Dorr raised his hands to get everyone's attention. "We need to steal every engineer not already working on a critical project and get him or her down here to build more fission mines. Once the next shipment of gel arrives, we should have enough materials to make a thousand mines and get them deployed in just a few days."

Natalia knocked on Rick's door.

"Come in," Rick said.

The Marine guards opened the doors, and Natalia entered.

"Mr. President, Director O'Connor wants a vid-conference with you."

"When?" Rick asked.

"Now. He's waiting for you already."

Rick nodded. He activated the vid-monitor, and Natalia left the office.

"Good morning, Director O'Connor," Rick said when the man's face appeared on the monitor.

"Good morning, Mr. President," O'Connor said, smiling. "I wanted you to be the first to know. Your son has already made a tremendous contribution to our planetary defense efforts."

Rick was delighted to hear that. "How?"

O'Connor filled Rick in on Bret's idea for increasing the fission yield in the nebula mines. O'Connor then showed Rick the images and analysis from the prototype test earlier that morning.

"That's unbelievable!" Rick exclaimed.

O'Connor nodded enthusiastically. "Not only is the device more powerful, but it's easier and faster to build. We'll have nebula minefields finished ahead of schedule, and it'll take fewer mines to get it done. Your son's idea may be the deciding factor in the fight to come."

"Thank you for sharing this with me, Director O'Connor," Rick said. "Does Admiral Longstreet know?"

"He's my next call, Mr. President."

Rick nodded. "Then don't let me keep you."

"Of course, Mr. President," O'Connor said smoothly. "Good day, sir."

The vid-conference ended and the vid-monitor went blank.

Rick couldn't stop smiling. *Look at what Bret has already accomplished. That's my boy!*

Bret pulled out his com-dev and typed a quick message to Jen. "Can't stop thinking about last night. Already having a great day at work and feel like celebrating tonight. Any chance of you joining me?"

A moment later, Jen replied. "Yes, yes, yes! My place again?"

Bret smiled. "Good idea," he typed. "No privacy at my place. I'll see you after work."

Jen sent a message back quickly. "Perfect. Dinner first, celebrating second. Deal?"

"Deal," Bret typed. He sent the message and put his com-dev back in his pocket.

O'Connor ended the vid-conference with Admiral Longstreet, picked up his com-dev, and dialed Natalia's number. "I want to see you tonight," he said when she answered. "Are you free?"

"For you? Of course I am," Natalia purred.

"Good. I have a bottle that I've been saving for a special occasion. I'll bring it with me. 9:30?"

"I'll be waiting," Natalia replied.

O'Conner ended the call and leaned back in his chair. *It's a good day to celebrate.* He reached up and put his hand around the pendant that Fleming had given him. *It's too bad that this will be the last time I visit Natalia's bed. She's a wonderful girl, and the sex is truly exquisite. But at least I'll have one more night of pleasure with her before the end of the world. Maybe I'll push the button just as I climax – go out with a bang, as they say. Or maybe I'll wait until the aliens arrive. I'll have to see how I feel tonight.*

Cindy spent all day with Colten and the ranchers, preparing the additional pastures that would be used by the cattle aboard the twelve freighters arriving from Equus 4 and Baris 8. Most of her volunteers were busy setting up temporary shelters for the ranchers who'd be arriving in two days, but Cindy and the rest of the volunteers were digging fencepost holes, setting the posts, and building the fences.

Cindy's ribs weren't hurting as much as they had been, but she still had to be careful bending over. Colten stayed close to her, ready to help if the pain in her ribs or abdomen made it impossible for her to work.

Beth visited the ranching complex just before mid-day to inspect the progress. She had been spending most of her time at the farming complex, overseeing the farmers who were getting ready to start planting the seeds and seedlings.

"We have five freighters arriving the day after tomorrow," Beth said as she and Cindy walked along the new fence lines. "They'll have mostly cotton and other plants that can be used to make fabrics."

"I thought that there were eight freighters coming from Darius 13 and Felis 5," Cindy commented.

"There are," Beth confirmed, "But three of the freighters are filled with cloth, already-made clothing items, and equipment for making cloth and clothes. They're landing on the western continent where we're building the industrial complex."

Cindy nodded. "We have twelve freighters landing the day after tomorrow. I haven't seen the inventory yet, but it's going to be crazy around here. Are there any volunteers you can spare to help out over here?"

"I'll see what I can do," Beth promised. "Oh, by the way, the construction materials from Darius 8 have landed and are being unloaded. I'll have a team of construction workers bring supplies here tomorrow to start working on permanent housing, barns, and other facilities that the ranches will need."

"That'll be great, Mom!" Cindy said. "I don't need anything big, but it needs to have an office that I can use to coordinate the volunteers and ranchers."

Beth looked at her daughter. "You're planning to stay here?"

Cindy nodded. "I've found my place, Mom."

"You're only sixteen."

"And I'm one of the few surviving humans in the galaxy," Cindy countered. "My age doesn't matter. We all have to work if we're going to survive and rebuild. This is what I want to do. I'm learning about cattle ranching, and so far, I'm good at it. Colten is teaching me everything he knows about being a rancher."

"Is this about Colten, Cindy?" Beth asked gently.

Cindy shook her head. "No, Mom. It's about me and what I can do to help out. I know that you'll eventually go back to the capital to be with Dad, but I'm staying here. I don't think I can go back to my old life now."

Beth smiled. "All right, Cindy. I'll make sure that they build something for you. But don't make any final plans yet. Give ranching a try, and then let's talk about it in a couple of months to see if it's still what you want to do."

Cindy gave Beth a hug. "Thanks, Mom!"

They walked to the transport waiting to take Beth back to the farming complex. "Take care of yourself, Cindy," Beth said as she boarded the transport. "I love you."

"I love you, too, Mom," Cindy said. "Tell Dad that I love him when you talk to him next time. And don't forget about sending me more volunteers."

Beth nodded and waved as the hatch closed. Cindy backed up as the transport lifted off and streaked away.

Colten walked up to her and handed her a canteen of water. "What did you tell her?" he asked.

"That I'm staying here to learn ranching."

'How did she take it?"

Cindy smiled. "I think she's worried that I'm being impetuous. She wants me to learn as much as I can, but she wants us to talk about it again in a couple of months."

Colten nodded as they walked back to the new fences. "That gives us plenty of time to get you trained, so you can show her how good a rancher you are."

Cindy laughed. Looking around, she asked, "Are we going to be ready to handle the twelve freighters arriving in two days?"

"Do we have a choice?" Colten asked.

"No."

"Then we'll be ready."

Bret arrived at Jen's building as the sun disappeared below the horizon. One of the additional Marine escorts rode up the elevator with him again and delivered him to her door.

When she opened the door, Bret saw that she had already changed clothes. She wore shorts and a lose-fitting shirt, and she was barefoot.

"Hi!" she said, giving him a kiss and pulling him inside. "I heard about why we're celebrating. It was in this afternoon's defense briefing. That's amazing!"

Bret smiled. "The idea just came to me…"

"Don't be modest," Jen said, laughing. "You had a great idea. I had a great idea, too."

"And what was that?" Bret asked, putting his arms around her waist.

"Move in with me."

Bret stared at her. "Are you sure? Isn't it a bit soon?"

Jen sat down on the couch and pulled him down next to her. "Look, Bret, after all that's happened, I don't want to waste a minute of the time that we have left. You and I both know that the aliens are eventually going to find us. If this is the end, I want to spend every remaining moment with you. If we survive, I want us to be together for the rest of our lives – on our terms. It's like you said to me. If I want something, I'm going to ask for it. This is what I want."

Bret gazed into Jen's eyes. *She's all alone. Her family was on Trinity 5, and they're dead now. But I don't think loneliness is why she wants this. I think she really loves me and wants to spend the rest of her life with someone she loves. I love her. I've been crazy about her for two years. We like the same things, we get along great, and she makes me feel like the most special man in the galaxy. And she's right; everything changed when the Confederation was attacked. We're writing new rules because it's a different world now.*

"I have two conditions," Bret said.

Jen smiled and said, "Name them."

"First, we have to tell my family."

"Okay," Jen said, nodding. "And the second condition?"

"I want to have time for my art. You and my family are the most important things to me, and the job seems to be going well, but I can't give up my art completely."

Jen laughed. "I love your art, and I don't want you to give it up. I agree to your conditions."

She got up and walked over to her vid-com console.

"What are you doing?" Bret asked, getting up and joining her.

"I'm calling your family," Jen replied. "Can you think of a reason not to tell them now?"

Bret was about to protest, but looking at her made him change his mind. *I want to spend every moment with you, too.*

"Call them," he said.

Natalia filled their glasses from the bottle that O'Connor brought with him. She handed him his glass and adjusted her pillows so she could sit up and drink without spilling the wine on her breasts again.

As O'Connor took a sip, Natalia couldn't help notice the new pendant he wore. "What's that around your neck, Allan?"

O'Connor held it up. "Peter Fleming gave this to me. This, my dear, is how I'll deny the aliens their prize. It's the detonator transmitter for the fusion bombs that Peter placed around the refineries, mines, and Olympium ore deposits."

He opened the covering, exposing the button. "So much power in such a small pendant. I just push this button, and boom! The Olympium is destroyed forever. Bacchus 12 will disintegrate a day later from the chain reaction. The aliens will get nothing."

He closed the covering. "I'll wear this until the time to use it."

Natalia looked confused. "Even when we're..."

O'Connor smiled. "Yes, even when we're in the throes of passion. Who knows, perhaps the sex will be so great that I'll decide to push the button tonight. That would be a climax for the history books, don't you think?"

You are insane, Allan! You've turned into a madman. You're not the man who swept me off my feet and made me fall in love with him. You're a monster, and you have to be stopped.

"But who'd be left to write or read it?" she purred, fighting to remain calm as she traced a fingernail along the edge of his chest.

O'Conner looked at her. "Good point, my dear." He reached for her, and she spilled some of the wine on her breasts. He bent down and licked it off as Natalia hastily placed the glasses on the table next to her side of the bed.

Rick has to know about the pendant. And somehow I have to keep Allan from pushing that button tonight.

CHAPTER 22

Rick and Beth had been on their vid-conference for nearly two hours. It was late, but they didn't want to end their conversation. They missed each other too much.

Rick was amused. "So Cindy has found herself a rancher and wants to become one herself?"

Beth nodded. "This isn't the same Cindy that you know. I think she's serious. For now, she's going to stay down here, helping the ranchers and learning to be one."

"Well, good for her," Rick said.

"Now what's this about Bret moving in with Jen Peterson?" Beth asked. "I read your note, but there weren't any details.

Rick grinned. "Bret wanted to tell both of us at the same time, but you were tied up and he didn't want the news to wait. He's spent the last couple of nights with her. He's been crazy about her for years, and evidently she feels the same way for him. They've made their choice. I don't see how we can talk him out of it. You know how headstrong he can be."

"What's happened to our children?" Beth asked.

"The world changed, and they were forced to grow up very quickly. I think we should support them. It's that or risk losing them, and I'm not ready for that. They're both behaving responsibly and have jobs that are important. I don't think we could have asked for a better outcome."

Beth sighed. "I'm not ready."

"It doesn't matter if we're ready or not. They think they're ready, and given the circumstances, I'm not willing to tell them that they're wrong."

Beth smiled a tired smile. "When did you get so good with our kids?"

"I had a good teacher," Rick replied.

Beth stifled a yawn. Rick leaned closer to the vid-monitor. "Get some sleep, honey. You've got a busy few days ahead of you."

"You, too, Rick. I wish I were there with you."

"So do I," Rick said. "I need your strength."

They talked for a minute longer before ending the vid-conference.

Rick looked at the clock on his desk. It read 2:30 in the morning. *I need to get some sleep.*

He was just about to get up and go to his quarters downstairs when the com-dev signaled an incoming call. *Who the hell is calling me at this hour?*

He looked at the caller information and saw that it was Natalia. *This can't be good.*

"Hello?"

Natalia looked over at O'Connor, sleeping deeply on the other side of the bed. She carefully got out of bed, grabbed her com-dev, and snuck out of the bedroom. She closed the door and crept down the hallway to her living room. *I have to tell Rick about Allan's plan now. I can't wait until morning.*

She dialed Rick's number and waited for him to answer.

"Hello?" It was Rick's voice.

"Rick, it's Natalia," she whispered into the com-dev. "I have to talk to you."

"What's wrong, Natalia?" Rick asked.

"It's Allan. He's ready to destroy the Olympium. Peter Fleming placed fusion bombs near all of the refineries, mines, and Olympium deposits. They're armed. Allan has the detonator transmitter on a pendant around his neck. He never takes it off. He's planning to detonate the bombs as soon as the aliens breach the Bacchus system so they can watch the Olympium be destroyed. I'm terrified, Rick. He's gone completely mad!"

"Is he there with you?" Rick asked.

"Yes," Natalia whispered.

Natalia heard O'Connor stirring. "Natalia, where did you go, my dear?" he asked.

"Rick, I have to go." Natalia ended the call, stuffed the com-dev between the cushions of her couch, and ran to the kitchen.

"Just getting some water, darling," she said.

She filled a glass with water from the kitchen tap. When she turned around, O'Connor stood there.

"What are you doing, Natalia?" he asked. Natalia felt a coldness coming from him.

"I told you I'm getting some water," she replied, holding up the glass. "See?"

"And who were you talking to just then?"

"I wasn't talking to anyone, darling. I was humming. That's the only sound you heard coming out of me."

O'Connor took a step forward. "Don't lie to me, Natalia. You were talking to someone. Who was it?"

"You were having a dream, Allan. That's all." Natalia took a drink of water and put the glass on the counter. She tried to remain calm, but her heart raced and her breathing deepened.

O'Connor smiled and cocked his head. Natalia thought he looked like a snake about to strike. She was right.

O'Connor's hand flew and struck her across the face. She winced and cried out in pain. She dropped to one knee, holding her cheek in her hand.

"Allan…"

He grabbed her arm and forced her to her feet. "Who were you talking to?" he demanded again.

His grip on her arm hurt Natalia. He shook her.

He put his face close to hers and hissed, "Who were you talking to?"

"You're hurting me, Allan. Stop!" she pleaded.

He struck her again.

She sobbed uncontrollably by this time. "L-l-l-let go of me, A-Allan," she whimpered.

"Not until you tell me who you were talking to."

Natalia tried to pull away. O'Connor grabbed her by the throat and squeezed with both hands. "Tell me, Natalia."

Natalia couldn't believe what was happening to her. Fear took over as O'Connor's thumbs pressed against her throat. Her knees buckled; only O'Connor's grip kept her upright. She tried to scream, but no sound came. She clawed at his face, but he just tightened his grip. She tried to hit him, but he just squeezed tighter. She couldn't breathe. Her vision blurred, and she felt her body going limp.

I loved you, you bastard!

Darkness took her.

O'Connor looked down at the lifeless form on the kitchen floor.

"Look at what you made me do, my dear. Such a waste."

O'Connor spent the next thirty minutes washing the glasses, making the bed, and wiping down all of the surfaces in the apartment to remove his fingerprints. Once he was done, he looked at Natalia's body on the floor.

Where do I put you, my dear? He searched the apartment for a place that would keep her hidden should anyone come looking for her. When he checked the storage closet at the back of the apartment, he noticed a recycling chute. *Trash removal from the privacy on one's own home. How convenient. And how perfect!* He returned to the kitchen, carried Natalia's body to the recycling chute, and dumped her in. He heard her body falling down the chute to the central bin in the building's basement. Then he looked for Natalia's com-dev.

After several minutes of searching, he gave up. *It's not here. Maybe she really wasn't talking to anyone at all. Oh well, it's not like I was coming back here again.*

He left her apartment. His private security detail waited for him in the sitting area by the elevator. They jumped to their feet when they saw him.

"Good morning, Director O'Connor," the head of his security detail said.

"Hmmmm," O'Connor replied.

They rode down the elevator in silence. Once they were inside the vehicle, the driver asked, "Where to, Director O'Connor?"

"The office," O'Connor replied.

As the vehicle sped off into the night, O'Connor reached for the pendant and stroked it with his thumb.

Rick stared at the com-dev and then put it down.

I wonder what happened. I guess I'll find out in the morning.

He picked up the com-dev and called Admiral Longstreet. When the Admiral answered, Rick filled him in on what Natalia had told him.

"Do we know any more than that, Mr. President?"

"No. I'm going to tell Bret to keep an eye on O'Connor. You and I need to make certain that O'Connor doesn't find out when the aliens have breached the Bacchus system. We have to give Bret and his Marine escorts time to get that pendant away from O'Connor before he can detonate the bombs."

"Why not just take grab the pendant now?" Longstreet asked.

"Because we don't know if that's the only detonator, and we don't know where the bombs are."

"Can't we arrest him and take the pendant that way?"

"We don't have proof that he's done anything wrong," Rick reminded him. "We only have Natalia's word. Besides, it would take the entire planetary Marine garrison to breach the Advanced Weapons Division's campus, and he'd see us coming miles away. He'd set off the bombs, and that would be the end of everything."

"So it's up to our inside man?" Longstreet asked.

"Unfortunately, yes," Rick replied.

Once Rick hung up from the Admiral, he sent Bret a message. "Stop by my office before you go to work. I have news to share with you."

Rick put the com-dev down again. *I hope my son is ready for what I'm going to ask him to do. Our safety depends on him.*

Bret woke the next morning alone. He got up and went looking for Jen. He found her in the kitchen, making breakfast.

"What's this?" he asked, coming up behind her and kissing her neck.

"It's our first breakfast as an official couple," Jen replied. "I wanted to do something special."

"What can I do to help?"

"Sit down and let me do this for you," Jen replied.

Bret complied. "I've never had someone make breakfast for me wearing just a shirt," he said, smiling.

"There are lots of firsts waiting for you," Jen said, wiggling at him.

She turned around to face him. "By the way, your com-dev's beeping. I think you have a message."

He got up and took his com-dev out of pocket of his pants, which were draped over the back of the couch. He saw that the message was from his father.

"It's from my Dad. I need to call him back."

"Don't be long," Jem said.

Bret sat down in an overstuffed chair near Jen's front door. He entered his Dad's number.

"Good morning, Son," Rick said when he answered.

"Good morning, Dad," Bret answered. "I got your message. I don't know if I can get over there before I have to be at work. Can you tell me the news over the com-dev? Or do you want me to come by after work?"

There was a pause. Then Rick said, "Enter scrambler code four into your com-dev."

Bret was surprised. This meant that the news was highly classified. He entered the code and heard the com-dev make a clicking noise confirming the security protocol.

"Okay, Dad. What's up?"

Rick told him about O'Connor's pendant and his plans to detonate the Olympium.

"Is Natalia sure that's what he said he was going to do?" Bret asked.

"It's what she told me. I've been trying to reach her, but I can't get through. I'll talk to her when she gets in, but for now we have to proceed as if she gave us the right information."

"What do you want me to do?"

"As soon as we detect aliens breaching the Bacchus system, I'm going to alert you. You'll have about fifteen minutes before O'Connor hears the news. You have to get that pendant away from him and have your Marine guards place him under arrest before he discovers that the aliens are here and decides to detonate the bombs."

"That's not much time," Bret noted.

"I know, Son. I hate putting this on you, but you're the only person on that campus I trust."

"I'll do my best, Dad."

Bret ended the call and sat back down at the table.

Jen served breakfast and sat across from him. "What did your Dad want?"

Bret looked up and smiled at Jen. "I can't talk about it. I'll be able to tell you later, but not now."

Jen nodded. "I understand."

Bret reached across the table and took her hand in his. "Thank you for breakfast."

"You're welcome," she said, sounding happy. "Now, eat. You don't want to be late for work."

"Yes, dear."

The freighters and escort ships left the surface of Darius 13 on schedule. They rendezvoused with the *Hercules* and the *Edinburgh* thirty minutes later. After making certain that there was no alien presence in the Darius system, the ships activated their main engines and headed for Bacchus 12.

The *Hercules* had been hurt badly in her skirmish with the alien ships over Darius 8, and it was thanks to the skill of her crew that she'd be able to make it to Bacchus 12 at all. Temporary repairs had been made all over the ship, but more permanent repairs were required if the *Hercules* were going to be of any use in a battle.

"Is there any movement from the alien ships?" Admiral Flynt asked her scanner technician.

"No, Admiral," the scanner technician replied. "They're holding the same positions as before."

"Are all of the search-and-rescue missions heading back to Bacchus 12?" she asked.

"Yes, Admiral. We're the last ships to end our mission and return home."

Flynt nodded. *If all of our ships are heading back, and the alien ships haven't moved, then they haven't detected us, and they haven't found the star charts that will lead them to Bacchus. With any luck, most of our repairs will be finished before we have to fight again.*

Natalia had scheduled a meeting between Rick and Archbishop Canterbury for late that afternoon. As Rick left his office at 6:00, he noticed that she was still not at her desk. He had been concerned about her absence up until then, but now he was really worried. *O'Connor was with her when she called me, and now she's disappeared. Where is she? I'm going to send someone to check on her.*

As he rode down the elevator to the waiting vehicle, he said to the head of his security detail, "Send some Marines to Natalia's apartment, and find out if she's all right. If she's not there, then initiate a search. Find her."

"Yes, Mr. President."

Rick entered the vehicle, and the motorcade left the Planetary Administration Building for the headquarters of the Interplanetary Ecumenical Church.

Rick arrived at the cathedral at sunset. As he walked up the steps to the main entrance, Fleet Marine guards took up positions around the perimeter of the huge structure near the center of the city. Rick returned the salute of the sergeant who held the door open for him.

The main lights in the sanctuary were dark, but the artificial illumination behind the stained glass created a soft glow that allowed Rick to see where he was walking. He strode down the main aisle toward the pulpit and through the doors to the right of the dais. He followed the dimly-lit corridor past the church offices until he reached a large door at the end. He knocked softly and waited.

"Enter," he heard the Archbishop say.

He opened the door and stepped inside. The private office of the Archbishop was a large room made of polished hardwood and pressed stone. Deep crimson rugs covered the floors. At one end of the office sat an ornately carved wooden desk that Rick imagined would take at least five people to lift. In the center of the room were several chairs and couches covered in deep green leather. At the far end of the room was a great fireplace with a fire burning. The fire was the only light in the room.

Archbishop Canterbury sat in one of the chairs closest to the fireplace, sipping an amber liquid from a cut-glass tumbler. He didn't look up as Rick entered the room and closed the door.

"You missed the last several Cabinet meetings, Archbishop," Rick said as he crossed the room.

Realizing who was there, the Archbishop started to rise, but Rick motioned for the man to keep his seat. "I'm sorry, Mr. President." The Archbishop reached for another tumbler to pour Rick a drink. "I seem to have lost all sense of the passage of time lately."

Rick accepted the tumbler filled with the amber liquid and sat down next to the clergyman. He looked at the man's face and saw that the Archbishop was clearly disturbed about something. He took a sip, wondering how to start the conversation.

"Do you study history, Mr. President? Earth history, I mean."

"I did when I was younger," Rick replied. "I don't have much time for that these days."

The Archbishop nodded, never taking his eyes off the fire. "I've been reading the church histories for the past few days, looking for some insight into how to better help the people. But I'm at a loss to know what to do."

"What's the problem?" Rick asked.

The Archbishop looked at Rick. "Do you believe in God, Mr. President?"

"Of course I do," Rick replied.

"Do you think whoever is attacking us does?"

"I don't know," Rick confessed. "Why?"

"Is their God better than our God?"

"I thought there was only one God," Rick pointed out.

"That's the problem, Mr. President."

"I don't understand."

The Archbishop sighed and took a sip of his drink. "Did you know that, before the cataclysm, there were people on Earth who thought that heaven floated in the clouds above the Earth and hell was a lake of fire deep inside the Earth's core?"

Rick shook his head. "No, I didn't."

"Before man began exploring the stars, we preached that there was only one God in the universe, even though we acted like

213

our God was just the god of our planet. Paradise and perdition were part of the planet, God walked among the people of Earth for a brief span, and no one put much real thought into the nature of a truly universal God.

"But then we discovered how to reach out and explore other planets. There was a crisis of faith among many of the religions on Earth. If people died on another planet, would their soul come back to Earth to go to heaven or hell? If there were life on other planets, where did their souls go after death? Did each planet have its own heaven and hell? If so, did each planet have its own God? Was the concept of one universal God wrong, or was our view of heaven and hell wrong?"

"I forgot that there used to be multiple religions on Earth," Rick said. "How did the crisis get solved?"

"There were great divisions between the various religions," the Archbishop replied, "but no urgency to do anything about it... until it was discovered that Earth's core was collapsing and the planet would destroy itself. What started as a crisis of faith became all-out religious hysteria.

"Once the decision was made to evacuate Earth, the different religions realized that the problem could no longer be ignored. A council was called to discuss the implications that leaving Earth would have on the religious doctrines."

"What happened?" Rick asked.

"Some religions simply couldn't let go of their 'holy places' on Earth. They felt that to abandon the holy places was to abandon God. They stormed out of the council meeting and refused to be part of anything that forced them to leave Earth or change their views. The rest of the religions worked to bring their doctrines closer together. What came out of those discussions were the tenants of the Interplanetary Ecumenical Church that we brought with us to the Confederation – one universal God, heaven and hell are planes of existence and not physical locations tied to any one planet. We dedicated ourselves to helping mankind live God-centered lives and comforting those in need."

"What about the religions who walked out of the council?" Rick asked. "What happened to their believers?"

"When Earth was evacuated, they remained behind. More than two billion people stayed on Earth, convinced that the planet was blessed and could never be destroyed – in spite of all evidence showing that Earth was tearing itself apart. The science ships, which monitored Earth's last days, watched as the planet broke apart into millions of asteroids, tearing away the atmosphere and exposing those people to the vacuum of space. Everyone who stayed on Earth died horribly and needlessly."

Rick took a drink. "I had no idea so many people remained behind."

The Archbishop nodded absently. "Such a waste," he said softly.

"So what does this have to do with whether the aliens who attacked the other Confederation planets believe in God?" Rick asked.

"Do you believe we've done something that deserves divine punishment, Mr. President?"

"No."

"Then why was ninety percent of our species just wiped out? That's what the people are asking, and they're looking to me for answers. What do I tell them?"

Rick thought about this for a moment. "Do the people believe that we're being punished?"

"They don't know what to believe, Mr. President. And frankly, neither do I."

"I thought God only punished the wicked," Rick pointed out.

"That's what we teach," the Archbishop acknowledged. "The exodus from Earth forced man to stop focusing on himself and start focusing on the survival of mankind. We're as far from being wicked as we've ever been as a species."

"Then why would God punish us?" Rick asked.

"I don't know. That's the problem."

"Do you believe that God has abandoned us?"

The Archbishop shook his head. "I believe that God is active in our lives. He would never abandon us."

"Does he love whoever attacked us more?"

"If there is one God who created the universe, why would he love one species above another?" the Archbishop countered.

Rick shrugged. "I don't know. We don't know if our attackers even believe in God."

"That doesn't matter," the Archbishop said. "God believes in us regardless of whether or not we believe in him."

"Then what's the problem?" Rick asked, grateful that the Archbishop's thoughts were going where Rick was leading.

"Have you ever heard the expression, 'If God be for us, who can be against us'?"

Rick nodded.

"If that's true, then doesn't the recent crisis mean that God has turned his back on us?"

"Why?" Rick asked. "We're still alive."

"But what about all those who died?" the Archbishop asked.

"Just because a lot of people died, it doesn't mean that God is taking sides against us. We're still here. Survivors from the other planets have started arriving. This planet has everything we need to sustain life indefinitely. Agricultural systems are being set up to feed us. We have abundant natural resources. Now, if we hadn't discovered the Bacchus system after the Confederation was founded, we wouldn't have a home right now. The human race would be all but extinct. Doesn't it stand to reason that God hasn't abandoned us, given that we've been given everything we need to survive?"

The Archbishop stared at Rick for several moments. "I hadn't considered that," he said finally.

"I know it's hard to focus on the positive with everything that's going on right now," Rick said. "But now more than ever, that's exactly what we need to get the people focused on. It's proper to mourn the loss of everyone killed in the attacks, but not to the point that we lose sight of the fact that we were spared. I don't know what will happen tomorrow, but for today, we're safe, and we're alive. And that's something that demands gratitude, not consternation."

The Archbishop nodded, and a faint smile appeared on his lips. "You always were a good student, Mr. President. I never realized that you had become a great teacher."

Rick finished his drink and stood up. "I had good teachers, Archbishop. You were one of them. If this was my chance to return the favor, then that's something else for me to be grateful about."

The Archbishop stood up and held out his hand. "Thank you, Mr. President," he said as he shook Rick's hand. "You've given me clarity on the situation."

"My pleasure. Now make sure you don't miss any more Cabinet meetings. I need you to help provide clarity to *my* issues."

The Archbishop laughed and walked Rick to the door. "Good night, Mr. President."

"Good night, Nigel."

CHAPTER 23

Cindy and Colten walked in the light from five of Bacchus 12's moons that had risen above the southern continent. The planetary rings glowed brightly in the night sky.

Cindy had just finished meeting with the volunteers and refugees that would be helping to unload the freighters landing tomorrow. Twelve freighters were bringing livestock, equipment, and ranchers to the southern continent. But the temporary shelters weren't finished, and Cindy knew that they wouldn't be ready for several more days. *We'll have to make do with what's already completed and hope that the rest of the shelters are finished quickly.*

"Are you ready for tomorrow?" Colten asked.

"Not really," Cindy replied. "But I wasn't ready when your freighter arrived, either, and I got through that. We'll make it work somehow."

"Is there anything I can do?"

Cindy stopped and faced him. "Just hold me."

Colten put his arms around her. "I can do that," he whispered.

The *Hercules* approached the space dock above Bacchus 12. Once moored with its engines shut down, teams of personnel from the Advanced Weapons Division boarded her and began assessing the damage.

Weapons specialists also boarded the ship to download the data from the ship's battle with the alien ships. This was the first time that the new weapons systems had been used in combat, and the data would help the engineers assess the performance of the new plasma cannons and torpedo launchers.

Repair crews began replacing the damaged hull plating, so damaged sections of the ship could be repressurized. Additional deck plates were added to strengthen vulnerable parts of the hull, based on the firing patterns of the alien weapons.

Admiral Flynt was impressed with the speed and quality of the repair work. She left her executive officer in charge of the ship and shuttled down to Bacchus 12 to be debriefed by Admiral Longstreet and Admiral Marshall, who had returned with the *Waterloo* a few hours earlier.

Rick left his quarters and headed for the elevators. The head of his security detail met him when he arrived.

"Good morning, Mr. President," he said.

"Good morning," Rick responded, returning the Marine's salute. "Is there any word on Natalia?"

The Marine stiffened, and the expression on his face turned serious. "They found her body at the bottom of the recycle chute in her building, Mr. President. It looks like she was strangled. She was naked, and it's clear that she'd had sex shortly before her death. Teams searched her apartment, but someone had cleaned it. There was no evidence of a struggle or of who might have been in the apartment with her. The bed even had clean sheets."

I don't believe it. Not Natalia! She was like a daughter to me!

Rick nodded slowly and wiped his eyes. *O'Connor did this. He may have cleaned up after himself, but there's no doubt in my mind that he killed her. Once he's arrested, he'll face a murder charge along with the other charges we're preparing. He'll pay for this.*

"I want a full investigation," Rick said grimly. "She was a valuable member of my staff, and I want whoever did this brought to justice."

"Yes, Mr. President."

Bret walked into the upper level of the Fission Development facility and headed for his workstation. The place seemed deserted. He glanced through the window of the warehouse as he passed it on the way to see if the engineers were in the meeting room. He couldn't believe his eyes.

The warehouse floor was filled with new fission mines using the irradiated Olympium gel. *Jason must have every engineer on campus working on the mines.*

Jason Dorr walked around the corner and saw Bret looking at the mines. "Impressive, isn't?"

Bret nodded. "I can't believe you have so many mines finished."

"They're a lot easier to make now, thanks to you. The Minesetters are coming in a few hours to load these and deploy them in the nebulas."

"I wish we had time to make thirty times that many," Bret said, following Dorr down the hall. "I'd like to have more mines out there. Those nebulas are millions of miles across."

"I know, but we're going to keep building and deploying more mines until we run out of materials. And the guidance system should help make a difference. It triangulates with the proximity detectors outside the nebula to determine where an enemy ship has entered. The mines in that area will congregate and detonate, letting the shockwave do the work. It's not perfect, but because of the currents within the nebulas, it's the best we could come up with."

Bret nodded. He followed Dorr to the Clean Room.

Dorr motioned for Bret to enter. "It's time for you to learn how to build a fission core with your own hands."

The first four freighters landed before noon at the temporary spaceport near the ranching complex. Cindy's volunteers were ready, and the refugee ranchers were assigned to temporary housing in record time. The ranchers then gathered around their freighters to receive instructions.

Tucker McNabb, Colten's father, instructed the cattle ranchers how he wanted the cows and bulls unloaded. "My ranchers will show you where to take the cows once they're unloaded," he told them. "Save the bulls for last, and triple-check their harnesses. One got loose on the first freighter and nearly crushed a young lady. We don't want a repeat of that."

The cattle were being unloaded and led to their pens when the next four freighters landed. The last four freighters landed late in the afternoon, and soon they were being unloaded.

Once each freighter was emptied, it lifted off and headed for the western continent. Fleet Command had decided to keep as many freighters as possible away from the main spaceports in case of attack.

It was well after midnight when Cindy talked to her mother. "Thanks for the extra volunteers," she said. "There's no way we could have gotten the freighters unloaded this quickly without them."

"You're welcome," Beth said. "You sound tired."

"I'm exhausted," Cindy said. "There are thousands of cows and every other kind of animal we need for food. We also have hundreds of horses for the ranchers to use. I'm going to start learning to ride tomorrow."

"That sounds like fun," Beth commented. "I haven't ridden in years, but I remember how enjoyable it was."

"Colten's letting me ride one of his horses. His family brought ten with them on the first freighter."

"Just remember that they're large animals, and it's a long way down if you fall off."

Cindy laughed. "I'm not worried about falling, Mom. I just don't want to look bad in front of the volunteers."

"Or in front of Colten?" Beth asked.

"That, too," Cindy replied.

By the time Bret arrived at Jen's apartment that night, he had helped build the fission cores of over a hundred mines. The Minesetters had come and gone multiple times, and within hours of them emptying the warehouse, the engineers had the warehouse filled with mines again.

I can't believe the number of mines we're able to build in a day. If we can keep building mines for at least another two days, we should have enough mines to prevent the alien armada from reaching us through the nebulas.

He rode up the elevator with one of the additional Marine escorts. He used his key for the first time and entered the apartment he now shared with Jen. He set his bags down and closed the door.

"Jen, I'm home," he called.

Jen came out and saw the bags on the floor. "What are those?" she asked.

"I went by the house and picked up my clothes," he replied, giving her a kiss. "I'm starting to run out. I'll go by tomorrow and get the rest of my things, including my art supplies."

Jen smiled. "Perfect timing. I just finished clearing out space for you in the closet and my dresser. Bring the bags, and I'll help you put everything away."

Bret followed her to the bedroom. Not much was put away that night, but neither Bret nor Jen seemed to mind. There were more important things that they wanted to do in the bedroom.

The next morning, Rick met with Admirals Longstreet, Marshall, and Flynt, and General Monroe in the Situation Room.

"How bad is it, Admiral Longstreet?" Rick asked.

"We don't know yet, Mr. President. Alien ships have redeployed from the Baris and Piris systems. They appear to be heading for the Trinity system. There's no movement yet in the Manis or the Equus systems. We can't tell if they're concentrating their armada, or if the ships are moving for another reason."

"How are the defense preparations going?" Rick asked.

Longstreet pointed to the holographic project of the Bacchus system. "All of the Fleet ships, except for the *Hercules*, have been refueled and resupplied. The *Ticonderoga* and *Normandy* are deploying with their task forces this morning, and the *Waterloo* will deploy to Bacchus 11 this afternoon. Admiral Marshall will take command of the *Yorktown*, and it will deploy this evening. I'll remain here at Fleet Command to coordinate our forces."

"What about the *Hercules*?"

Admiral Longstreet looked over at Admiral Flynt. "Repairs are proceeding, Mr. President," Flynt replied. "Most of the hull damage has been repaired, and the decompressed compartments have been repressurized. They're working on the weapons systems now and repairing life support and several other systems that were severely damaged. She'll be ready for service in a day or so."

Rick nodded. "What about the unmanned defenses?"

"The minefields along the debris field are completed, Mr. President," Longstreet reported. "Orbital platforms and weapons systems mounted on moons and asteroids are also completed and in position. The nebula minefields are nearing completion. They're hoping to have the last mines in place late tomorrow."

Rick looked around the room. "Is there anything that we haven't done?"

The Fleet officers shook their heads. "We ask ourselves that question several times a day, Mr. President," Longstreet said. "We can't think of anything that we've missed. This is the best strategy we can devise with the ships and resources that we have to work with."

"Is there anything we can do to offer protection to our civilian population in the case of an attack?"

Longstreet shook his head. "Based on an analysis of the planets the aliens attacked, we have no shelters that will protect against their weapons. Our only hope is to destroy them before they reach the planet."

Rick stood. "Keep me posted. I'll have to address the people once we know that the aliens are coming. I can't hold that information from them."

"Yes, Mr. President," the Fleet officers said.

Four hours later, Rick was back in the Situation Room. Admiral Longstreet and General Monroe were the only senior officers there. Admirals Marshall and Flynt had left earlier in the day to rejoin their ships.

"Mr. President, the alien ships in the Manis and Equus systems have redeployed to the Trinity system. They're concentrating their armada."

"Have they started heading here?" Rick asked, feeling numb.

Longstreet shook his head. "Not yet, but it's just a matter of time."

"Let me know the minute that armada moves," Rick said.

Rick left the situation room. He walked to Jen's office and stuck his head inside. "I need to see you in my office."

Jen jumped up and followed Rick down the hall. Once inside, Rick gestured for her to sit.

"I'm going to have to make a planet-wide announcement very soon," Rick said. "The alien armada has concentrated near the Trinity system. Once it starts moving in this direction, we'll have about a day before it arrives and tries to penetrate our defenses."

Rick watched Jen put her hand to her mouth. *She knows that the battle is coming.*

"It's important that the announcement reach everyone on the planet... except for the Advanced Weapons Division campus. I need you to block them from seeing the announcement and any news reports about the announcement."

"Why is that, Mr. President?" Jen asked, regaining her composure.

Rick filled her in on O'Connor's plans and Bret's assignment to retrieve the detonator transmitter.

Jen now understood what Bret couldn't talk to her about. "I understand, Mr. President, but what about the Advanced Weapons Division employees who will be at home when the announcement is made? Won't they tell O'Connor about it when they get to work tomorrow?"

"Possibly, but Bret and his Marine escorts should be in position by then."

Jen nodded. "I'll have everything ready for you, Mr. President."

"Thank you, Jen."

They both sat in silence for a minute.

"Is there something else that you wanted?" she asked.

Rick nodded. "How are things between you and Bret?"

"Wonderful!" She beamed. "He's the greatest guy I've ever known."

Rick nodded. "I'm happy for the two of you. I hope..." Rick couldn't finish the sentence. He couldn't bring himself to say it out loud – his fear that this might be the end of mankind.

Jen leaned forward. "I know, Mr. President. So do I."

Admiral Longstreet entered Rick's office an hour later.

"It's confirmed, Mr. President. The alien armada is moving this way. It'll be here tomorrow."

"God help us," Rick said.

Longstreet left to inform the rest of the Confederation Fleet.

Rick walked over to the vid-com console and entered the com-dev codes for Beth, Cindy, and Bret.

When they answered their com-devs, Rick told them that the alien armada was coming.

"Beth, and I want you and Cindy to remain on the southern continent."

Both Cindy and Beth began to protest, but Rick cut them off. "No arguments. You'll be safer down there. I want you as far away from the capital as you can get."

Cindy and Beth reluctantly agreed.

"I'm making an announcement to the people in a few minutes. Tell your volunteers and the refugees to watch it."

Beth and Cindy were crying when Rick disconnected them from the call.

"Bret, if O'Connor's going to make a move to detonate the bombs, it will either be tonight or tomorrow. According to Natalia, he'll wait until the aliens are here. He wants them to see the Olympium destroyed. Are you and your Marine escorts ready?"

"Yes, sir," Bret replied. "We're ready."

"Good. According to Natalia, Peter Fleming is the one who planted the bombs. He knows where they are, and he knows how to deactivate them. Make sure your Marines detain him."

"I will."

"Thank you, Son. Good luck to you."

"Good luck to us all, Dad."

Rick ended the call, and then he called Jen. When she answered, he said, "Jen, it's time."

All vid-monitors on the planet turned on. The Confederation seal was displayed in the center of the screen, with the words "Stand By For An Important Announcement" flashing on the bottom. A moment later, Rick's face appeared. He stod in the media room one level below his office. The wall behind him was a deep red, and the Confederation seal hung just behind his head.

"Good evening, people of Bacchus 12. A short while ago, Fleet Command notified me that the alien ships, operating in the other Confederation star systems, have congregated and are heading toward Bacchus. They've managed to locate us, and their armada is coming for the Olympium. We are now in a state of emergency.

"The alien armada will reach the outer rim of the Bacchus system by this time tomorrow. Fleet Command and the Advanced Weapons Division have taken every possible measure to defend our planet against alien attack. I urge all of you to pray that those measures will be sufficient to save us.

"Government facilities and the Advanced Weapons Division campus will remain open and operational, but all other businesses in the capital are to close and remain closed until after the crisis is over. Please keep the streets clear, so military and emergency vehicles can go where they're needed.

"My fellow citizens of the Confederation, I ask that you remain calm. No good can come from panicking. Further communications may not be possible. Good night. God bless."

CHAPTER 24

Rick walked into the Situation Room before dawn, followed by Enrique and Karl. It was filled with Fleet officers and technicians reviewing holographic projections and entering information into their net-devs.

"Place all orbital platforms on automatic controls if the alien armada gets past the *Yorktown* and the *Hercules*," Admiral Longstreet ordered the Fleet personnel manning the targeting controls of the plasma cannons and torpedo launchers around the planet. "I don't want them left on manual control if the aliens should hit this building."

"Yes, Admiral," they responded.

Rick, Enrique, and Karl took their seats. "Good morning, Admiral," Rick said.

"Good morning, Mr. President," Longstreet responded.

None of the Fleet personnel jumped to their feet or stood at attention. Rick had given orders that, until the crisis was over, Fleet and Marine personnel were not to stop what they were doing just to give Rick a salute or show him any other military courtesy.

The large holographic projection in the center of the room showed the Bacchus system, the position of all Fleet ships and planetary defenses, and the approximate location of the enemy armada.

"Is the projection accurate?" Rick asked. "Do they have that many ships approaching Bacchus?"

Longstreet nodded. "I'm afraid so, Mr. President. It was confirmed by the orbital probes around Trinity 7 after the alien armada concentrated."

The door to the Situation Room opened, and Archbishop Canterbury cautiously entered. "May I join you, Mr. President?" He seemed unsure of himself.

Rick smiled and gestured for him to take a seat. "You're welcome here, Archbishop."

Once the Archbishop had sat down, Rick leaned over. "Why are you here, Nigel? I thought you'd be tending to your flocks."

"The church is vacant, Mr. President, as are the streets. I thought my prayers would be more useful here than in an empty building in the center of a deserted city."

"Thank you for coming," Rick said, patting the clergyman on the hand. "If there ever were a time to pray for divine intervention, this is it."

Bret and his two Marine escorts walked across the main floor lobby of the Advanced Weapons Division's central office. The level of activity around them seemed normal.

"It's like they don't know that the alien armada is approaching," Burgess whispered.

"Didn't they see the announcement?" Nesbit asked.

Bret shook his head. "No. My Dad blocked the announcement from all of the vid-monitors on the campus. All news reports about the announcement were also blocked. Dad wanted to give us time to find and arrest Peter Fleming and Director O'Connor."

"Peter Fleming?" Burgess asked.

Bret nodded. "Fleming placed the fusion bombs for O'Connor. He's the only one who knows where they are and how to defuse them."

Just outside the rear entrance of the central office building was a landing pad that could handle shuttles and mid-sized Scout-class ships. Bret looked out the windows and saw a Scout ship landing on the pad. It was similar to the one he and Burgess had used to escape from Manis 2.

The doors of one of the elevators in the center of the lobby opened, and Bret saw Peter Fleming get out and head for the rear entrance. *Where is he going?*

Bret pointed to Fleming. "There's Peter Fleming," he said to his Marine guards. "Arrest him!"

Burgess and Nesbit chased after Fleming, unslinging their weapons as they ran. Bret followed close behind.

Burgess reached Fleming just as the man was about to board the Scout ship. He grabbed Fleming by the collar and yanked him back, forcing him onto the landing pad.

Bret stood over him. "Peter Fleming, you're under arrest for sabotage, the attempted illegal use of nuclear weapons, and conspiracy to commit mass murder on a planetary scale."

Fleming squirmed as Burgess put restraints around the wrists of the Director of Mining Operations. "Let me go! You have to let me get away from here!"

Burgess hauled Fleming to his feet. Bret saw Fleming's face filled with fear – almost terror.

"Why do we have to let you go?" Bret demanded.

"He's crazy. He's going to blow up the planet. I need to get out of there. You can come with me! There's a research station on Bacchus 10. It has enough supplies for us to survive for years. Please, you have to let me go!"

"Who's crazy? O'Connor?" Bret asked. "We know that you planted fission bombs around the Olympium refineries, mines, and ore deposits. But I thought that it would take a day for the planet to disintegrate. Why are you trying to get away from here so quickly?"

"Because I also planted a bomb on *this* campus," Fleming said, trembling. "No one knows except for the Director and me. It's one of the fusion mines, and it's in the warehouse with the other fusion mines. When it goes off, it will level this campus *and* the capital. He knows that the aliens are coming. He's going to detonate the bombs!"

"How does he know that the aliens are coming?" Bret demanded.

"He has the Situation Room at the Planetary Administration Building bugged!" Fleming struggled to break free from the restraints.

Bret looked at Nesbit and Burgess. *There's no time left. We have to get that detonator away from O'Conner.*

"How do I get to O'Connor's office?" Bret demanded.

"You can't," Fleming answered. "The elevator requires a special keycard to access that floor, and his office door only opens from the inside."

"No one can get into the office unless he opens the door?" Bret shouted, grabbing Fleming by the lapels and shaking him.

"His secretary can, but she'll never open the door for you."

"We'll see about that. Do *you* have a keycard that will get us to O'Connor's floor?"

Fleming stared wide-eyed at Bret, but he didn't say anything.

"Corporal Burgess, shoot him in the shoulder," Bret ordered.

Burgess pushed the muzzle of his weapon against Fleming's left shoulder.

"Wait, wait, wait!" Fleming shouted. "It's in my shirt pocket. The code is 11287643."

Bret reached into Fleming's shirt pocket and found the keycard.

"Can you disarm the fusion mine on this campus?" Bret asked.

Fleming shook his head frantically. "There's not enough time. I'd have to remove the core, and that takes at least an hour."

Bret pointed to Nesbit. "You stay here and watch Fleming." Gesturing to the Scout ship, he added, "And make sure that shuttle doesn't take off."

"Yes, sir!" Nesbit grabbed Fleming by his arm.

Bret turned to Burgess. "Follow me. We're going after O'Conner and the detonator transmitter."

"Good luck, sir," Nesbit shouted as Bret ran for the elevators with Burgess close on his heels.

Bret hit the elevator call button, and the doors opened on the elevator that Fleming had exited a few minutes earlier. Once inside, Bret looked for the keycard reader. He found it and inserted the card.

"Enter access code," the computer said.

Bret entered 11287643 into the keypad. The elevator immediately began moving upward.

Bret looked at Burgess. "Do you have an extra sidearm, Corporal?"

Burgess nodded. He reached down to one of the lower pockets on his trousers. He reached in and withdrew a small pistol. He handed it to Bret. "It's loaded and ready to fire, sir. Just point and shoot."

Bret tucked the pistol into the waistband of his pants near the center of his back.

The elevator continued to climb toward the top floor of the central office building.

Rick looked sharply over to the Fleet personnel manning the proximity detector controls. An alarm sounded. The holographic image in the center of the room updated, showing the alien armada just reaching the edge of the Bacchus system. Proximity detectors along the outer debris field were highlighted.

"Five alien ships are attempting to enter the debris field," one of the proximity detector technicians reported.

"Are they entering anywhere near the two safe passages?" Longstreet demanded.

"No, Admiral. They're attempting to breach in an area of heavy debris."

"Which ships are closest?" Longstreet asked, staring at the projection.

"The *St. Petersburg* and the *Montreal*, Admiral," one of the Fleet tactical officers responded.

"Contact the *St. Petersburg* and the *Montreal*, and order them to deploy to a position just this side of the debris field from where the alien ships entered. Tell them to fire on any ship that makes it through."

One of the communications technicians responded. "Yes, Admiral."

Longstreet turned to Rick. "The aliens aren't entering through one of the safe passages. It may be that the star charts they found didn't show where the entrances to those passages are located. The first ships they're sending in are coming through a very dangerous point of entry. They may not survive the debris field, but it's best to prepare for the worst."

Rick nodded.

After ten minutes, the communications technician reported, "Message from the *St. Petersburg*, Admiral. They report a large explosion inside the debris field. It looks like one of the alien ships collided with an asteroid."

Longstreet nodded. "Very well."

Twenty minutes later, the communications technician looked up again. "Admiral, the *Montreal* reports another large explosion inside the debris field. The *St. Petersburg* reports two small explosions, but they cannot confirm whether they're from the same ship or different ships."

Another fifteen minutes passed before either the *St. Petersburg* or the *Montreal* reported anything. "Admiral, two alien ships emerging from the debris field. The *St. Petersburg* and the *Montreal* are opening fire. They indicate that the alien ships are the same configuration as the ones the *Hercules* engaged over Darius 8."

Longstreet nodded. "Not their Capital Ships. That's a sound strategy. Don't risk the big ships until you find a safe way into the star system."

Battle reports came in as the two Fleet ships fired on the aliens. The *St. Petersburg* destroyed the first alien ship, and then it moved to help the *Montreal* finish off the second alien ship.

"Both alien ships are destroyed, Admiral," the communications technician reported.

"Very well. Order the *St. Petersburg* and the *Montreal* to hold their positions in case any of the other alien ships survived the debris field."

"Yes, Admiral."

Longstreet looked at Rick. "So much for round one."

Rick nodded. *There are many rounds left before this fight is over.*

The elevator doors opened, and Bret and Burgess exited at a run. Bret looked around for a sign that would point them to O'Connor's office. He found it and led Burgess down the hallway to the left.

At the end of the hallway was a massive reception area. In the center was a single desk with an attractive woman sitting behind it.

Bret pointed his gun at her. "Get up and step away from the desk. Don't touch anything or my Marine friend and I will shoot you."

The woman's hand hovered above her security console. She looked at Bret's gun pointed at her and pulled her hand away from it. She stood and backed away from her desk.

"Where is the control that opens Director O'Connor's door?" Bret demanded.

"Inside Director O'Connor's office," she replied with contempt.

Bret stepped toward her. "Don't lie to me. I know you have the only other control to open that door. Where is it?"

The woman stared at Bret defiantly.

"Corporal Burgess, what kind of gunshot produces the most pain and the slowest death?" Bret asked.

"A shot to the stomach, sir," Burgess replied coldly. "It'll take her hours to die, and it will hurt worse than anything she's ever felt before."

Bret lowered his gun to point at her abdomen. "About here?"

Burgess nodded. "That'll do it, sir."

Bret leaned toward the woman. "Don't think for one second that I won't do it," he growled softly. "For the last time, where is the control that opens Director O'Connor's office?"

The woman stared at Bret, warily eyed his gun, and looked back at him. Her shoulders slumped, and she pointed to her desk. "It's underneath the counter, just to the left of the net-dev keyboard."

Bret walked around the desk and crouched down so he could see the control. "Here?" he asked her.

She nodded.

"If you're lying and this button does anything else, I will shoot you in the gut and leave you to bleed out. Understand?"

She nodded.

"Bind her hands," Bret ordered Burgess.

The Corporal pulled her arms behind her back and put restraints around her wrists. Then he forced her to sit against the far wall.

"Ready?" Bret asked when Burgess joined him at the desk.

"Ready, sir," Burgess acknowledged.

Bret pushed the button. The double doors against the far wall swung open, and Bret and Burgess ran through them into O'Connor's office.

Proximity detectors lit up on the holographic projection. The aliens were attempting to breach the debris field in four places. Longstreet ordered Fleet ships to intercept any aliens that made it through. Several of the alien ships were destroyed, but a few made it through and were immediately fired upon by the Fleet.

"We've lost the *Edinburgh*," the Fleet tactical officer announced.

Rick looked at the projection and saw one of the Fleet ships disappear. Several smaller Cruisers attacked the alien ship, and after nearly twenty minutes, the alien ship disappeared from the projection, along with six Cruisers.

"We're beating them back, but we're losing too many ships," Longstreet commented. "And they're still not committing their Capital Ships to the fight."

Before Rick could comment, the Fleet tactical officer looked up. "Admiral, enemy ships detected inside one of the safe passages. They'll reach the minefield in fifteen minutes."

"Which Battleship is closest?" Longstreet asked.

"The *Ticonderoga*, Admiral," the Fleet tactical officer responded.

"Notify the *Ticonderoga* to be ready. With any luck, the aliens won't get past the mines."

"Yes, Admiral."

Proximity detector alarms went off again, and the projection highlighted where the alien ships had been detected.

"Admiral, alien ships detected inside the other safe passage through the debris field. They'll reach the minefield in twenty minutes. I'll alert the *Normandy* to be ready."

"They're coming at us from all sides," Longstreet noted. "But where's their main force going to strike?"

Rick shook his head and watched the projection as alien ships closed in on the *Ticonderoga* and the *Normandy*.

Director O'Connor stood in front of the windows overlooking the Advanced Weapons Division campus. His left hand hovered near his neck. Voices were coming from the net-dev on his desk, and Bret recognized Admiral Longstreet's voice giving orders to the *Ticonderoga* and the *Normandy* about aliens approaching the minefields.

Bret saw O'Connor's hand. *He must be holding the detonator transmitter.*

"What the hell is it, Gabrielle?" O'Connor demanded irritably. "I told you that I don't want to be disturbed."

Bret ran toward O'Connor as Burgess aimed his weapon at the Director of the Advanced Weapons Division.

O'Connor saw Bret's reflection in the window glass and turned to see what was going on. His eyes opened wide as he saw Bret running toward him and the Marine's rifle leveling at him.

"No!" he shouted.

Bret leaped into the air and dove for O'Connor. He grabbed the pendant, snapping its chain just as Burgess fired his weapon. Bret and O'Connor hit the floor, and the window exploded from the gunshot. Shards of glass flew everywhere as the window disintegrated from floor to ceiling. Bret's weapon slipped from his waistband and skidded across the floor, landing just out of reach.

"You are not going to stop me from doing what I have to do," O'Connor shouted at Bret. "I must keep the aliens from getting my Olympium."

Bret struggled to hold onto the pendant as he shook the glass off his back. He felt O'Connor trying to open the covering on the bottom of the pendant, and he moved his thumb over the covering so it couldn't open.

"You're going to let the aliens win!" O'Connor said, trying to snatch the pendant from Bret's hand. "I have to do this!"

"Like you had to kill Natalia?" Bret said through clenched teeth as he struck O'Connor in the groin with his knee. "Did you have to do that, too?"

"She betrayed me." O'Connor grunted in pain as Bret's knee hit his groin again.

Burgess didn't have a clear shot at O'Connor. Every time he was about to shoot, Bret got in the way. *Damn!*

He started moving around the desk to help Bret, but he heard running feet behind him. Turning, he saw several security officers approaching O'Connor's office with their guns drawn.

"Stand down!" Burgess ordered. "We're here on orders from the president. Director O'Connor is under arrest."

The security officers didn't seem to care. They opened fire.

Burgess returned fire and dropped to one knee to make himself a smaller target. The security officers took cover in the reception area and continued firing.

Burgess heard Bret and O'Connor struggling behind him. "Hurry up, sir. I can't hold them off for long."

Bret struggled to his feet – his hand never leaving the pendant. O'Connor stood and grabbed Bret's throat with his free hand. Bret twisted away and drove his elbow into O'Connor's stomach.

"I thought choking people was something you only did to women," Bret shouted with contempt.

O'Connor tried to kick him, and Bret side-stepped out of the way, almost losing his grip on the pendant. Bret's free hand closed around the pendant, and he pulled it with all of his might.

O'Connor's free hand also grabbed the pendant, and both men struggled to take it away from the other. They were moving dangerously close to the opening where the window had been.

Bret noticed his weapon of the floor, and he tried to maneuver O'Connor closer to it. *I need to get him close enough so I can reach it.*

O'Connor pulled both of his hands straight up, causing Bret's thumb to move off of the covering at the bottom of the pendant. Bret felt the covering move. He struggled to keep O'Connor from pressing the now exposed button. O'Connor spun around, accidently kicking Bret's weapon. Bret heard it land in the corner behind O'Connor's desk.

Bret looked at the shattered window. *I can't let him detonate the mines. Whatever it takes, he's not pushing that button.* Bret twisted and began forcing O'Connor back toward the window.

Burgess dove forward so he was flat on the floor. The security officers were hiding behind the chairs in the reception area, but

Burgess saw that the officers' legs were exposed. He fired at the open space underneath each of the chairs.

It worked. The security officers stopped firing and were writhing in pain from the wounds to their legs.

"Toss your weapons to me," Burgess ordered.

The security officers complied. Burgess jumped to his feet and kicked the weapons into O'Connor's office. He was about to check on the wounded security officers when he heard Bret and O'Connor still struggling behind him. He turned and saw that Bret and O'Connor were precariously close to the broken window.

Bret forced O'Connor closer to the opening. O'Connor must have realized what Bret was doing. Keeping his right hand on the pendent, he put his left hand on Bret's chest – pushing him back. Bret also let go with his right hand and reached around O'Connor's back, keeping them together and pressing the pendant between them.

"You're not pushing that button, Director."

O'Connor struggled to break free from Bret as his heel reached the edge of the opening in his office wall. A few inches more, and he and Bret would fall twenty-five stories to the ground below.

Bret knew that he was about to fall, but all he could think about was keeping O'Connor from pushing the button. He felt O'Connor's weight shift, and knew that it was too late to pull back. He felt himself being carried out of the window, but he kept his hand over the pendant.

As Bret lurched forward, he saw the look of panic on O'Connor's face. O'Connor released the pendant and tried to grab the edge of the window to keep from falling. It was too late. He couldn't reach the edge, and his arms flailed as he grasped for anything to save him.

Bret felt something yank at his waist. A moment later, he was back inside O'Connor's office with the pendant in his hand.

"Are you all right, sir?" Burgess asked excitedly, letting go of Bret's belt.

Bret was shaking. *Burgess saved my life! Again!* He grabbed Burgess and hugged him. "Thank you!"

"You're welcome, sir," Burgess said.

Bret looked at the pendant in his hand and saw that the button was still exposed. He closed the cover on the pendant and put it in his pocket. Then he stepped over to the window, putting a hand on the edge to keep himself from losing his balance.

O'Connor had hit the ground next to the landing pad where Nesbit guarded Fleming and the Scout ship. It was obvious that O'Connor hadn't survived the fall.

"Good riddance," Bret commented, pulling back from the window.

Bret recovered his weapon, and they left O'Connor's office. Burgess checked on the wounded security officers, and then he removed Gabrielle's wrist restraints.

"Thank you for your cooperation, ma'am," he said as he helped her to her feet. "But I don't think your boss is going to need you for the rest of the day. You should call for medics to tend to your wounded security officers."

Bret and Burgess rode down the elevator to get Nesbit and Fleming. When Bret reached them, he grabbed Fleming by the shoulder.

"You're going to jail. And if we survive the alien attack, you're going to take us to every one of those bombs you placed, and you're going to disarm them. After that, we'll decide what we're going to do with you. Understand?"

Fleming nodded, glancing at the body of his former boss lying on the ground nearby.

Bret shoved Fleming at Nesbit, who grabbed his prisoner by the arm. Bret led them through the lobby of the central office building to their vehicle in the main parking lot.

Rick's con-dev notified him of an incoming call. He saw that it was Bret.

"What's up, Son?" he asked.

"O'Connor is dead. We have the pendant."

"Are you all right?"

"I'm fine, Dad, thanks to Corporal Burgess. This is the second time he's saved my life."

"Who killed O'Connor?" Rick asked.

"You could say that it was gravity, but Corporal Burgess and I helped. We also arrested Peter Fleming. It turns out that he rigged a fusion mine to destroy the Advanced Weapons Division's facilities. If it had gone off, it would have taken out this campus *and* the capital."

"You did great work, Son," Rick said, feeling pride in his son. "But you should take shelter as quickly as possible."

"Has it started?" Bret asked.

"Yes."

"Understood. Good luck, Dad. I love you."

"I love you too, Son."

Rick put his com-dev back in his pocket. He looked at the projection in the center of the room and saw proximity detectors going off all around Bacchus.

"Admiral," the proximity detector technician reported, "enemy ships breaching the debris field in multiple places. More enemy ships are entering the two safe passages, in spite of the fact that the mines destroyed the first ships they sent in."

More proximity detector alarms sounded. "Admiral, their Capital Ships are on the move."

"Where?" Longstreet demanded.

"The nebulas, Admiral. They're sending the bulk of their ships through the nebulas!"

CHAPTER 25

Rick watched as the holographic projection showed the positions of the alien ships. There were scores of red images being projected all over the Bacchus system. Most were still inside the debris field or the nebula, but several had breached the debris field and were engaging Fleet ships along the outer rim of the Bacchus system.

Nearly a dozen more alien ships managed to slip past the minefields along the two safe passages, and they were engaging the *Normandy* and the *Ticonderoga* battlegroups.

"Admiral," the Fleet tactical officer shouted. "Four alien ships have slipped past our outer defenses."

"Alert the *Yorktown* and the *Hercules*," Longstreet ordered. "And notify the *Waterloo* to prepare to intercept any ships approaching Bacchus 12 from her direction.

"Yes, Admiral."

The proximity detectors detected more alien ships entering the two safe passages through the debris field.

Longstreet looked at the projection. "How long will it take the alien armada to pass through the nebulas?"

The Fleet tactical officer responded. "Given the debris and the currents through the gas cloud, it could take nearly an hour."

"When will the alien ships be in range of the nebula mines?"

"Twenty minutes," the Fleet tactical officer replied. "The mines are triangulating with the proximity detectors based on where the alien ships entered the nebulas. Once they've moved into position, they'll detonate."

"Keep me posted on those mines," Longstreet ordered.

"Yes, Admiral."

Both the *Ticonderoga* and *Normandy* were heavily damaged. They were forced to withdraw from the outer rim and redeploy to Bacchus 12. So far, the Fleet had lost four Heavy Cruisers, seven Cruisers, three Destroyers, two Frigates, and one Fast Attack ship during the battle. The alien ships were still entering the Bacchus system through the debris field. Eleven medium-size alien ships were heading for Bacchus 12.

"Issue the recall order," Longstreet said. "All ships are to immediately fall back to the defense of Bacchus 12."

"Yes, Admiral," the communications technician responded.

Rick watched the projection closely. Nineteen alien ships now approached Bacchus 12, but the Capital Ships and the rest of the alien armada were still inside the nebulas.

What are they waiting for?

Longstreet consulted with the Fleet tactical officer. Then the senior Fleet commander issued new orders.

"Have all unmanned weapon systems open fire as soon as the enemy ships are in range. Hold all Fleet ships in reserve until the aliens have passed the *Hercules* and the *Yorktown*. Then hit the ships with everything we've got."

The technicians operating the unmanned weapons around Bacchus 12 activated the targeting systems, waiting to open fire.

Twenty minutes passed. The lead alien ships approaching the planet came into range of the orbiting plasma cannons and torpedo launchers. The technicians activated the firing controls.

Blueish-white streams of plasma energy struck the two lead ships, splitting them open from their bows to the middle of their hulls. Nuclear torpedoes finished off the two alien ships, which exploded in purple flame just beyond the planetary rings.

A cheer went up from the Fleet personnel in the room. Additional plasma cannons opened firing on the approaching aliens, attacking at them from all directions. The aliens fired back at the plasma cannons, but torpedoes knocked out the forward guns of many of the alien ships.

Eight alien ships were damaged or destroyed. The remaining eleven ships changed course to approach Bacchus 12 from different directions. One alien ship headed for the space dock, but it split in half and exploded when the space dock's ten plasma canons opened fire at the same time.

Plasma cannons and torpedo launchers, fired from asteroids in the planetary rings, hit the redeploying alien ships hard. Two alien ships were hit near their fuel cells, causing them to explode instantaneously.

The battle continued. The Capital Ships inside the nebulas were still nowhere to be seen.

The Fleet tactical officer turned toward Admiral Longstreet. "Admiral, the nebula mines have finished triangulating the rest of the alien armada and are in position."

"Detonate the mines!" Longstreet ordered.

Hundreds of blinding lights appeared inside both nebulas. The holographic projection of the Bacchus system showed where the detonations had taken place and where the shockwaves were heading.

Rick was amazed at the magnitude of the shockwaves. They crossed each other multiple times as they radiated from their initial points of detonation. *How could any ship survive that?*

The projection showed Minesetters and Scout ships racing toward the nebulas to assess the damage to the alien armada. Proximity detectors registered no ships escaping from the Bacchus system, and the scanners on the Fleet ships detected no ships coming through the nebulas.

"Did we destroy their Capital Ships?" Rick asked. "Did the mines destroy all of the alien ships coming through the nebulas?"

"Unknown, Mr. President," Longstreet replied. "But we still have eight alien ships above the planet to deal with."

Turning to the Fleet personnel, he said, "Order all Fleet ships to attack. Maintain plasma cannon fire from the space dock and the orbital platforms."

Admiral Marshall was in the command chair on the *Yorktown* when the order to attack came in.

He activated his communications console. "*Yorktown* battlegroup, open fire and engage the enemy!"

The *Yorktown* and its escort ships left their hiding place behind one of Bacchus 12's moons and attacked the closest alien ship. The *Yorktown* was aided by several orbiting plasma cannons, and the alien ship was soon destroyed. The battlegroup moved to its next target.

Rick watched the projection as it displayed the battle going on above the planet. The *Hercules* had engaged an enemy ship, but her repairs had not been completed, and she was forced to withdraw before inflicting sufficient damage on the enemy ship. The *Waterloo* moved into position and continued the fight.

"There are only six alien ships remaining above Bacchus 12," Longstreet said to Rick. "Do we let them withdraw or continue attacking?"

These bastards destroyed twenty-one planets, killing billions of innocent people. They don't deserve any mercy from us. We can't let them return to their home planet and build another fleet to come after us. We have to end this with an indisputable victory.

Rick shook his head. "No, Admiral. No quarter will be given. Destroy them all."

"Yes, Mr. President."

Rick thought he saw a smile on the Admiral's face.

The Fleet ships were not powerful enough to destroy the remaining alien ships without suffering heavy damage, but the orbiting plasma cannons were. Longstreet ordered the Fleet ships to break off the attack, and he ordered the technicians manning the plasma cannon and torpedo launcher controls to end the battle.

The technicians had been redeploying the plasma cannons that were not mounted on asteroids or moons. They were now in perfect position to attack the remaining alien ships. All remaining plasma cannons opened fire at the same time.

The alien ships tried to escape, but plasma cannons hidden in the planetary rings opened fire and forced the aliens into a tight cluster. Hundreds of torpedoes detonated inside and around the cluster, setting off a chain reaction. The alien fuel cells were hit.

The remaining alien ships exploded, sending wreckage and debris in all directions.

"Admiral, all alien ships destroyed," the Fleet tactical officer reported.

No alien ships appeared on the holographic projection.

"What about the nebulas?" Longstreet asked. "Did any of their Capital Ships survive?"

"No alien ships detected inside the nebulas, Admiral. No signals, no engine trails, nothing. If they were inside the blast radius of the nebula mines, there shouldn't be anything left of them."

Longstreet nodded. "Continue monitoring the nebulas. Order all ships that sustained heavy damage to head for the space dock for repairs. All remaining ships are to stay on high alert in case any alien ships survived in the nebulas or in the debris fields. Unmanned planetary defenses are to also remain on high alert."

"Yes, Admiral."

Eight hours later, Rick and Admiral Longstreet addressed the Confederation Council. The session was broadcast across the planet and the Fleet.

Admiral Longstreet gave an overview of the battle. At the end of his comments, he said, "The alien ships have all been destroyed. It was a compete victory, but it was a costly one. The Fleet had lost seven of its twelve Heavy Cruisers, ten of its eighteen Cruisers, six of its nineteen Destroyers, four of its twelve Frigates, and two Fast Attack ships during the battle. One Fleet Carrier suffered extensive damage, and two Battleships require major repairs. More than half of the fusion mines deployed along the two safe passages through the debris field were detonated, and nearly a thousand fission mines in the nebulas were detonated.

"Our defenses are below half-strength, and the lives lost aboard our ships are irreplaceable. But we will rebuild."

Longstreet paused. "This victory would not have been possible if it weren't for the brave men and women who risked their lives to keep this planet safe. Their dedication, determination, and extraordinary courage are a testament to the strength of the human spirit. They are an example to us all. Those who perished will be remembered. Those who survived have earned our respect and our undying gratitude.

The chamber erupted into applause as Admiral Longstreet took his seat. Rick stood and walked to the podium.

"We face an uncertain future," he said to the Council. "But we *have* a future."

The Council Chamber welcomed that statement with a standing ovation.

Rick continued. "Now is the time to rebuild. There are still survivors on the other Confederation planets that must be brought here. Equipment, livestock, plants, and spare parts must be rescued. Ships on those planets can be salvaged and used to repair and strengthen our Fleet. The Advanced Weapons Division will continue to reinforce our planetary defenses and create new weapons that can be used to protect us the next time we face a threat like this one.

"My fellow citizens of the Confederation, we are alive. We have faced devastating adversity, and we have survived. We have come through the long night of the alien threat, and we stand at the dawn of a new day for us. The alien threat is gone for now, and we are left with the lesson that this crisis has taught us: by working together, we can accomplish anything! God bless the brave men and women who fought and died to protect us, and God bless us all as we embark on the next great adventure of mankind – our future!"

Bret and Jen were waiting for Rick when he left the Council Chamber.

"Great speech, Dad," Bret said.

"Thanks, Son."

"So what happens now?" Jen asked.

"The search-and-rescue missions continue," Rick replied. "We have to save what's left of humanity and bring them here to start over. We have industries to relocate, ships to repair, and lives to rebuild. It'll take years, but we'll get it done."

They walked down the corridor. "I think it's time for me to visit the farms and the ranches that Beth and Cindy have been working on," Rick said as they reached the elevators. "Want to come with me?"

Bret smiled. "Sure! When are you going?"

"Tomorrow morning." Looking at Jen, he added, "I want you to come with us, Jen. You're part of the family now, and I want you included in family activities."

"Thank you, Mr. President," Jen said happily.

Rick's transport landed at the spaceport near the ranches at mid-morning. Beth, Cindy, and Colten were there to meet Rick when he arrived with Bret and Jen.

Beth came around and hugged Rick, giving him a kiss.

"I just want to hold you for a week," Rick whispered in her ear.

"Me, too," Beth said nuzzling his cheek with her nose.

Rick felt a tapping on his shoulder.

"My turn," Cindy said.

Beth smiled and stepped back.

"I've missed you, Daddy," Cindy said as she hugged Rick. Then she introduced Colten.

"This is the man who saved me from the bull on the freighter," she explained as Colten shook his hand. "He's been teaching me about ranching and how to ride horses."

Rick nodded, not taking his eyes off Colten. "I'm happy that you're safe and that you've agreed to help build the new ranches here on Bacchus 12, Colten. I've never seen my daughter this happy before. You've introduced her to a whole new world."

"It's my pleasure, Mr. President. She's wonderful, and she's a fast learner. She knows her way around the animals like she was born to this."

Rick smiled. Then he leaned in and whispered so no one else could hear. "See those Marines that are part of Cindy's protective detail?"

Colten nodded.

"They're job is to protect her from any threats. Do you know what that includes?"

Colten shook his head.

"Anyone who hurts her. Understand? Now, It's clear to me that Cindy likes you and that you like her. So don't hurt her, okay? I don't want to have to get the Marines involved. Do you?"

Colten shook his head. "That won't happen, sir."

Rick straightened. "I don't expect it to, but I thought you should know what I expect from someone my daughter is spending so much time with."

"I understand, sir," Colten confirmed, shaking Rick's hand again.

"Perfect!" Rick said. "Why don't you show me around so I can see what's been done so far?"

They walked toward the ranching complex so Colten could show Rick the progress being made.

"So, how are you doing, Mr. Savior-of-the-planet?" Beth asked, holding his hand as they walked.

"Exhausted. I just want to spend some time with my family before I have to get back to work. I need to find a replacement for Natalia. She was the best, and I miss her terribly. I can't seem to stay organized without her. At least she got justice when O'Connor was killed. And speaking of that, I need to appoint a new Director of the Advanced Weapons Division, a person who will work well with the government. The search-and-rescue missions to all Confederation planets need to be coordinated... oh, and Archbishop Canterbury wants us to declare a day of Thanksgiving and have a huge church service to celebrate our survival. It's a busy time."

"And it always will be, Mr. President. You wouldn't have it any other way. I told you that you were the right person for the job."

"I couldn't have done it without you. And what you and Cindy have accomplished down here is nothing short of miraculous."

Rick and his family sat at a table near one of the cattle pastures. Beth and Cindy had arranged for them to have lunch together. Bret and Jen were laughing, Cindy and Colten were telling everyone about ranching and riding horses. Beth looked at her husband with pride and love in her eyes.

The last time we were all together for a meal, Bret and I were arguing, Cindy had her nose buried in her net-dev, and Beth was frantically trying to play referee between us all. Now look at everyone. Bret is working, and he created the weapon system that saved the planet. He's in love and living with his girlfriend as they start their life together. Cindy recruited, organized, and led thousands of volunteers to help Beth create a new agricultural system on this planet. She's becoming a rancher and has found a guy that she wants to spend the rest of her life with. Beth is working again, and her work will ensure that the remnants of mankind don't starve. What a difference a few weeks can make!

He leaned back and just smiled. *My family is all right. My planet is safe. Mankind is safe. This is what I have to be grateful for.*

Rick looked up at the planetary rings visible in the sky. *What a wonderful day this is!*

The End

ABOUT THE AUTHOR

Award-winning author William Speir was born in Birmingham, Alabama in 1962, attended the University of Alabama, and graduated from the University of Alabama at Birmingham in 1984. He spent over 25 years in corporate America, serving as a management consultant, consulting practice leader, IT executive, and HR/ Payroll executive for top tier consulting firms and Fortune 100 companies.

During William's corporate career, he published several articles on leadership and the human impact of organizational/technology change. His first experience with book publishing was with a series of ten textbooks he authored about field artillery in the 19th century. These textbooks were later consolidated into a single volume and re-published in 2015 as *Muzzle-Loading Artillery for Reenactors*.

In addition to his artillery manual, William has published 14 novels, including an 8-book action-adventure series (*The Knights of the Saltire Series*), four historical novels (*King's Ransom*, *The Saga of Asbjorn Thorleikson*, *Nicaea – The Rise of the Imperial Church*, and *Arthur, King*), one fantasy novel (*The Kingstone of Airmid*), and one science fiction novel (*The Olympium of Bacchus 12*).

William is a 5-time Royal Palm Literary Award winner: 2014 Second Place Unpublished Historical Fiction for *King's Ransom*, 2015 Second Place Unpublished Historical Fiction for *The Saga of Asbjorn Thorleikson*, 2017 Second Place Published Historical Fiction for *Arthur, King*, 2017 First Place Published Historical Fiction for *Nicaea – The Rise of the Imperial Church*, and 2017 First Place Published Science Fiction for *The Olympium of Bacchus 12*.

For more information about William Speir, please visit his website at WilliamSpeir.com.

Progressive Rising Phoenix Press is an independent publisher. We offer wholesale discounts and multiple binding options with no minimum purchases for schools, libraries, book clubs, and retail vendors. We also offer rewards for libraries, schools, independent book stores, and book clubs. Please visit our website and wholesale discount page at:

www.ProgressiveRisingPhoenix.com

Progressive Rising Phoenix Press is adding new titles from our award-winning authors on a regular basis and has books in the following genres: children's chapter books and picture books, middle grade, young adult, action adventure, mystery and suspense, contemporary fiction, romance, historical fiction, fantasy, science fiction, and non-fiction covering a variety of topics from military to inspirational to biographical. Visit our website to see our updated catalogue of titles.

www.ingramcontent.com/pod-product-compliance
Lightning Source LLC
Chambersburg PA
CBHW050502260626
47157CB00004B/1151